MW00880045

UNTOUCHED

UNTOUCHED

THE GIRL IN THE BOX
BOOK TWO

Robert J. Crane

UNTOUCHED
THE GIRL IN THE BOX, BOOK 2

Robert J. Crane
Copyright © 2012
All Rights Reserved.

AUTHOR'S NOTE

This book is a work of fiction. Names, characters, places and incidents are products of the author's imagination or are used fictitiously. Any resemblance to actual events or locales or persons, living or dead, is entirely coincidental.

Contact Robert J. Crane via email at
cyrusdavidon@gmail.com

Layout provided by **Everything Indie**
http://www.everything-indie.com

Acknowledgments

Who's in charge of this mad house of literary achievement (or mediocrity, depending on your perspective)? Well, technically, as the author, I am. But that's not the whole story.

Shannon Garza once more gave me her whole-hearted effort at making sure my characters didn't jump the emotional shark, as it were. She gave detailed feedback and commentary that allowed me to keep a pulse on how everyone was feeling, what everyone was doing, and how it all fit together to create a reading experience, and for that, I owe her my thanks.

Debra Wesley once more came to the rescue with countless technical details and thought of things I didn't even consider.

More thanks also to Calvin Sams, who once more read the draft and provided some additional critique.

We also had a new addition this round, the great Robin McDermott, who took time away from her busy life as a new mommy to parse the book, and she found some insights that no one else did.

Lastly in the editorial department, but certainly not leastly, muchas gracias to my esteemed Editor-in-Chief, Heather Rodefer, who not only finds my errors and corrects my grammar, but also found the flaming man in the cover art for this work! That's why she's the Editor-in-Chief.

The cover was put together by Karri Klawitter (artbykarri.com) using a work done by user dmv-bros on dreamstime. I don't know who dmv-bros is, but I know Karri did an amazing job turning it into a fantastic cover.

My apologies to the city of Glencoe, Minnesota. It was nothing personal; it was down to either you or Norwood Young America, Minnesota, and frankly, look at the name on them! You expect me to type that over and over? Simplicity was your undoing. Accept it with grace and move on.

My mom marvels at my ability to churn out books (frankly, so do I, but let's not look gift equines in the oral cavity, okay?) and recently asked me how it came to be, since neither she nor my father have even the remotest interest in writing. The answer is this - my mom has read more books than any other person I've ever met. If she ever created a Goodreads profile and plugged in all the books she's read, it'd crash the site (thanks for not doing that, mom). My father, on the other hand, is not much of a reader, but is quite the wordsmith. He makes up rhymes and turns phrases just for the fun of it. Nothing narrative, just idle amusement. But when you combine my mother's love of story and my dad's enjoyment of messing around with words...well, you get me. Someone who wants to write a lot of novels. For their respective contributions to my career path, I owe them my thanks.

Finally, we come to my wife and kids. Once more, I owe them everything, because without them, I wouldn't be doing this.

Prologue

Above the Podkannaya Tuguska River
Russian Empire
June 30, 1908

His skin was wreathed in flames, burning red and yellow, as he streaked across the early morning sky. Aleksandr Timofeyevich Gavrikov was not yet eighteen. *I can't believe I killed her*, he thought. *I have done murder.*

The air felt cold in spite of the fact that his skin was covered by a solid inch of fire. How *is that possible?* he wondered. The wind that whipped across his face did not affect the flames. *This is unlike anything I have ever seen...unlike anything Father has ever seen too, I think...* The smell of rank, stale water rose up from below him in the swamps. A river cut the land, the shine of the rising sun refracting off it. He was several hundred feet up, flying—*as though I were a bird*, he thought. *Without flapping my arms, I can fly! Just like Father.*

He felt a thrum in his heart at that thought. *He will hurt me for this; worse than he ever has before. Perhaps things would have been different if mother had lived,* he thought for the thousandth time, then dismissed it. *I am on fire and flying through the air and I have done murder. Had mother lived long enough to see this, the shock would have killed her.*

Seventeen years, he reflected. *Seventeen years of hell for me and Klementina. But no more.* The flames on his skin burned brighter as he thought about it, of all the abuses, the beatings, the nights he heard Klementina squealing and crying when their father went to her—

The flames that covered him changed, grew hotter. The cold air was warming around him, and he hovered a few feet above the water, staring at himself, his reflection, in the river below. *How many times, Klementina? How many times did he hurt you?* He and Klementina were forced to stay on the farm on all but the rarest of occasions. His sister was fair—*beautiful*, he thought. More beautiful than the peasant girls he had seen when they had gone into Kirensk. Her green eyes were hued with some blue, and her skin was tanned and freckled. Her blond hair hung about her shoulders as she carried buckets of water in from the well. She was far, far more beautiful than the girls he had seen in Kirensk.

He drifted close to the surface of the water, looking at himself. No skin was visible; he was a glowing fire, shaped like a man. *What...am I? Even Father does not burst into flames when he flies...*

"Aleksandr!" The word crackled through the air, and panic ran through him. He whipped his head around to see his father flying toward him from above, eyes narrowed, his teeth bared in rage.

I will get such a beating for this, Aleksandr thought. *I will be chained and locked in the shed for a week.*

He remembered the time when he'd had courage. A year earlier he had awoken to hear Klementina crying, his father slapping her in the only bedroom of their farmhouse. It happened so often, and every night it had, he turned over, shut his eyes tight, and covered his ears with his old, threadbare pillow. It almost shut out the cries of his sister and the primal, disgusting grunts of his father.

He had thought he couldn't bear it any longer. He had run into the room in the middle of the night and grasped his father by the shoulders, throwing him off Klementina. She huddled, clutching a sheet to her, moaning and sobbing, her eyes wide with fear. The first two punches had been so satisfying; he heard his father's nose break, watched the blood run down his lip. Then the drunken eyes had focused on him, and his father had brought a hand across his face in fury.

Aleksandr had gone flying across the room. After landing, he could dimly hear Klementina crying, saw her covering herself with the blanket as his father approached him. He could smell the awful night smells, the stink of sweat and fear. The blood was slick and running across his eye as his father leaned down to him. With another punch, everything went dark.

When he awoke, it was midday, hot, and he was chained to a stake in the middle of the shed. No water, no food, until after dark when Klementina came to him, bringing him some crumbs of supper and something to drink. Her eyes were black and swollen, and a trail of dried blood led from one of her nostrils to her upper lip.

He had not intervened since.

"Aleksandr!" The shout came again, and Aleksandr turned, blasting away from the river, up into the air above. The chill was back, the coolness of early morning, but this time it was fused with the tickle of the flames that wreathed him. His father was following, he knew. *He won't let me go. Not after what I've done.*

He climbed higher and higher in the sky, felt the chill increase. He looked down, and the Tunguska River was so far below that it was but a line. He felt the flames start to die, saw his skin peeking out from beneath the place where the fire had burned so hard only a minute earlier. *He'll catch me. He'll lock me away. I won't be able to stop him.*

The air was thin, and he couldn't breathe. He gasped for breath, but it didn't seem to help. He looked back; father was gaining on him, coming up behind him, his face fixed, eyes blazing in a way that told Aleksandr that this might be the last time...

He felt his father's hand close around his arm, felt it tighten, then felt the bone crack, and Aleksandr Timofeyevich Gavrikov tried to cry out with a breath he didn't have. His father had broken his arm, and the excruciating sensation felt as though someone had jammed a knife into his upper arm and twisted. He felt the pull of his father's strength, dragging him down, down, down. He fought, he struggled, but without breath he failed, sagging. He was pulled down, and after a moment he felt his breath return, felt the chill start to fade.

Felt the heat under his skin return.

"You have killed her!" His father's words were barely audible over the wind as they descended. "Your sister is dead because of you!"

"I did not mean to," Aleksandr's words came out ragged. "She touched me and..."

"You killed her," his father said again, and backhanded him across the face with his free hand. The smell of the swamp water below reminded him of the night smells, of the fear.

The heat under Aleksandr's skin grew, his breaths grew deeper and less forced. *He beats me during the day and tortures Klementina at night.* "You will never be able to hurt her again."

Another backhand was his reward. "I never hurt her!"

"You hurt her all the time." Aleksandr heard a menace in his own voice that had never been there before. It reminded him of the time he'd had courage. The heat underneath his skin was unbearable; it was burning, aching to get out. "I may have killed her this morning, but you have killed her every night since she was a girl."

"LIAR!" His father struck him again, and the heat became intense within him. His eyes were burning, his skin was burning, and suddenly it was on fire again, and his flesh was covered in flames. "What...?!"

His father yelped and his hand withdrew. Aleksandr felt himself fall for a second before he took over and felt the power of his own flight return. He hovered a few feet from his father, staring at the old man with unfettered contempt. "You have flown for as long as I can remember, Father." The menace was there. The courage was in his voice. His father was cradling his hand, a blackened, burned husk of what it had been: a strong, powerful limb that he used to beat his children. "It appears that I have taken more from you than I would have imagined."

"You are my son," came the ghostly reply.

"I am not. I am my mother's son." He felt the heat, still under his skin, even as the fire raged on top of it. "I am my sister's brother. I am Aleksandr; not Timofeyevich nor Gavrikov, because I want nothing of yours that I don't need." Without hesitation he flew at his father, slammed into him, and the searing under his skin unleashed as they fell toward the earth below. *Seventeen years of hell*, he thought, and it all came out at once—a torrent of rage, fire, flame, an explosion of his anger. He watched his father's skin blacken, his eyes disappear in the initial flash of heat, watched his flesh burn away, then the bone turn to ash and then dust.

The world went white all around, the trees below were like little pieces of tinder in the wind, picked up and flung through the air, the landscape flattening for miles in every direction. A screeching sound filled his ears, and cracks like thunder went off one after another.

When it was all over, Aleksandr Timofeyevich Gavrikov was no more.

And Aleksandr flew off, taking the only thing of his father's that he wanted.

The gift of flight.

Chapter 1

Sienna Nealon
Present Day

I awoke in a cold sweat. The red light of the clock told me it was close to five A.M., and my eyes searched the room around me, trying to acclimate after another nightmare. I worked to get my breathing under control as I sat up, walls spinning around me. The only other light came from the windows and the far distant lamps that lit the Directorate campus.

The Directorate. That's where I was. A secret organization dedicated to policing humans with powers beyond the norm— metas, they were called. I still wasn't sure I believed that the Directorate did what they claimed to, but I had very little evidence as yet of what their true intentions might be. All I knew was that so far they'd helped me when no one else had.

I still didn't trust them.

My breathing returned to normal. I blinked my eyes a few times to adjust to the darkness and then I stood, letting my feet touch the soft, carpeted floor. The room smelled sterile, with just a hint of dust from what I assumed was the reconstruction it had undergone. I looked back through the glass, which was flawless, having been replaced only a couple days ago. Hard to believe it was such a short time.

Until a little over a week ago, I had been a prisoner in my own home for over ten years. Mom kept me from leaving with a simple threat: if I got out of line, was disobedient in some way, offended her or didn't mind my manners, she locked me in a six-foot-tall metal sarcophagus. It certainly kept me from running. The drywall dust had a light and pleasant smell compared to the stench of being locked in that metal box for days at a time.

I had left my house in a rush, pursued by agents of the Directorate, who, at the time, I thought had ill intentions toward me. I'd met a guy named Reed who also helped me. Good looking, in a tall, dark and handsome kind of way, if you're into that. I kind of am. Maybe. He helped me get away from the Directorate for a while, but we got attacked by a beast.

The beast's name was Wolfe. He had lived for thousands of years, had killed countless people before we crossed paths, and after we tangled, he became obsessed with me. Everyone tells me I 'm strong. Wolfe was stronger. So much stronger that it wasn't even a contest. He manhandled me, humiliated me, bent me, broke me, cut through a dozen or more armed Directorate guards, and left me in a bloody heap more than once.

I shook away the thought of Wolfe as I padded, barefoot, into the bathroom. I felt the cool night air against my skin. I was wearing only a bra and panties, less than I had ever worn to bed in my life, but there was a reason for it beyond simple tactile pleasure.

When I squared off against Wolfe for the last time, it was because he had held the entire city of Minneapolis hostage, leaving a trail of dead bodies until I came out of hiding and faced him. The Directorate higher-ups, Old Man Winter, his gal Friday Ariadne, and even one of the agents, Zack (he's a cutie, that one) begged me not to go up against Wolfe again. They urged me to wait until their highly trained team of metas, M-Squad, returned from a mission so they could handle it. But people were dying, and Wolfe seemed unstoppable. Since all he wanted was me, I went to give him what he wanted.

Meta powers are twofold. One, they have enhanced strength, speed, dexterity—attributes far above a normal human's. I can lift heavy objects, run faster and farther, leap fences, and essentially do stuff that makes everyone but Superman look pathetic. I was reminded of this again as I went to take a drink of water after washing my hands and I accidentally burst the bottle, soaking the bathroom floor, the sink, and myself.

I shouldn't think about Wolfe while I'm taking a drink. Or handling anything delicate, come to think of it. But these days, it's hard not to think about him all the time.

The second set of powers a meta possesses is unique to each one, to his or her type of metahuman. Wolfe, for instance, had skin that was highly adaptable to damage. If he got shot, the next time it happened he was able to take a greater amount of that kind of damage. I saw a shotgun go off at point blank range and leave nothing but red marks on his skin.

It was in my final confrontation with Wolfe that I had discovered my other power. I am a succubus, possessed of the ability to drain a soul, or the essence of a person, with nothing but the touch of my skin. He had me in a chokehold, but I touched him, and he screamed, and I drained the life out of him.

Hence the bra and panties for sleepwear. If anyone came for me during the night, I wanted to be able to defend myself. I didn't think anyone would, but when you've been imprisoned in your own home for twelve years and then turned loose in a world where everyone wants a piece of you, it's easy to develop a sense of paranoia. Except it's not paranoia when they're actually after you.

I sighed, feeling the water dripping down my skin. I looked at myself in the mirror. I didn't know for certain, but I was pretty sure my meta powers also included enhanced hearing, smell, sight, taste, and feeling, because it felt like I could see every detail of the water drops that were tracing their way down my pale belly.

I wasn't very tall, about five foot four, and my brown hair was tangled from the way I slept on it. My eyes looked more blue than green, and I had acquired a couple of small freckles since the last time I had studied myself in the mirror. I had yet to see the sun, but I had spent enough time outside that they had formed, one on my cheek and one on the tip of my nose. I stripped, removing the wet clothing, and toweled off before I turned off the light.

As I turned to leave, something in the mirror caught my attention. A flash of black eyes, tangled, matted, dirty hair, far different than the slight mess that mine was, and a vision of wicked teeth, the type a predator would use to rip and shred its prey. The eyes watched me, and I could almost taste the desire for my blood—and something else, less savory.

So pretty, the voice came. *So pure and sweet and untouched.*

"Dammit, Wolfe," I said, my words coming out as close to a growl as I could imagine, "Can't you just go away?"

The unfortunate side effect of my power, one which I had told no one about yet, was that I now had Wolfe bouncing around in my head. He gave a running commentary on my life; his thoughts ranged from the mundane to the disgusting, and I got all of them— unfiltered, profane, and revolting. Living a life cooped up with my mother had kept me more or less innocent, and having this diseased freak sharing my skull was giving me nightmares, both figurative and literal, as I got to witness his crimes every night as I slept. And there were so many.

Can't go away, he whispered back. *You and Wolfe are bound together, little doll. Intertwined.*

I resisted the urge to vomit in my mouth and flipped the light switch, casting the bathroom in the bright aura of the overhead lamps. The reflection of Wolfe was gone from the mirror.

Such sweetness, he intoned, his words growing with verve in my head. *Wolfe would have touched you, Wolfe would have made you scream with pleasure—*

"You would have died," I said to my reflection, as though I could sense his presence behind my eyes. "Oh, wait," I said with mock joy, "You did. And it couldn't have happened to a more disgusting creature." I thought about it for a beat. "Actually, you dying did make me scream with pleasure—"

I felt a searing pain in my skull, one that dropped me to my knees. With my eyes almost squinted shut, I could only see blurry shapes in the mirror; one was flesh-toned, on its knees, the other was behind me, stalking back and forth—

I turned, but there was no one there. I fell back on my haunches, felt the cold linoleum of the bathroom floor against my backside, and lay down, closing my eyes and putting a hand over my throbbing head. "You're such a bastard," I said. "Why don't you tell me what you know about my mother?"

I stared at the ceiling, waiting to see if Wolfe would reply. He didn't.

Mom had gone missing about a week before the Directorate had ousted me from my house. Everyone here denied knowing anything about her disappearance. Wolfe knew something, I suspected, but in the last day or so of sharing skull space with me, he'd been cagey.

He was there, I could feel him, skulking in my brain. The headache was his doing. Whenever he had a burst of strong emotion, I felt its effects. Yesterday, when I was leaving the medical unit, a stay caused by my last fight with Wolfe, Ariadne had offered me different options of where I could stay on the Directorate campus.

"We have a variety of dorm rooms," she said, talking in a quiet voice, as though I were too brittle to be exposed to words spoken at normal volume. "Or, if you would feel safer, you could stay in the secure room in the Headquarters basement—"

"How about the dorm room I stayed in before?" I asked her, not sure where the question came from.

"The one where Wolfe...attacked you?" She took a step back, her eyes wide. "I assumed that there would be bad memories associated with...that place."

I had felt a little thrill run through me, a surge of pleasure at the memory of what he'd done to me there. It wasn't my feeling, which would have been closer to nausea, but it was strong enough to overwhelm my own emotions. "Yeah," I said. "I'll stay there."

Ariadne didn't have the most expressive face; it was reserved most of the time, and her red hair was always the only splash of color in her drab attire. Still, on this occasion, she had emotion—concern. For me.

"I'll be fine," I said. "He's dead. Nothing to fear from him now."

Oh, but there is. I ignored him.

Ariadne's fashion sense was prosaic; it was as if the dull and dreary winter weather was her inspiration. Wolfe threw out an uncharitable and crass thought about what he'd do to liven up her look and I ignored it even though it caused a vein in my eye to pulse. She didn't argue with me anymore after that, just let me go to my room—to rest, I told her. I didn't, though, not the rest of that day. Not until well after nightfall, and then I was plagued by the nightmares that had caused me to wake in a sweat.

The linoleum on the floor was causing my body to ache, and I felt a throbbing in my head. I sat up, felt the pain Wolfe had inflicted fade, and grabbed hold of the counter, pulling up to my feet. I stared once more into the mirror, looking at myself, my face, my eyes. There were bags underneath them; I looked tired.

I turned out the bathroom light and walked back out into the room, heading to the closet. The feeling that Wolfe had been watching me while I was nude left me unsettled; I dressed in silence, slipping on a long-sleeved sweatshirt and jeans.

The air was warm enough; I could feel an unseen heater fighting against the chill of the winter outside. The window was one-way, Ariadne had told me, a type of special glass that was tinted so that whatever happened inside could not be seen from outside, even if the lights were on. I had walked around the dormitory building and couldn't see anything but my own reflection, even at night, when I knew there were lights on inside.

I walked to the window with confidence that I was unseen. The ground was covered in snow, at least a foot deep if not more; the only disruption to its smooth, unblemished surface was the place a few hundred feet away where a path had been cut with a snow blower so people could walk and some footprints that were not fresh—mine. Far in the distance lurked a pine forest, the green needles blending with the black of night.

The sky seemed lighter than I remembered it being a few minutes ago. I stared out and saw a flat spot next to the headquarters building with heavy lights sticking up out of the snow around it, reminding me of a baseball game I'd seen on TV that was played at night.

I watched, looking through the dark, and saw figures standing on the concrete—the red hair of Ariadne was visible even at this distance. Old Man Winter was with her, towering above her small frame, and it looked like the wind was swirling snow around his legs.

Old Man Winter was the boss of the Directorate. Ridiculously tall, he looked like he was in his seventies, and his face looked as though it had been carved out of rock that had been exposed to the elements for too long. His eyes were the most piercing blue you could imagine, though even I couldn't see them at this distance. Standing next to him was a shorter man, a fatter one, and I knew it was Kurt Hannegan.

Kurt and I had a history of antipathy. He'd been the one that had helped me deliver myself to Wolfe, unbeknownst to Old Man Winter and Ariadne. Kurt and I had no love lost, not since our first encounter when he broke into my house and I pummeled him. If that wasn't enough, since I arrived at the Directorate I had caused the deaths of quite a few of his fellow human agents. None of them were intentional but I doubt it mattered to him; he didn't like me before that, and it wasn't the sort of thing that was going to put me on his good side.

The three of them stood to one side of the lighted area. The wind was blowing hard, and with the exception of Old Man Winter, they were wearing heavy coats. I pressed a hand against the glass and felt the chill seep through; the temperature outside had to be below zero. Two more figures joined them, one from the Headquarters building, the other cutting across the snow from in the distance. Based on the shuffle of the steps, I knew that one was Dr. Ron Sessions, the lab geek that the Directorate kept on hand. The other was shorter, her frame undeniably female, dark hair whipping in the wind. I suspected it was Dr. Perugini, the woman who ran the medical unit and had treated me several times since I arrived. When she turned, I caught a glimpse of her chiseled features.

Once Sessions joined them, the five of them stood to one side of the patch. I watched, waiting for something to happen. Ariadne appeared to be speaking to Sessions and Perugini while Old Man Winter watched, his mouth unmoving, and Kurt stood to the side, stamping his feet to ward off the cold. I could feel Wolfe stirring in my brain, wondering what they were up to. His thoughts matched mine, but I was trying to mask my thoughts from him. I had my doubts that it was working.

What are they waiting for, little doll?

"I don't know," I said. "Why am I bothering to answer your sick ass?"

Hard to resist the Wolfe, isn't it?

"Don't think that just because you're in my head that you have any idea what I think." There was a flicker of movement outside, and Wolfe didn't bother answering.

A helicopter descended. I recognized the type, my photographic memory reconciling what I was seeing with what I had seen in movies. It was a Black Hawk, and I could see the doors open as they descended. I saw a figure emerge, hanging out the door while waiting for the helicopter to touch down, a figure that was shorter than Old Man Winter by a lot. It was all I needed to see, and I had grabbed my coat and was slinging it on as I ran out the door.

Zack had returned.

Chapter 2

I barely remembered to put my boots on before I was off and running. On the way out of the dormitory building I felt the cold air slap me in the face, but I didn't care.

Little doll seems very happy to see the flimsy agent. Wolfe wonders if she knows how useless the little man is to her, he breaks so easy, he would burn if she touched him...

"Shut up," I said as my feet found the path and I loped along, barely keeping myself from dropping to all fours the way Wolfe's instincts were compelling me to. "I'm not a dog," I snapped to the voice in my head. "I can't run on my hands and feet the way you can—could."

But it would be so good to see you on hands and knees again... A wave of revulsion washed over me and I tried to ignore it as I cut through the wintery air. *Why is this little man so important to make you run out in the middle of the night?*

"He's not..." I stopped talking when I realized I was giving the psycho in my head more fodder for taunting me. Besides, why was I running to see Zack? When last we had parted, it had been after he had extracted a promise from me to not go after Wolfe, a promise I had broken. Afterward, I had spent some time examining my thinking behind that promise and found it lacking; I believed I made it because Zack was hot. Tall, with tousled hair, brown eyes and in amazing shape. Downside: I suspected he was spying on me for Old Man Winter and Ariadne.

At that moment, I didn't care. Of all the people I had met since leaving my house, Zack was the one I felt most connected to. After he left, things around the Directorate got much worse and—I hated to admit it—I missed having someone to talk to who was close to my own age. It's not like I had a ton of time to get used to it before he left, but still...I missed him. I felt a tingle of amusement that I knew came from Wolfe, and wished, not for the first time, that I could mentally slap the hell out of him.

I covered the ground between the dorm and the helipad quickly, arriving just after the helicopter set down. None of the observers noticed me as I slipped up behind them and I felt a thrill of predatory success as I stared at their backs and realized I could kill every last one of them.

I would have been disturbed by that, but Wolfe's thoughts were bleeding into mine with such regularity that unless he "spoke" in my head, I couldn't be sure whether it genuinely came from me.

I lurked behind them, and saw Ariadne say something to Dr. Perugini that caused Old Man Winter to look back at them both. "He was stable for transit," Ariadne said, then the rotors cut out her next words before I caught a few more, "...amazed they were able to catch him, really." Old Man Winter looked past Ariadne and noticed me. He stared, his eyes into mine, before nodding in acknowledgment. He spoke, something low, but loud enough that those around him heard it and looked, each of them finding me in turn.

I moved forward to join them, figuring that lurking in the shadows was a pointless game. I saw Zack, dressed in a paramilitary uniform, olive green overalls with a tactical vest, a submachine gun slung under his arm, and a headset covering his ears. He stepped down and tossed the headset back into the chopper. I could see him saying something to the figures inside.

He turned and strode across the pad to Old Man Winter. I half-expected him to salute, as though I were watching a war movie, but he leaned in and whispered something to his boss. While he did so, others were stepping out of the Black Hawk, four of them, in quick fashion. M-Squad, I figured.

A stir of interest from Wolfe kept me watching them rather than Zack. The first one off the chopper was a man. He had a jaw that looked like it had been carved from an iron bar. It extended down, giving him the look of someone who perpetually stuck his chin out. His skin was dark, his hair black and short, military-style, stubble on the sides and just a patch of black on top. I couldn't tell what color eyes he had because of the dark, but they were moving fast and they were focused. They found me in the dark, surveyed me—not in the dirty way Wolfe had, but as a potential opponent.

The next off the Black Hawk was a woman. Her hair was short, blond, cropped in one of those boyish, pixie styles of someone who has no time and no interest in impressing anyone with it. Her facial structure was pronounced, Nordic, but her skin was tanned. She saw me, too, and watched me for long enough to do an assessment of her own. She was so severe, I wondered if she ever smiled.

The third off the chopper was a man with long, gray hair and a beard that matched it. The rotor blades stirred his silver locks, blowing them into his eyes, but it didn't seem to distract him. He gave me the same once-over as the others and halted by the door to the chopper.

The last guy off surprised me. I'm not going to mince words: he was fat. Not the size of a house or anything, but he was a big boy. The others were muscular, but his belly hung out under his fatigues. He was laughing about something as his feet hit the ground, but none of his teammates were laughing with him. His grin was not a happy one; for some reason I got a little dash of an unsettling feeling from looking at him.

He reached into the chopper and pulled something out, slinging it over his shoulder to carry. It was a tube, about six feet long, a couple feet wide and a foot deep. It reminded me of an oversized coffin at first glance.

Actually, it reminded me of the box my mother used to put me in, but smaller and more compact.

The big guy joined his comrades and the four of them walked across the helipad as the Black Hawk spun up the rotors and lifted back into the air. I turned my attention to Old Man Winter, who had finished his conversation with Zack.

Zack moved to talk to Kurt. The two of them were partners the day they came to collect me from my house. I didn't know if they still worked together, because they'd had something of a falling out after Kurt tried to hit me at one point. I wasn't sure if Zack knew what had happened since then, but I doubt he'd be excited to know that his partner had driven me to an encounter with Wolfe.

I caught a subtle look as he was talking to Kurt. He held eye contact for just a second longer than he had to, and I saw a smile.

Ariadne broke away from the crowd and walked over to me. "You should be sleeping," she said, resting a careful, gloved hand on my shoulder.

"Am I not allowed to be here?" My words came out more bitter than I had intended. I thought that was because of Wolfe's influence, but given my past history with Ariadne, there was a strong possibility that it was all me.

"No," she said, remaining cool in spite of my acrid tone, "I just meant that I assumed you would be resting."

"I heal fast." I looked past her, trying to catch Zack's eye again. "I've rested enough, anyway." That was more defensive.

"I heard you broke into the cafeteria after it closed and took some food." She watched for my reaction.

I froze, trying to keep my eyes from widening. Had I done that? I managed to speak after a short pause that I hoped she attributed to my guilt at being found out. "It's better for all involved if I don't have to go to the cafeteria when I don't want to. Safer, really. It's like a public service." With the flight of the Black Hawk, things had gotten quieter on the helipad. "I'm surprised you don't have a helipad on the roof of Headquarters." I was desperate to change the subject by that point.

"We do." Ariadne crossed her arms and looked back at M-Squad. "But it'll be easier for Clary to carry his...cargo..." She nodded to the burden that the fat guy was carrying over his shoulder, "...to the science labs without having to navigate an elevator or stairwell."

"Big guy like that?" I inclined my head toward the coffin. "He looks like he can carry a lead casket for a ways." I stared at the object, but he had it inclined so that I couldn't see anything but the bottom and sides. I was beyond curious about what it contained; I wondered if it was the mysterious reason why M-Squad had been in South America for so long.

"I'm sure he can. But it's delicate, and it would be best if it were undamaged." She smiled, a tight, insincere one that told me worlds about how much of my question she was avoiding answering.

"Hey." Zack appeared in front of me, Kurt a few steps behind him.

"Hey," I said, feeling like the single greatest idiot in the world for repeating his greeting back to him. Genius level IQ, and I was still reduced to this by a boy. FML. (Yes, I know what it means.)

"I heard you broke your promise." He didn't come off as accusatory, which surprised me, and yet, didn't. If he was spying on me, getting into an argument seemed counterproductive. "But I also heard you killed Wolfe, so...good job." On the other hand, maybe he was just happy that Wolfe was dead. I knew I was.

If I was dead, I wouldn't be talking to you.

Shut up, I thought with all my might. I must have grimaced while thinking it, because Zack raised an eyebrow. "Yeah...I'm sorry. I just couldn't wait for you guys to get back." I looked away from him.

"Damn shame you killed Wolfe," the fat guy from M-Squad said, loud enough that it told me he'd been eavesdropping. I turned to find him leering at me; well, not so much me as my body; his eyes were looking below the equator and moving up slowly. "I was looking forward to tangling with him. But if he can get himself killed by a little girl, " he said with a laugh that sounded like a bark, " I guess he wasn't so tough, was he?"

"You're a moron, Clary," said the leader, the first guy off the helicopter from M-Squad. "You're just lucky most people judge by appearances, like you do, and write your fat ass off or you'd be dead ten times over."

"You think I'm fat?" One of Clary's eyes had squinted, drawing his puffy cheek up his face and causing it to wrinkle. "This is three hundred and twenty pounds of ripped steel." He waved a hand over his body. "And the ladies love it."

"The next lady to love your body will be the first, I'd wager." I said it before I knew I had, and heard the snickers from M-Squad, Dr. Perugini and Zack. Even Kurt seemed amused by my barb. The old guy in M-Squad let a low, rolling guffaw of purest amusement. "Unless you're resorting to picking up lovers from the graveyard," I said, pointing at the object on his shoulder, "in which case they're not loving you so much as—"

Clary turned a bright red and I watched him clutch the coffin a little tighter, and he let out a loud grunt. "I'm not gonna sit here and be insulted by some tweener punkass bitch."

"Yeah, you've got important things to do," the older guy spoke up. "You were talking about your damned motorcycle the whole time we were gone. You gonna go ride your 'phat hog'?"

Clary's embarrassment turned to glee. "Naw, your mom said she's busy tonight." He let out a high, long burst of laughter, one that was obviously fake, and turned to Dr. Sessions, slapping him on his skinny back and nearly waylaying the good doctor. "Come on, Doc, this son of a bitch is getting heavy."

I watched Doc Sessions nod and turn, leading the way toward the science building, Clary in tow and Perugini following behind them. When he turned to follow Sessions, the coffin dipped and I saw the top of it for the first time as he repositioned it to carry it like a backpack. It was flat, with a small window, just enough to show something glowing within, like fire in a bottle. He dipped it lower, and I saw something else—

Eyes. There were eyes staring at me from within. Plaintive, begging, filled with a fear that I knew all too well; the fear of a captive confined, one who might never take another free breath again.

Chapter 3

"Who is that?" I asked Ariadne. I turned and caught a flash of her face pinched as though she had just pulled a splinter from her finger. I turned to Zack, and he looked away.

"Aleksandr Timofeyevich Gavrikov," the leader of M-Squad said to me. "One of the most dangerous metas you'll ever meet." He nodded at the capsule on Clary's back. "That's a containment cell Dr. Sessions designed to keep metas that have high energy projection abilities under control—without it Gavrikov could fry everyone."

"How'd you catch him, then?" I didn't throw any undue sarcasm into the words; I was curious.

"By not getting anywhere near him," the Nordic woman said, a slight smirk curling her flat lips.

"I think introductions are in order," Ariadne said. "Sienna Nealon, this is Roberto Bastian," she nodded to the leader, then to the woman, "Eve Kappler and Glen Parks," she indicated the older guy, who gave me a genuine smile, one that (surprisingly) didn't creep me out. "And of course the other gentleman," she strained at the word, "was Clyde Clary."

"Don't call him Clyde," Parks said, his gray beard reminding me of a thousand grandfathers I'd seen on TV. "It doesn't bring out the sparkling side of his personality."

"Sure it does," Eve said. "He sparkles like broken glass—then cuts you." Her smile became a smirk, a self-satisfied look that either Wolfe or I found insufferable and wanted to destroy along with the rest of her sculpted face. I think that was Wolfe. Mostly.

"Sir." Roberto turned to Old Man Winter. "Would you like us

to make our report now or in the morning?"

Old Man Winter kept his silence. Everyone waited for his pronouncement, which came with all the gravity his position and deep voice afforded. "Come to my office at noon. We have other matters to discuss."

"Yes, sir." Roberto saluted, then nodded to Glen and Eve, and the three of them headed toward the dormitory building, Kurt in tow.

I looked back to Clary and Sessions, almost to the science building now. The capsule carrying Aleksandr Gavrikov looked heavy, and Clary was struggling to readjust it again. *Let him loose*, Wolfe said from somewhere in the depths of my brain.

Shut up, I told him, as if that would work.

If you let him loose, Wolfe will tell you what he knows about your mommy.

Son of a bitch. That immediately put me on guard; if Wolfe wanted someone out of confinement, there was no stronger indication that said person should remain under lock and key, preferably buried under several tons of soil, indefinitely.

You don't know anything, I thought back to him. *You're just lying to get your way.*

He was quiet for a split second, and a thought floated to the surface of my mind. *3586 Curie Way, Bloomington, Minnesota.*

I blinked, and Ariadne caught it. "Tired?"

"No." My mind was racing. "Just remembering something. Wolfe mentioned an address—3586 Curie Way in Bloomington. Is that close?" It wasn't a lie; I didn't say when he had mentioned it.

Zack, Ariadne and Old Man Winter were the only ones remaining on the helipad. Zack was the one who answered. "It's about forty minutes away. Ten minutes south of your house."

"Wolfe gave you this address?" Ariadne looked skeptical. Old Man Winter looked blank, as always.

"He did."

"Why would he give you an address?" Her eyes were narrowed, and you could see her crunching the odds in her head—wondering if it was some sort of trap. Leave it to Ariadne to ask the tough questions I wanted to avoid. I guess it could have been a trap, but if it was, it seemed counterproductive for Wolfe to kill me, since he lived in my head. I had this feeling that even after thousands of years of life, he was clinging to even this little half-life in my skull like lint clings to a sweater.

I chose my words carefully so as to avoid a flat-out lie. "I don't think he intended for me to survive our final encounter." True enough. "So anything he mentioned wouldn't have mattered, would it?"

I looked from her to Old Man Winter then Zack. All three of them were studying me with varying degrees of suspicion, which worried me. Even though what I was saying was technically true, I was leaving a lot out—lying by omission. Based on my experience with Mom, who could always tell when I was being false, I was a bad liar. Ariadne shot a look at Old Man Winter, who had a cocked eyebrow and very little else to tell me what was going through his mind. Zack was looking at the snow.

"Zack," Old Man Winter spoke. "You and Kurt will take Sienna to the address she provided." He turned, gracefully for a man with such a tall frame, and lumbered down the path to Headquarters.

The worry was evident on Ariadne's face. "Be careful," she said to Zack and me before following Old Man Winter.

Zack had his cell phone out and was already talking on it. I could tell it was Kurt by the way he was speaking. His cheeks were red and he shivered as he ended the conversation; I realized for the first time he wasn't wearing a coat. "You're cold," I said, feeling a blush for being so stupid as to state the obvious.

"Yeah, I should have grabbed a coat at the airport before we got on the chopper, but for some reason it slipped my mind. Was in a hurry to get back here, I guess." He cast a sidelong look at the retreating backs of Ariadne and Old Man Winter. "I get the feeling that you're not telling us everything you know about that address."

"Oh, no," I said, "I've told you all I know about the address; it's as much of a mystery to me as it is to you."

"And Wolfe just...gave it to you?" His brow was furrowed and one eye seemed to be more closed than the other.

Now I had to be even more careful if I was going to avoid outright lying. "He hurt me pretty bad during the last fight, slammed me through a concrete wall." I tried to recall the final battle. "I don't know; maybe he was talking to someone else. I think I lost consciousness for a few minutes at that point." That was true.

"I see," he said. Doubt flowed through his words, and he wasn't looking at me. I felt a drop in my stomach. I hated lying to him, but I had to know what was at Wolfe's address. "Kurt's meeting us in the garage in five minutes."

I needed to know where Mom was, and I was sure that Wolfe knew something he wasn't telling me. I doubted she was there, but I also didn't think he'd give me the address if there wasn't some hint as to her whereabouts. Damn him; he was dead and he was still toying with me. I had to wonder if I'd ever be free of him.

I fell into step beside Zack, feeling the wind play through my hair, hoping it was blowing it in a sexy way. I self-consciously ran my fingers through it and found it to be tangled instead. I yanked my hand down as he turned to look at me, and I swore I could hear Wolfe's cackle ring through my head. In that moment I regretted he no longer had a physical body because I wanted more than anything to kick him in the balls.

"I have to ask," Zack started, and he looked at me, those brown eyes shining in the light of the helipad's spotlights, "Did you know you could beat Wolfe when you went after him?"

"What?" I was caught off guard by the question. I hoped it

showed on my face. "No, I didn't think I had a chance against him. That afternoon I watched him wipe out a SWAT team and a half-dozen police officers without taking so much as a scratch. I didn't think anything could kill him." I lowered my head, and felt a tingle of fear at the memory. "That's why I went. Only I could stop him."

"That's pretty damn brave," Zack said with a shake of his head. "I don't know too many people who'd throw themselves into the fire like that."

"It didn't feel brave." I felt a cold unrelated to the weather, something much deeper inside. "Someone who was brave would have confronted their problem long before I did, long before all those people died. What I did felt inevitable—and I just wanted it over."

"Most people," he said, "Wouldn't have forced a confrontation with that maniac after their first encounter with him. You did." He shook his head, I think in amazement. "How many eight-een-year-olds—"

"I'm still seventeen."

"How many seventeen-year-olds do you think would get choked out by some lunatic and then willingly go back for another round?" He laughed. "You're brave, Sienna. Maybe the bravest person I've ever met."

I felt a thrill at his words, then felt it go as I recalled the cold facts of the situation. "Yeah, but that second round cost you guys eight people. All so I could try and fight him."

"You didn't know that was going to happen."

"But I should have!" I felt hot, like something under my sweater was causing my skin to catch fire. "I was so focused on myself, trying to get what I wanted that I didn't worry about any-one else." I thought about that day, and suddenly it felt a little too close to what was happening now. Wolfe played his game and he did it his way; it was not unreasonable to think he might have allies left behind at the address he gave me, or a trap, or worse. I looked back at Zack, watched the mist from my breath blow in the air. "I need you to take me to the address and then wait in the car."

"Are you kidding?" His reaction was immediate dismissal. He didn't get angry, he scoffed. "I'm not letting you go in alone."

"I have to." I stopped walking, and he took another couple steps before he realized I wasn't alongside him and stopped too. "Wolfe doesn't play nice."

"I'm not helpless," Zack still stayed away from anger, but I could see the beginnings of annoyance in the way his eyes were wrinkling at the sides and how his mouth had moved from a smile to a flat line. "I can hold my own in a fight. Just because I'm not a meta—"

"It's not that you're not a meta." I aimed for gentle, soothing words. "If Wolfe set a claymore mine as a trap and it blows off my foot, it grows back." I gestured at him. "You'd never walk again."

I could see the wheels spinning as he struggled to put together an effective response. He started to say something, then stopped short, frustration pinching his handsome features. "I can't let you go in by yourself." His words came out mangled, as if he was at war internally. "But you have a point. Wolfe's not known for being subtle with his violence, so..." he took on the air of a man proposing a bitter compromise, "I'd be willing to let you lead the way while Kurt and I follow at a safe distance."

"A mile?"

"About ten feet. I doubt Wolfe bothered with explosives." He was firm; there was no more room to negotiate. I nodded and started to walk again. "And you don't know," he said, falling into step beside me.

"Don't know what?" I asked, confused.

"You don't know what would happen if you got an arm or a leg blown off. Yeah, it may grow back, or it may not."

"I heal pretty fast," I said. "I've regrown an awful lot of skin since I met you."

"Ouch."

"That's what I said." Deadpan. Perfect. He grinned at my wisecrack and I smiled back.

He walked a few more paces and I saw him gnaw on his lower lip. He turned his head to look at me. "You don't blame me for all the hell you've been through since..."

"Since you and Kurt rousted me out into the world?" I shrugged. "If it wasn't you, it was gonna be Reed or Wolfe. Reed might have been gentler," I needled him, giving him a wry smile, "but it all worked out, I suppose." Except I now had a psychotic mutant squatting in my brain.

"Yeah." He opened the door to the parking garage and held it for me. "I guess it did."

I heard Zack beside me, the squeak of the rubber soles of his boots on the tile floors, heard his breathing. I caught a whiff of his cologne and took a deep breath through my nose. I could feel the heat from the exchange positioned in the entrance nearby blowing on me.

Kurt Hannegan was waiting by the car, a thoroughly disgusted look marring his otherwise ugly face. I put my emotional turmoil to the side, because however bad I was feeling, I wanted to make sure that Hannegan felt worse. Again, if I could blame this on Wolfe, I would, but the truth is I loved pissing him off.

"Let's get this over with," he said with a grunt. He was wearing a tweed suit coat with brown patches on the elbow and a brown tie to contrast with his white shirt and dark pants. He had tried to comb the meager hair he had left on the sides of his head to the top in an attempt to...I dunno, revive the glory days, I guess, but it failed.

"You mean you haven't been looking forward to this?" I said, feigning hurt. "Kurt, didn't you miss me?"

"No."

"Sure you did," I said. "You missed me with your little pop-gun the first time we met. I think it's a metaphor for our entire relationship."

He looked at me, wary. "That I'll always be shooting at you?"

"And I'll always be dodging and kicking your ass."

We got in and he drove out of the garage without another word. It was a heated structure, with space enough for a couple hundred cars. The Directorate maintained a fleet of vehicles, along with the countless other things they kept—Black Hawk helicopters, weird and experimental weaponry, a host of agents, facilities all over the U.S. and the world. I had to wonder who funded it all, who ran the whole show, and what the real purpose was, if it was something different than what I'd been told.

Kurt kept the speedometer pushing eighty most of the way. We streaked through the farmland that surrounded the Directorate, zipping along a state highway until we got on the freeway loop that circled Minneapolis and St. Paul. We headed east, as the sky showed the faintest hint of lightening in that direction.

After about twenty minutes we exited onto a street that held houses on one side and warehouses on the other. My pulse quickened as we neared our destination; I didn't think we'd find Mom, but I wondered what Wolfe was playing at. If he'd given me the address, there had to be a reason for it. It couldn't just be a dead end.

We turned onto a side street filled with small warehouses, all gray, all run down and drab, and Kurt stopped the car. We all stared at one in particular, with shiny brass numbers reading 3586 hanging on its dingy concrete block walls above a steel door.

I was out of the car a few seconds after it stopped, Zack and Kurt hurrying behind me. When I looked back, Kurt was looking around, nervous, and had his hand resting on his gut. I assumed it was because it was within easy reach of his gun, but maybe he just liked it there.

"We're gonna need a minute to pick the lock," Zack said when we reached the door. I shook my head, grabbed the handle and pulled. I heard a creaking before the mechanism broke free, the metal handle tearing from the door. I reached inside and pushed the guts of the lock out, then ripped the door open. I didn't wait for either of them to comment before I walked in, pausing inside to give my eyes a chance to adjust to the dimness.

It was all one big room with concrete floors and corrugated metal walls. There was a lump over in the far corner and I went toward it. The soles of my boots tapped against the bare concrete and each step sounded like doom as it echoed off the metal walls. As I got closer to the shape, my hand came up to cover my nose; a horrible smell filled the air and it got worse as I got closer and closer.

Zack and Kurt had flashlights on behind me, and I gestured for one of them to hand me theirs. Zack did. The beam played along the ground as I went toward the mass. It was big enough to be a person, it wasn't moving, and I hoped I wasn't about to find one of Wolfe's greatest hits.

"It smells like he killed something in here." Kurt gagged as he spoke, the choked glottal stop sound sending an echo of its own off the walls.

"Maybe he's keeping trophies," Zack said.

"You mean...body parts?" Hannegan didn't bother to hide his revulsion at the thought.

"I don't think Wolfe was a collector," I said. I knew it somehow, the same way I knew everything else, even though he wasn't talking to me right now. He was watching, waiting for me to find out what he'd left for me. I kicked the lump with my toe. It didn't move or squirm or anything. I knelt down, the flashlight shaking a little, and pushed at it. It was soft, cloth, and filthy.

I grasped it and it lifted with ease, a blanket all balled up. I shook it and it unfurled, and I sighed as I realized what it was.

"Bedding?" Kurt asked. "Is that...is that his bed?"

"Yeah. All balled up, like he was a hamster or something." I felt Wolfe bristle at my comparison, but I was annoyed. I shook it again out of a sense of irritation, and something came loose within the depths; I felt it moving inside. I shook it again and felt it tumble down, falling out of the sodden, filthy blanket.

I tossed the bedding aside and stooped to retrieve what dropped. It was a purse. Black, leather, no longer than my arm and with a broken strap. I opened it and shined the light inside. Frustrated, I turned it upside down and let the contents spill out to the floor. Lipstick, a cell phone, a few other odds and ends, and a wallet.

I picked up the wallet and noticed the name on the driver's license before I saw the face: Brittany Eccleston.

The picture was of my mom.

Chapter 4

"How did you get this?" I mumbled the words, but I knew Kurt and Zack could hear them. I just hoped they assumed I misspoke or was talking rhetorically to Wolfe, who, as far as they knew, was not there.

Many, many stories I could tell you...but I have my price. The words were taunting, teasing. I killed him and he was still an absolute shit to me. At least he wasn't around to physically abuse me anymore.

"You think he got your mom?" Zack's voice was laden with concern, and it sounded genuine.

Kurt was more analytical. "No way to tell without more evidence." He pointed. "The strap's broken; he could have just ripped it off of her. The I.D. has her address on it, " he nodded to me. "This explains how he found her."

I wondered if I could chance another interrogatory toward Wolfe without attracting the curiosity of Zack and Kurt, but I decided against it. He'd wanted me to find this, to get curious, so I would do what he wanted. Maybe he knew more, maybe he didn't. All I was certain of was that he wanted Aleksandr Gavrikov out of that containment cell, and that scared me.

"Anything else in here?" It was Zack who asked the question, but Kurt who started shining his light around. The warehouse looked empty, abandoned.

"I don't see anything." I shone my flashlight to the corners, but all I saw were metal walls, through and through. I turned and started to say something but stopped and froze in fear as Kurt Hannegan got slapped down hard. The big man hit his knees and an arm wrapped around his neck. I watched his face turn red as he was dragged back to his feet, his portly body interposed between us and his assailant.

"Hi, Sienna," came a mild voice, a familiar one.

I shone the flashlight at the man who held Kurt. "Reed, what are you doing?"

I hadn't seen him since the day I killed Wolfe; he had fled from the basement before the Directorate arrived. He was muscular and it showed, even through his leather jacket. His dark skin stood out in contrast to Hannegan's face, which was turning red. His long brown hair was in a ponytail and he held a gun pointed at me then Zack, in turn.

"Well, well," Zack said, his own gun out and pointed at Reed. "If it isn't your old friend."

"Friend, enemy," I said, wary, "when they're pointing a gun at you, what's the difference?"

"A friend doesn't pull the trigger." Reed clubbed Kurt on the head, and I watched the big man's eyes roll up as he went unconscious. Zack tensed, as though he were about to shoot, but Reed held the gun up in surrender as he let Hannegan sink to the ground, letting him slide to the floor gently. "I have to talk to Sienna." He looked at me. "I don't want your boyfriend listening in either, but I'm willing to let him walk away instead of sending him off into the clouds."

"You can try—" Zack snapped.

"I can do it," Reed said. "You eager to cross me? I'm a meta, you're a Directorate agent. Do you want to find out what my power is just so you can try to keep her from having a conversation?"

Zack did not flinch nor lower his weapon. "You want to talk to her? Talk. She's right there."

"If I wanted the entire Directorate leadership to hear what I have to say to her, I'd visit your campus." Reed's lip curled at the end.

"You should come visit. I'd love to see you out there; it'd be fun to watch M-Squad beat you down and throw you in a holding cell for interrogation." Zack's eyes were narrowed, the gun still pointed at Reed. "I'm not letting her out of my sight."

"I'll go over to the corner with him, we'll talk," I said to Zack, who looked sidelong at me, mutinous. "It'll be fine. " I worried when he didn't blink, but he finally gave me a subtle nod of the head. He kept the gun pointed, following Reed, who joined me in a corner. "All right," I said when we were out of Zack's earshot, "what's so damned important that you had to crack Hannegan over the head?"

"That?" Reed chucked a thumb over his shoulder where Zack was nudging Kurt with his foot, trying to rouse him without taking the gun off Reed. "That was for him driving you back to your house when you went after Wolfe the last time." Reed's expression darkened. "It was only because you discovered your power that you even survived." He glanced back to Hannegan, who had yet to stir. "But you're still hanging around with him—with them."

"I haven't been presented with any other options," I said, bitterness inflecting my tone. "In case you forgot, right after I killed Wolfe, you freaked out on me and bailed."

"I didn't bail on you," he said. "I got the hell out of there before the Directorate decided to make me a test subject."

"You yelled at me."

"I'm sorry," he said with sincerity, " but I didn't want to get my soul drained. Besides," he looked wary, "I suspect your head is full enough now without me adding another voice to the chorus."

My eyes widened and I felt my jaw drop in shock. "You know?"

"If the Directorate had experience with incubi or succubi, they'd know too," Reed said. "They're trying to view metas through a scientific lens, and there's not one big enough yet to explain how metas work. Take this Gavrikov they just caught, for example," he said with a smile. "Explain to me scientifically how someone can fly without wings or sprout fire from their skin without burning it off?" He shrugged. "Maybe there's a scientific explanation, but it's so far outside our grasp right now that we might as well be talking about myth and magic, like the ancients used to describe us."

"How did you know about Gavrikov?" I kept my voice hushed.

"Everyone in the meta world knows about Gavrikov. He's been a legend and a whisper since he detonated in Russia a hundred plus years ago."

I squinted at him, trying to recall. "The Tunguska blast? I read that was a meteor."

His smile grew deeper. "There was no meteor; there was Gavrikov." He shrugged. "Or so the rumor goes."

"How goes the rumor about me?" I tightened my jaw.

He nodded, the smile sticking in place on his face, but no longer sincere. "It goes that your mother, Sierra Nealon, who everyone thought was dead, is a succubus, and has a daughter just like her. Whip smart, stronger than any other ten metas combined, and currently hiding behind the tender mercies of Old Man Winter in Minneapolis."

I absorbed his words. People whom I had never met were discussing me, as though I were some commodity waiting to be bartered. "How did you know I was here?"

"I've been watching the place for a few days, waiting for..." he hesitated, "...someone. Wolfe didn't bother to cover his tracks, so I expect the police will be here in the next day or so." He cast a look around. "Hope you found what you were looking for, because this is likely your last shot at this place."

I held up my mom's purse and I.D. "Know anything about my mom?"

Reed was cool when he answered. "A few things. Where she worked, known associates from before she disappeared, that sort of stuff." He looked back to Kurt, who was sitting up now. "Nothing I can share while you're still with them."

"You got a better deal for me?" I stared him down. "Because as I recall, when Wolfe was hot on my heels, you told me to stay put."

He shrugged. "Here in the U.S., I don't have a quarter of the force the Directorate could use to defend you. In fact, I'm with an organization that's big overseas, not so much here. The Directorate is king of meta activity on this continent, for now. But if you want to come with me..."

"Where?"

"Can't say until you decide to come along." He shrugged again. "Sorry for the secrecy, but we're not on the Directorate's radar and I'm of a mind to keep it that way."

I looked at him pityingly. "You just knocked out one of their agents; I think you're on their radar now."

"Heh, maybe me," he said, "but not we. They don't know who I work for. And I suspect it'll remain that way for some time."

I looked at him, a hard, long look. "Forget the background stuff. Do you know where my mom is?"

I saw pity flood his face, along with a sincere regret. "I don't. I'm sorry. If I knew anything that I thought would help, I'd tell you, but I don't. There are a lot of people looking for her, and not just from the Directorate. All the major players have people in town, but I think she's gone quiet. Maybe Wolfe got after her, maybe something else spooked her, but if she could disappear for all those years with you, she can hide even better without someone else to slow her down. Not to say you slowed her down."

"No, it's fine," I said. "I'm sure I did; it's probably why I was locked away all those years, to keep her profile low."

"Or to keep you out of harm's way." His voice got softer and his eyes lost their gleam. "These people that are after you now? At least you have the power to fight back. Imagine Wolfe coming after you when you were seven."

I shuddered, and deep inside felt Wolfe stir with interest at that idea. A few images floated to the surface of my mind, of places I'd never been, people I'd never met—young girls, all. I could taste bile rising in the back of my mouth and wished for nothing so much as the ability to drive his frightening psyche from my head. "That would have been bad. So what now for you?"

"I'll be around," he said. "I assume you're not taking me up on my offer?"

I lowered my voice even more. "Can you get this maniac out of my head?"

He looked over to where Zack and Kurt were waiting for me. "I don't think so. Once he's in, he's part of you from now on." He shrugged. "There aren't many experts on what you're going through, and I don't work with any. Counting you, there are three succubi on record. Only a couple of incubi."

I rubbed my head. "I'm losing my mind. I don't know how any of this works." I snorted in wry amusement. "I don't even know how my mom had me without killing my father, whoever he was." I thought about it for a moment. "Hell, maybe she did." I shook my head. "I know nothing about myself, where I came from, who my mother really is. You can tell me a little more, but I'd have to leave and go somewhere mysterious, somewhere outside the country?" He looked at me and nodded, and I knew he realized my decision was made. "Sorry," I said. "I think I'm gonna stick it out here a while longer."

"I figured. Like I said, I'll be around." He smiled, and with a gloved hand he brushed my cheek, sending a tingle through me. "You know how to get in touch with me." He turned and started away.

"Bad choice of words," I said to him with an impish smile. "I think the last thing you want is me touching you."

"There are worse ways to go." He laughed, shook his head, and disappeared out the door.

Chapter 5

After I watched him leave, I returned to where Zack and Kurt waited for me. The older man held his head, and let out a near hissing sound when I approached. "Every time I go somewhere with you..." he said.

"You blame this on me? Last time we went somewhere together, I believe you made it out just fine." I smiled, and a look of panic crossed his features; the eyes widened, his mouth opened slightly and I would have bet his mouth was drier than the air outside. He looked at Zack, who was frowning. "I don't see anything else," I said, changing the subject to spare Kurt. "We can leave."

"Let me be the first to say, 'Thank God' at the thought of getting outta here," Kurt said with a grunt. He led the way, and I looked around, not quite forlorn but wondering if I was missing something, some subtle clue that might tell me more about where Mom was. I stared at the dark corners of the warehouse, as though I could sift the secrets out of the shadows if I only concentrated long enough.

"Come on," Zack said. I looked back to find him standing behind me, and his eyes were warm. He put a hand on my shoulder, and even through the heavy cloth I felt the gentle pressure. I didn't want to but I felt myself involuntarily close my eyes and wondered what it would feel like without his glove or my coat and shirt.

I forced a smile and buried that thought as Kurt yelled from the door. "Come on!" Without waiting for us, he pushed through to outside. Zack and I were only a few steps behind him as the door started to close, but before it did something silvery appeared with a flash and hit Kurt, sending the older man spiraling out of our field of vision.

I hesitated but was quicker to move than Zack. I burst out the door, felt my shoes hit the snow, the frigid air slamming me in the face followed by a metal-encased hand cracking me in the cheek. My feet left the ground and I landed in the snow. My jaw was on fire, and I felt the biting cold of the wet mush run down my collar. Before I had time to cry out, something punched me in the back of the head, and I felt a hand lift me to my feet.

I was dazed, but even so I recognized that what was in front of me seemed wrong. It was shaped like a man, but covered in metal. The figure was angular and the chest was boxy, like a robot I'd seen once in a movie. The head was roughly cylindrical with a rounded dome, giving me a flashback to the time Mom let me watch Iron Man on TV. I saw a metal fist raise and I squirmed to get out of the grasp of the metal man before the blow reached me.

I felt my coat rip along the collar as I pulled down and put my weight into it. Much as I might wish I was lighter when I looked in the mirror, I was thankful at that moment that I didn't look like a model as I slipped underneath the punch he had leveled at me. The metal man followed through and I heard a crunch. I rolled across the snow and to my feet, looking back to see he'd buried his hand in the concrete wall all the way to the elbow.

As he struggled to pull his hand back out, I realized he was grunting, which meant he wasn't a robot. I can't tell you how thankful I was in that moment; I was afraid that someone had perfected some sort of seeker droid and turned it loose on me. "All right, Full Metal Jackass," I said to him. "You want a fight, you sucker-punching Tony Stark wannabe?" I cracked my knuckles. "I'll give you a fight."

I darted low as he came at me again. I could tell from his breathing that the armor had some weight and heft to it. His fist whistled through the air in front of my face as he winged another punch at me. After it passed, I raised up and gave him a solid kick to the gut, just like I would have back when Mom and I broke boards in the basement. After all, I was a super-powerful meta, right? I should be able to break through steel; I had before, after all.

I heard a crack as I connected and realized that something had broken, all right—but I was pretty sure it was my foot. Full Metal Jackass went staggering back and fell over, which was the only saving grace in the whole thing, because I dropped to the ground, clutching at my foot, which felt like I had slammed it in a door well over a hundred times. I let out a stream of curses as I went down.

As I lay on the ground, clutching my appendage and plumbing the depths of my error in judgment, I tried to roll over. I had enough presence of mind to realize that the metallic monkey wasn't going to be down for as long as I was and that I needed to do something to avoid him and that screaming and rolling around wasn't going to do it. I got to one knee as I saw him rising to his feet, a hulking metal goliath. His eyes were two slits, and behind them I could see pupils staring back at me as I rested my weight on one leg. I raised my hand in a defensive posture that was purely for show; I doubted I'd be able to effectively evade him while hobbling.

"Hey Man of Steel!" Zack's shout caused him to turn. I saw Zack holding a very familiar weapon in both his hands. He'd been to the trunk of the car, clearly. "I bet you think you're invincible, beating up a girl like that. Boy, are you in for a shock."

I cringed, partly from his pun, partly from the ache in my foot as Zack discharged the weapon into the metal-suited man. A forked bolt of lightning arced from the barrel and made contact with the front plate of Full Metal Jackass's armor. The metal man shuddered only slightly, and then took a menacing step toward Zack, then another, before breaking into a run toward him, the electricity diffusing harmlessly off the metal as though it weren't conducting it.

I took two aggressive hops forward before the metallic tool could get any momentum and slammed into him with my shoulder, knocking him face-first into the snow. I saw a joint open between his helmet and his neck as he fell, a patch of exposed skin no wider than my fist that showed a strip of weathered flesh. I reared back, letting fly a punch aimed at the open spot. I connected and heard him shout in pain as his face slammed into his helmet, which impacted into the snow.

He started to stir and the gap in his armor closed as he lifted his head, making him effectively invulnerable again. "Let's get outta here," I said to Zack and limped my way to Kurt, slinging his bulky ass over my shoulder in a fireman's carry. I made my way to the car one hobbled step at a time. I threw Kurt in the back seat unceremoniously and heard him let out a moan as he landed on the padded cloth. I slipped into the passenger seat as Zack tossed the gun onto the floorboard at my feet.

In the rearview mirror I could see Full Metal Jackass rising to his feet as Zack floored the car. He didn't chase us, but his eye slits were watching as we slid out of the parking lot, following us until we rounded the corner and disappeared from his sight.

Chapter 6

"Do you want to grab some breakfast with me?" Zack's words shocked me enough that I think my head spun. The ride back to the Directorate had been long and filled with Kurt's surliness. I didn't even bother to defend myself as he loosed a profanity-laden tirade about Reed colluding with me that lasted until we were well out into the farmland. I felt fortunate Zack was driving because with the fat man wailing and gnashing his teeth as he was, I had no faith he could have driven the car without putting us into a snowy ditch.

I blinked at Zack, amazed that he would offer after what had just happened, and I wondered if my head was twitching like Dr. Sessions did, brain trying to understand the question that was posed. "You want me to go like this?" I gestured to my coat, which was shredded from the collar to halfway down the back and hung open, the zipper ripped from the seam. My shirt and jeans were soaked and filthy, my hair was still wet from the snow in the parking lot and I could feel the grains of dirt in it. I couldn't see my cheek but the throbbing in it told me that I had a bruise of no small scale where I had been punched.

"You look fine and the cafeteria's bound to be open by now." He smiled at me and I felt my better judgment slipping away. "I'm starving. The last leg of the flight feels like the longest trip I've ever taken. Facing off with your friends in the warehouse didn't help matters at all." His voice hit a sour note and I couldn't tell if it was because of Reed or the armored ass.

"Friends? I don't know if you saw, but that armored tool damned near took my head off." I snorted, more from annoyance than anything, and it faded fast. "All right," I said, taken aback by his...I don't know, boyish charm. I felt my stomach roll over and knew that either I was hungry or Wolfe was reacting to my mooning over Zack. Forgotten was the fact that I avoided the cafeteria and the people who visited it, those people who hated me so. I watched Kurt limp off toward the medical unit for a once-over by Dr. Perugini.

The cafeteria was showing the first signs of life when we entered, with workers behind the glass counter adding food to the display and a few people already sitting at tables. The cafeteria was huge, a massive structure with glass windows for walls that stretched a hundred feet into the air on two sides, giving it an open feeling. I looked at the edges of the room and realized for the first time that the panes along the perimeter were doors that could be opened to what I presumed was a patio outside; with the snow covering the ground it was impossible to tell, but it seemed like there was an eating area out there.

The framework of the whole thing was metal struts that held the glass in place. I wondered idly if one could climb it, then wondered why I'd ever need to. I decided that I could, probably with ease, because the segments were no more than four- or five-foot square. On the opposite side of the room I shifted my attention to the cafeteria workers. When they saw me enter the line with Zack, several of them scowled. After we had collected our food, I let Zack lead me to a table by the windows, in the corner.

Others were here, a half dozen people scattered throughout the cafeteria. One caught my eye; a young man who I'd had words with in the past, here in this room. He'd been the only one in this place with enough guts to confront me after the first incident where I'd gotten agents killed. Everyone else had just gossiped behind my back. He had a rounded nose and his dark hair was curly and cut short. He hadn't caught sight of me yet, and was focused on the doll he was sitting across from.

When I thought of her as a doll, I shuddered. Damn Wolfe. She was tanned, with blond hair that fell below her shoulders, and green eyes that seemed very alight. Her smile was wide and genuine, and left me with the feeling that she had too many teeth, or they were too big for her mouth, or something. I wasn't jealous of her good looks, really. Well, not much anyway.

"Scott," Zack called out, stirring the young man out of his conversation. He turned and saw Zack and broke into a wide grin as he stood. Zack put his tray down and they did one of those manly greetings where they gripped hands and bumped shoulders.

The man he called Scott shook his head, his smile still wide. "When did you get back?" I wondered how well they knew each other.

"Just now." He nodded to me. "Have you met Sienna Nealon yet?"

Scott's features tensed and he looked me over. "Briefly."

I felt a flash of annoyance as I remembered what I probably looked like. "Have we met?" I kept a straight face. "I don't recall."

"My God," the girl next to Scott breathed. "What happened to you?"

"I got into a fight with a guy who thought he was the Black Knight," I quipped. "It turns out he didn't get so much as a flesh wound, but maybe next time things will be different."

"Sienna, this is Scott Byerly," Zack said. "He might be in training with the agents soon." Zack nodded back at me. "You better watch out, Sienna's pretty powerful. If she decided to go into training I think she'd give you a run for your money."

"Is that so?" Scott's reply was cool, far cooler than I would have given him credit for. He seemed like a hothead based on our first meeting. "I heard she might have some power, but there was a rumor she didn't have the..." He paused, as if searching for the right word, "...motivation to use it."

Courage, he means. Wolfe was so helpful. I was seeing red, and he was encouraging me to wrap this guy's head around the nearest table edge. I had to restrain myself to keep from showing Scotty Byerly exactly how motivated I was to use my power by throwing his limp and battered body through the nearest window. I wondered if I punted him how far he'd fly before landing headfirst in the snow like a lawn dart.

"Oh, she's motivated," Zack said before I could answer. "She killed that maniac Wolfe, you know."

"I heard about that!" Scott's companion bubbled with the enthusiasm he was lacking. "It's all everyone talks about since I got here, how this crazy meta killed dozens of agents and how she," she nodded at me, oh-so-helpfully, "went into a basement with him and was the only one to come out alive." Her eyes were as glowing as they had been when talking to him.

"This is Kat Forrest," Scott looked pained as he introduced her to us. "She just got here from our Arizona campus a few days ago."

Arizona Campus? I made a mental note to ask Zack about it later. Kat seemed to vibrate as she stuck out her hand for me to shake. I did, feeling the pressure of her grasp through the leather of my glove. "So glad to meet you," she squealed, and I could tell she meant it. "I don't know that I could have done what you did, facing off with that monster."

I pulled away as soon as I could, not wanting to find out if I could drain her soul through my gloves. "Thanks," I said, with as much sincerity as I possessed. "I'm surprised that everyone's talking about me in pleasant terms. It was my understanding that I wasn't very popular around here."

"Well, you're certainly popular to talk about," Kat said, almost gushing, "but I would have to say that the overall tone hasn't been terribly flattering." She looked a little chagrined, as though it was her sad duty to inform me that people hated me. "But it's difficult being the new kid in town, I know."

"Oh, you've had people say nasty things behind your back and send you a letter telling you that they hope you get raped to death, literally?" I kept my tone light and wore a smile, even as her face fell. Dark clouds gathered around Zack's eyes, and even Scott looked taken aback.

"Who did that?" Zack's voice was a low, strained murmur.

"I don't know. Does it matter?" I said.

"Yes. I want to know who it was," Zack said. I looked back at him, and his face was dark, as though he was in shadow.

"It wasn't the sort of work that the author would want to be associated with," I said.

"I wrote it," Scott said. "And it didn't say anything about anyone hoping you got raped to death. It said we all hated you for hiding while people were dying and we're rooting for him to turn you inside out."

I saw the punch coming, and I suspected that if Scott Byerly had any power as a meta, he did too. Zack took a long windup and swing that connected with Scott's jaw. The meta fell back, landing on his rump, his hand cupping his jaw lightly. "You done?" he asked, unconcerned.

"Maybe." Zack's hand quivered at his side.

"I didn't have to tell you." Scott sat on the floor, not bothering to get up.

"Which raises an interesting question," I said. "If you're so proud of what you did, why admit to it now when you left it unsigned before?"

"I'm not proud of it," he said with a shake of his head. "My aunt and uncle lived in Minnetonka. They got killed by that maniac while he was trying to root you out. And like I told you the last time we talked, I knew a lot of those agents that died for you."

"Which time?" I asked, voice laced with bitter irony.

He looked up at me, and I could see the loathing, the intensity with which he looked at me. "Both times."

"I was there." Zack's reply came out in staccato bursts, his whole face twitching with rage. "Sienna saved my life. I wouldn't have come out of that basement if she hadn't carried me out. I'd have been another body for Wolfe to torture."

It would have been so fun, Wolfe said in my head.

"Yeah, and?" Scott vaulted to his feet with the speed and agility of a meta. "There were a lot of other guys that didn't get carried out. Guys that we've known for a long time. Then she finally goes after him and miraculously kills him?" He smirked and I resisted the urge to give him a punch that I could guarantee he wouldn't see and would feel. "Why didn't she kill him sooner?" He threw his hands out. "Hell, HOW did she kill him? That's what I want to know—and nobody's saying a word about that."

"You want to see how I killed him?" There was enough menace in my voice that Byerly actually took a step back. "No? Then mind your own business." I wondered how much of his willingness to back down was based on the fact that I looked like I'd already been through at least one fight this morning.

I steered past him, guiding my tray toward the table in the corner that we'd been heading to before our detour. I sat down, my back to all of them, and started to attack my food with more violence than was necessary. It wasn't as if the eggs were going to stage an uprising and attack me, but I speared them on the end of my fork with enough vitriol to be certain.

Zack's tray hit the table in front of me a minute or so later. I'd heard him make a modicum of peace with Scott, enough that it sounded like they'd be on speaking terms but not enough that they'd be greeting each other like they did when we entered the cafeteria. He sat across from me and ripped into a strip of bacon with displaced anger. I didn't find it funny enough at the time to overcome my irritation with (still) being the most hated person on the campus.

"Amateur bullshit," Zack pronounced after throwing his bacon strip back on his plate.

"Excuse me?" I was halfway through a mouthful of eggs.

"When we take on the job of being an agent, it's understood that we're going up against metas. Most of them aren't that powerful. Some of them are." He stared at me, his eyes smoldering. "Policing metas is a dangerous business; especially since we have no powers and no way to know if we're up against an innocent person who's never done a violent thing in his life or the next psycho criminal who'll be glad to gut you and serve you for dinner." His eyes darted left and right. "It's a hazard of the business. Scott's got no right to take you to task for those guys dying."

"Maybe," I said, noncommittal. "You didn't have to deck him for it."

Zack licked his lips. "He didn't even feel it, did he?"

"Only a little," I said. "Why'd you do it?"

"Frustration." He let out a muted exhalation combined with an exasperated sigh. "I wanted to knock the crap out of Reed, too."

"Good job showing some restraint. If Reed really is a meta, he would have pummeled you, unlike your friend." My hand left my fork behind and I rubbed the bridge of my nose. "What happened in South America?"

"I went to find M-Squad." He put his hands on the table. "I found them."

"And a flaming metahuman in a casket." I stared him down and he tried to play it off but failed. "What happened? You got sent to retrieve them, but they were gone a long time; longer than Old Man Winter thought they'd be gone."

He concentrated, as though he were bringing up details of a story. "They were sent to our facility in the Andes Mountains."

"How many facilities does the Directorate have?" I crinkled my nose, trying to make it seem like an innocent question.

"Six in North America, two in South America, two in Europe, four in Asia, one in Australia, two in Africa." His eyes darted back and forth, looking up the whole time, as though he were trying to recall. "I think that's it. Anyway, they got sent down to the Andes facility—"

"For what?"

"Because the facility went dark. Completely offline, radio blackout, silence, dead air, all that. And we hadn't even had the facility that long—"

"What?" I frowned. "Was it new?"

"No, we took it over from someone else. Are you going to stop interrupting me so I can finish my story?"

"Sorry."

"So anyway, it went offline, and Old Man Winter had a suspicion he knew why, so he sent M-Squad down there with that coffin contraption after telling them about Gavrikov."

"I thought you said they went offline?"

"They did. Somehow he knew it was Gavrikov."

"How—"

"I don't know," Zack said, exasperated. "Because it's Old Man Winter, and he knows all kinds of things he shouldn't theoretically know. Do you want to hear the rest of the story?" I nodded, and he went on. "Gavrikov was there for some reason. He had come to the facility with something in mind. He killed the entire staff—about fifty people, in case you were wondering—and set up shop. Well, M-Squad started playing feint-and-parry, trying to get him boxed in so they could force a confrontation, but he wouldn't engage them directly."

He took a breath, and I jumped in. "Before, you said Gavrikov had energy projection capability..."

"Yeah, he flies and can throw fire. I heard from M-Squad he can even explode."

"Reed mentioned that Gavrikov was responsible for the Tunguska explosion in 1908."

I watched as Zack's jaw dropped open. "You told him about

us capturing Gavrikov?"

I shook my head. "He already knew."

Zack's mouth became a hard line, his eyes looked down at the table, and I could tell he was suppressing a kind of deep internal fury. It was the wrong moment for it, but I actually thought it was damned cute. Outwardly, I gave no sign. I hope. "How did he know?" he asked, restraining whatever anger he was feeling.

"I didn't ask."

"If ever you get a chance again," Zack said, measuring his words, "do ask. This is something that only a dozen people in the world knew as of this morning."

"Sure. Though I think you're naïve if you believe he'd tell me. So did he explode for you guys? Wipe out a few square miles of real estate in the Andes?"

Zack was distracted, but he went on. "Not quite, but I guess Clary had him pinned in a building at one point and he blew up, left nothing but a crater. It took Clary a while to climb out of that one. Anyway, Gavrikov has a shield of fire around his skin, so tranq darts can't make it through—"

"So how did they get him?" I was getting impatient. I blame Wolfe. He didn't have much to do with this one, actually, but I blame him anyway.

"It was pretty ingenious, I thought," Zack said with a smile. "He wasn't willing to leave the facility. He'd just fly to a different building whenever they came for him, throw some fire if they got close, do anything to keep them at bay while he jetted off—"

"He doesn't sound so dangerous," I said. "Except for the fifty people he killed, I suppose." I felt sheepish. *He sounds like fun*, Wolfe thought. *You should let him out.* I ignored him.

"Anyway," Zack went on, "they managed to set a trap for him when I got there. They used me as bait."

"What?!"

"Well, I went in and tried to reason with him, pinning him in place while the hammer fell. See, I was a new face—he'd seen them for weeks on end while they went back and forth. They tried to talk to him at first, too, I guess. Didn't work out. Anyway, once he figured out I was human, he shot at me like a missile— I mean, he was gonna kill me, but Clary was positioned perfectly, took the hit for me, got a hold of Gavrikov and managed to knock him unconscious."

I was going over what he had told me, but it didn't quite make sense. "How did Clary put a hand on Gavrikov if he had his fire shield up?"

Zack's smile was smug. "Clary can change his skin. In this case, he shifted into some kind of metal. It was actually dumb luck; Clary moves a lot slower than Gavrikov, and if he had been even an inch to either side, he wouldn't have been able to grab him and club him out." He leaned back in his chair. "After that, we stuffed him in the containment unit and carted him back here."

"Bravo," I said in a hushed voice, thinking of the containment unit. It was tiny, a coffin by any other name, a horrible, claustrophobic nightmare. I tried to think of Gavrikov's victims rather than about the means of his confinement. I forced a weak smile. "I'm sure the world is better off with one less monster wandering around."

"I think so," Zack said, eating another piece of bacon. The smell of my plate had stopped being appealing, so I watched him in silence as he ate, trying to think of something else to talk about. "You know," he said, "you still have quite a list to work through."

"List?" I stared at him, blankly.

"You know," he said. "Of things you haven't done—go to the movies, a mall, an amusement park..."

"Oh." I had forgotten that we had talked about that when last we saw each other. Nothing like having a mass murderer rattling around in your head to put some of the irrelevant things in perspective.

"You do still want to do those things, right?" He looked at me, all earnestness, and I couldn't flinch away from those eyes, those deep brown eyes, rimmed with concern. I got a sudden, uncomfortable feeling, like I was being put on the spot.

"Yeah," I said, and felt like my answer was burdened with a reluctance that seemed like metal scraping across stone. Slow and painful.

"How about this," he went on, "why don't we go out tonight—get dinner and see a movie. You can cross it off your list."

He smiled, and I felt my stomach twist. Did he just ask me out? Did I just get asked out for the first time? I blinked, almost in disbelief. Was it that he was spying for Ariadne and Old Man Winter that prompted this or had what he told Scott been true? Maybe he felt like he owed his life to me.

I mentally slapped myself. It wasn't like that, it couldn't be. After all, even if things went well and the date ended with a kiss, it wouldn't just be my first date—it'd be his last, and the next time I saw him would be at his funeral.

"Just friends," he added, as though that would make me feel better. It didn't. It made me feel a hell of a lot worse.

"Sure," I said with another weak smile. Wolfe was cackling again, that bastard. "Thanks for offering to...be my guide."

"It'll be fun." His phone rang and he answered, pulling it out of his pocket. "Yeah...I'm with her now, we're getting some breakfast. Sure, we'll see you in five." He finished his call and looked at me. "You're done, right?"

"What?" I didn't understand what he was asking until I looked down and saw my half-full plate. I hadn't taken a bite in several minutes. "Oh, yeah, I'm done."

"That was Ariadne. She wants us at Headquarters to talk about the warehouse."

"Okay." I stood, taking my tray with me to the nearest garbage can and dumping it in. I felt uneven; my head hurt a little, my heart hurt a lot, and I was once again suffering under the realization that my life had been so upended from what I was familiar with that I didn't know what I wanted.

I mean, even if he wanted me, I couldn't touch him, right?

Chapter 7

Ariadne's office was right next to Old Man Winter's in the Headquarters building. His was cold and Spartan, and I expected the same from her based on her wardrobe. When Zack knocked on the door and she called for us to enter, I was surprised.

Her office had the same view of the grounds as Old Man Winter's, but that was where the similarities ended. Whereas he had a desk that looked like it was made of a massive piece of natural stone stacked on top of two others, hers was a warm cherrywood, with a workstation and hutch against the left wall and a more formal desk between her and the two visitor chairs. There were pictures scattered around the office of Ariadne with other people, ones that looked a little like her—a man and a woman who were older, another that looked like her sister, and a few of her with her sister and some kids.

"Dear God," she said as I came into the room. "Are you all right?"

"I'm as fine as I've been since I've gotten here."

She beckoned for us to have a seat. "Can I get you something to drink?"

"I'll take a whiskey on the rocks," I said without blinking.

She froze. "I have soft drinks..."

"Bummer," I said. "What'd you want to see us about?"

"About the encounters at the warehouse, and uh..." she blinked and shook her head. "Something else."

"Great," I said without enthusiasm. "Let's start with the 'something else' that you don't really want to talk about and work our way back to the warehouse."

"Fine." She tried to smile but it was so fake that it fell apart after about two seconds. "We have a forensics lab that can analyze the personal items from your mother that you found in the warehouse."

"I'm not hearing the 'something else.'" I leaned back in her chair with exaggerated casualness.

"Very well." She rested her hands on the desk between us, folding them, for some reason bringing to my mind the idea that she must have been a goody-goody in school. "I've been ordered not to have them analyzed unless you agree to see our on-site psychologist."

"Beg pardon?" My tone carried more frozen bite than the worst wind I'd experienced thus far.

"The Director would like you to see our counselor," she said. "Understanding you've been through something of a ringer lately—"

"He wants me to submit to headshrinking?" My eyes were so narrow that I was surprised I could see anything out of them. "If he thinks I'm gonna do that, I submit to you that his head has been in the icebox for too damned long."

One of Ariadne's eyelids fluttered at my remark as she suppressed whatever her first response would have been. "He thinks," she said, pacing herself, "and I agree with him, that you've been under a great deal of stress and strain—"

"Most of which seems to be the fault of your Directorate."

"—and we are concerned with your long term health, mental as well as physical," she finished without stopping to answer my accusation. "We are willing to help you in the search for your mother, but we feel that you've been through a high level of trauma in the last few weeks, more than is healthy for anyone," she held up a hand and I restrained my sarcastic response, "let alone someone as young as yourself. This is not a negotiation. If you want our help, see our counselor." Her hands went back to being folded on her desk as she awaited my response.

I caught movement from Zack out of the corner of my eye. "It's not a bad idea." I turned to look at him, and I'm pretty sure my glare was more potent than any flame Aleksandr Gavrikov could have tossed out. "You've been through a lot—gaining powers, your mom disappearing, being locked in a metal box as punishment, being stalked by a psychopath, beaten, injured, watching a ton of people die and blaming yourself," he listed them as if he were ticking off points from a list. "It might not be a bad idea to talk to a professional about it."

"What will they tell me?" I felt the rage, but I leashed it. Wolfe was cackling, but I bade him shut up. "That it's normal to be stressed over being stalked by a psycho, imprisoned in your own house for over a decade, and finding out that you have superpowers?" I let the sarcasm fly. "I don't care what kind of shrink you've got, he's not qualified to deal with the crap I'd lay on him. I'd probably make him run screaming from the room, some of the stuff I could tell him."

Ariadne raised an eyebrow. "So you feel you should deal with these things on your own?"

I bit back an angry reply. Even with Wolfe circling in the back of my head, I knew there was truth to what she and Zack were saying. I had been through a lot, more than most people went through in their lives, I suspected. I'd been near death twice in the last week or so, had Mom vanish on me, and had a variety of other things, great and small, on my mind. I blinked. Actually, it *was* amazing I wasn't in pieces already, mentally. Maybe I was. I was hearing the voice of my greatest nemesis, after all, and he was dead.

"Fine," I conceded. "I will...talk to this...person." I said every word through gritted teeth. "When can you start looking over my mom's purse?"

"We've already started," Ariadne said. "Kurt had it delivered to the lab when he went to the medical unit. You'll get the results after the first session."

"Fine." I wasn't pouting, exactly. But close. "When can I meet with your psycho...analyzer?"

Ariadne's mouth was a thin line. "Right now. He's cleared his schedule to meet with you. He's in a different building." She looked to Zack. "Show her the way?" He nodded.

"What did you want to talk about regarding the warehouse?" I was in a little bit of a huff, but I wanted to get this over with so I could get the next thing over with. Actually, I just wanted to get the whole day over with at this point.

"Your friend Reed. And the new threat." Ariadne had turned wary again, like she was tiptoeing around what she wanted to say so as not to set me off.

"I've only met Reed twice," I said. Kind of sad, but that made him my oldest friend. "And I have no idea who this new guy is. Just for the record, I'm calling him 'Full Metal Jackass' because he's a sucker-punching douchebag, and I hope you'll join me in that by putting it on his official file or threat designator or whatever you use to keep track of metas that cross you."

"Duly noted. We have concerns." She folded her hands again.

"So do I," I agreed. "Most of them involve your fashion sense, with a few left to spare for the armor-clad whackjob that bitch slapped me around a parking lot this morning."

She sighed, bowing her head in utter resignation. "We'd like to know who Reed works for."

"So would I. But I'd also like to know who Wolfe worked for, who this new metal man is, who funds the Directorate, exactly how many factions are out there involved in this dustup over metas, what all their goals are..." I shrugged. "I asked him some of these questions, and he didn't answer, so I'm not sure how I can help you."

Ariadne hesitated. "You could tag him for us."

"Tag him?" I felt a laugh rising from within and I let it slip. "Is that a crude aphorism for sex? Because I think that would kill him before he could answer any of your questions." I couldn't bring myself to look at Zack after I said it. I wouldn't have gone there, but as conservatively as Ariadne dressed, I had a feeling the reaction would be worth it.

It was. She reddened, her face turning roughly the same shade as her hair. "I mean with a tracer bug, if you should run into him again." She reached into her top desk drawer and her hand emerged with a small wooden case. She snapped it open, revealing a pen. "When you hold the clicker, it launches a tracking beacon that only we can follow." She slid it across the desk. "It has a range of about twenty feet when it fires, so make sure you're aiming the pen properly. It will cling to almost any surface, and it has ten tracers within it."

"Tricky," I said. "Reed would be pissed if he found out I was tracking him. I think he'd be less offended if I tagged him the other, more lethal way."

"I think he knows how to find those," Zack said from beside me. I didn't dare look at him yet. We'd faced death together, but I didn't want to see his reaction to my references to sex for some reason. Dammit. "Kurt used one of those to tag the bumper of his car outside your house the day we met, and it went offline after he left us behind at the supermarket."

I stared at the pen, picking it up and cradling it in my fingers. It was small, black, and slightly rounded. Looked fancy. "I always wondered how you guys had found us there." I held it up. "I'm not going to promise that I'll use this because I still don't work for you guys. But I'll consider it."

"Fair enough," she said. "What will it take to get you to trust us?"

"I notice you didn't answer any of the questions I asked a minute ago about who the players are in this meta conflict." I stared her down, making her uncomfortable.

"You want answers," she said with a nod. "I think we can accommodate that request. Let me talk with the Director. It will be a long conversation though, so let's plan for it to happen tomorrow morning. There might be other things we can discuss by then."

"Just to be clear," I told her. "This isn't an 'all or nothing' proposition. You don't get my trust all in one move, but this will help. Be honest with me and you build your credibility."

"That's a two-way street," she said with a flush.

"Which is why I'm going to see your master of mind games." I stood and looked at Zack, now finally able to do so without profound embarrassment. "Care to show me the way to my mental doom?"

"You don't have to treat it like it's some awful, hellish scenario," Zack said once we were in the hallways outside Ariadne's office. "This is a good thing for you."

"Maybe. But it doesn't mean I want to do it." I was actually more scared that I'd inadvertantly let something slip that I shouldn't, like the fact that the first man I'd ever killed was a houseguest in my mind, spinning wheels and talking to me. Even for a recent arrival from recluse-hood like myself, that didn't seem normal. But then, neither did killing people with a touch.

"Life's about more than just doing what you want to do," Zack said, terse.

"That's the story of mine."

"Right," he said. "Just try and let Dr. Zollers help you. He's good; I've seen him myself."

"What for?" Now I was very curious.

"Standard procedure for agents," he said, just airily enough that I didn't believe him. "We're in a high-stress occupation, so before they put us on field duty we get a full evaluation, and the doctor counsels us throughout our careers."

"What do you talk to him about?"

"Normal stuff. The pressures that come with being on call 24/7, ready to round up and suppress any meta that steps out of line."

"Suppress?" I giggled. "You mean kill?"

"Or capture," he said, bristling.

I felt my face fall. "Like Gavrikov." I thought of that coffin that they put him in, and I felt a familiar kind of sick.

The regret was there, on his face. "Yeah. Like him."

"Are there more?" I looked at him. "Have you guys captured a lot of metas?"

"Yeah. Our facility in Arizona has a prison where they're kept. It's far out in the desert, middle of nowhere."

"What do they do, these metas? You know, to deserve confinement like Gavrikov?"

"Gavrikov is unique," Zack said in protest. "Most of the ones we have to confine—and it's very few, fortunately—are ones that are clear, obvious cases of metas using their powers to commit crimes. They're strong enough that law enforcement would have a hell of a time catching them."

"Like Wolfe?"

Zack cringed. "Not that bad. At least, none of the ones I've dealt with. Murderers, sure, some major thieves. But every one of them has committed enough crimes that you get the idea that they'll never be able to live in human society again without returning to the same behaviors."

"How many crimes is that?"

"Lots." He looked at me as we exited the Headquarters building, and he was all seriousness. "On average, twenty felony offenses, ranging from burglary to the big ones, the capital offenses, before we catch up with them."

"Do they get a trial?" Again, I was curious.

"Not really," he said. "Usually we've caught them in the act, and our forensics are better than average. But it wouldn't matter;

when we send them to Arizona, it's almost always for life."

"A life sentence," I mused. "So you guys are the judge, jury, and executioner."

"It's not like that." His voice lowered, and the defensiveness was on the rise within it. "These are criminals that the justice system couldn't contain if they wanted to."

"The government doesn't know about metas?" I shook my head. "They don't want to deal with them?"

"They know about them," Zack said. "I've heard they have a program in place for dealing with them if they catch them.

"And?"

"It's less charitable than ours. Our facility can allow even a truly dangerous meta some free rein, because our guards are metas and the staff are prepared. The government facility is a hole in the ground. They go in, they don't come out, and who knows if they're alive or dead." He looked at me. "You don't approve."

"I don't know," I said with a surprising lack of emotion one way or another. Bet I'd have felt different if I'd been in one of the Directorate's cells in Arizona. "I don't have a better solution, but I'm famed for my lack of trust."

"And?"

"Why would I trust you to faithfully execute a full criminal justice system, hidden where no one can observe or see it?" I shrugged. "I'm not going to get involved—for a myriad of reasons, including the fact that I'm one person, and I have no better solution—but it doesn't sound like a perfect use of power to me. It sounds worrisome, and seems like it has a high potential for abuse of prisoners and people. Kind of Draconian."

We lapsed into a vaguely comfortable silence, not saying anything as he led the way across the campus, which was just as well. If I hadn't been feeling so self-involved and worried about what was going on for myself, I might have thought more deeply about what Zack had been describing. It sounded ugly, but I had no time to worry about it.

He walked me to a building on a side of the campus I'd spent little time on. It was closest to the gymnasium but wasn't far from a host of buildings I'd never been in. Like the others, it wasn't marked well, I suspected on purpose. He held the door for me, which was a nice touch. I pretended to be too preoccupied to notice.

The hallways were long, brick, and like everywhere else in the Directorate they had a sterile scent to them. The building was older than HQ, the brick was faded, and it was quiet; only the hum of the overhead fluorescent lights could be heard. I wanted to believe I could hear the beating of my own heart, but I really couldn't. I was nervous, but not off the scale.

Zack stopped me at a solid wooden door. It had one of those silver name plates over it, and it read: Dr. Quinton Zollers, M.D. I grimaced inwardly. Not that I thought it would be easier, but having a psychologist without the M.D. appellation seemed less intimidating for some reason.

"You'll do fine," Zack said. In my nervous tension, I couldn't decide whether I wanted to kiss him or slap him, then remembered that they'd both have roughly the same effect. "Don't forget about our date tonight."

I froze. "Our what?"

"You know," he said, casual. "We're going to dinner, the movies, mall, all that?"

"Yes. Sorry."

"Not a problem," he said with a genuine smile. "You've got a lot on your mind. I'll come by your dorm at five to pick you up?"

"Sounds good," I said, relieved that he missed the source of my reluctance. After all, it was infinitely preferable that he thought I'd forgotten our rendezvous than that I was taken aback by him referring to it as a date. Because, of course, he meant nothing serious by it.

He was halfway down the hall and had not looked back when I reached for the door handle and swung it open. I found myself in a waiting room with chairs lined up against the walls and a fish tank in the corner. On the far wall was another door, solid, which I assumed led to the inner sanctum of Dr. Quinton Zollers, who would be helping me diagnose problems I didn't even recognize I had. I found myself surprised that Wolfe didn't have a funny comment for this situation, and then wondered if perhaps he was sleeping.

There wasn't another soul in the waiting room, so I made my way to the inner door and knocked, three sharp raps. A voice boomed out. "Sienna Nealon...come right in."

I took a deep breath, and swung the door open.

Chapter 8

Dr. Zollers rose to meet me when I entered the room and to his credit didn't blink at the sight of my torn clothing. I had expected one of those long fainting couches, facing away from the practitioner. Instead, I was surprised to find a few comfortable chairs and an office that was set up more like a living room. A couch sat in front of me, a full sized one, and three chairs sat across from it, with a coffee table in the middle. Sitting in one of the chairs was a shorter man with dark skin that spoke of his African heritage, a goatee, and eyes that glittered as though he knew the punch line to a joke he hadn't shared yet.

"Howdy," he said, not extending a hand, keeping them both clasped on the armrests of his seat. The faint smile he wore went well with his eyes, and he inclined his head in greeting. "It's my very great pleasure to meet you, Sienna."

"The feeling is..." I hesitated, and knew I was letting loose a little too much sarcasm, "...mutual."

"I kinda doubt that." He sat back down and pointed at the couch. "Have a seat."

"Right here?" I pointed to the couch he indicated.

"Wherever," he said with a slight shrug. Then, as if sensing that my immediate thought was that the bed back in my room seemed like a good option, he added, "In the office."

I snapped my fingers theatrically. "Damn." I sat on the couch and stared at him. He stared back, still wearing that smile.

"So. What do you want to talk about?"

"Oh, I don't know. How about the season the Vikings are having?"

He raised an eyebrow. "You a sports fan?"

"Nah. I just thought it'd be more fun than what Ariadne wants us to talk about."

"What do you think Ariadne wants us to talk about?" He gave me a shrewd look.

"This is gonna be a brutally long session if all you do is ask me questions every time I say things." My eyes searched the walls for a clock.

"Why would you think that all I would do is ask questions?" His smile got broader. "Talk about anything you'd like, we'll go from there."

"Let's talk about the Directorate. How long have you been here?"

He thought about it for a beat. "About three years."

"How many doctors do they have on staff here? I mean, Perugini, Sessions, you...do they have a full-time herpetologist too?"

He nodded without any hint of levity. "For the reptile metas, sure." After a moment in which I was sure he was dead serious, he laughed. "Kidding. I don't know. I pay less attention to their staffing than I do to their staff."

"And your job is to help them..." I tried to find a phrase that would fit and be insulting, but I failed, "...psychologically decompress?"

"That's a part of what I do," he said, his voice smooth. "Agents get put in stressful situations, they may have to use violence in their work, and it's something that stays with them. Also, the metas we have here sometimes go through a rough transition. Though," he said with a sense of irony, "usually not quite as rough as what's happened to you."

"I was gonna ask how you manage to keep any of them here if what happened to me was normal."

"You probably know this, but what happened to you was not 'normal,'" he said. "I've counseled a lot of metas who have come here after realizing that they won't be able to fit in with their former lives the way they thought they could before. None of them have been attacked the way you were—hunted by a psychotic super-meta who wanted to capture you."

"Kill me," I said in a whisper. "He wanted to kill me. But not right away."

He gave me a tight smile. "I heard, but it'd be indelicate of me to bring it up first. Still, I guess that makes you unique."

"I'd settle for less unique. It's probably less painful."

"But you don't get to choose, do you?" He leaned forward in his chair. "You're a succubus, the first of your kind of meta that the Directorate has seen. Top of the power scale when it comes to your strength and speed, and you've been granted a different power than someone who could, say, affect the temperature in the room or breathe life into the dead or put someone to sleep with a song."

"Different." I squirmed on the couch, feeling a sudden desire to burrow into it, away from this conversation. "That's one way to put it."

"How would you put it?" The way he asked it was so smooth, so empathetic, that it touched a nerve in me and I didn't try to dodge, I just answered.

"I would say..." I took a deep breath. "That I've been disconnected from people my whole life. First, because I was locked in a house with my mother, and now because I can't touch anybody without killing them. That I'm doomed to go through life untouched, like a porcelain figurine set up on a high shelf, so fragile it might break if anyone were to take it out." I tasted bitterness in my mouth. "Except I'm not the one that's fragile. Everyone else is."

He stared at me and then nodded, real slow. "I can see how you'd feel that way." He paused, as though steeling himself. "Can I ask about your mother?"

"She's missing."

"That's not what I was gonna ask." He didn't look away, even though I did. "If this is too deep for the first time we've talked, go ahead and stop me, okay? But I've heard rumors, and I'm wondering if they're true. Did your mother beat you? Lock you in metal coffin?"

"Yes," I said in a muted whisper, "that is too deep."

"Okay." He nodded, picking up a notebook and a pen. "How about this? Let's go back to what you want to talk about."

"Um. All right." I thought about it. "Do you have to report everything I say to Ariadne and Old Man Winter?"

He smiled, but it was overly cool. "Professionally, that would be unethical. You and I are stepping into the territory of doctor and patient, which means that there's confidentiality that extends to whatever we discuss in the course of that relationship. So, no—I'm not reporting to the higher-ups on what we talk about here, unless what we talk about here crosses the line—"

"Into something dangerous?" I asked, an odd sense of numbness falling upon me. "Into something threatening?"

"Exactly. Ariadne and Mr. Winter want to make sure that you're mentally healthy." His eyes were focused on me, but not in the uncomfortable way that Old Man Winter did. They were warm, and knowing, and that was why I couldn't meet them. "I don't think I'm revealing any big secrets when I say they have high hopes for you. The Directorate may be one of the only places you can safely exercise your powers in the world, that could give you a path, and some meaning if you wanted it."

"They want me to join M-Squad." I said it while looking at the laces of my shoes, studying a little piece of snow that had caught on the edge of the rubber sole and hadn't quite melted yet.

"They see a path there for you." He looked down at the notebook. "They see a natural fit with what your mother used to do in the old days for the Agency. From what I've heard, you have a certain fearless quality and tenacity that would serve you well in a variety of walks of life."

My mouth felt dry. "What if I don't know what walk of life I want to tread?"

He paused before answering. "Then I'd say you're probably an eighteen-year-old."

"I'm seventeen."

He laughed, a low, quiet one that actually brought a smile to my face. "From what I've heard, you have a lot of confidence—a lot of brass, I'd say—in standing up to adults who seem like authority figures. Not mouthy, pointless defiance. Rebellion is a natural teenage quality, but most teens are not gonna confront a guy like Erich Winter about much of anything."

He put down his pen and notebook on the table at his side and looked back at me. "You've got confidence in some areas that most others your age don't. But here's the thing about self-confidence: a lot of it comes from knowing who you are, and knowing that whatever problem that comes your way, you can solve it." I looked up and met his gaze. "So do you know who you are?"

I cleared my throat before answering, and it still came out crackly. "Not really."

He put his hands up. "There's your answer. If you don't know who you are, it's kind of tough to know what you want, at least on more than a basic 'eat-sleep-play' level."

"But wouldn't you think..." I swallowed hard before continuing, "after all I've been through, especially with the changes and revelations lately that I might have a hard time with that? That I might struggle with who I am and what I want?"

He laughed. "God, I hope so. Otherwise I'd be worried. Metas and humans aren't that different in a lot of the things they go through, but metas deal with their process of growing up differently when their powers start to manifest. Every human struggles to find their place in the world. Sometimes you feel like you're in control and in charge of your life and everything is grand. Other times you feel powerless and insignificant. If you didn't experience these same feelings of grandeur and wonder and worry...you wouldn't be human." His skin crinkled around his eyes with his smile. "Whatever else you may be, meta and all that, you are human. And normal, for what you've been through."

I felt a knot in my throat and a burning in my eyes. "I don't feel normal."

"Yeah," Zollers said with a drawl. "That's normal too." He leaned forward, features animated. "You've been through hell and a little more, but no teenager knows what 'normal' is. So," he finished with a smile, "in that regard you're as 'normal' as anyone else your age. Hell, most adults feel that way too, just not as consistently. Now...do you have anything else you want to talk about?"

I opened up, a little at a time. I didn't tell him everything (especially about Wolfe) but I did tell him a lot. An hour flew by as he asked me questions about life in our house, about being punished the way I was by Mom, about how I still missed her, even in spite of all that. About how I wanted some part of a normal life, or at least what I envisioned as a normal life in my TV-influenced brain.

I got close to letting it all go, but I just couldn't. I let him know more than almost anyone, which wasn't saying much, but there was something else, something below the surface that I couldn't define, and I wanted to keep it that way. For now, at least.

When I left, it was with another appointment scheduled for a couple of days later. I walked out of the doctor's office feeling much different than when I had gone in, lighter, somehow. As much as Zack wanted to talk to me, I couldn't have felt comfortable telling him even half the stuff I had talked to Dr. Zollers about. And I still hadn't told him the worst of it.

The sky was slightly brighter when I walked back outside, though there was still no break in the clouds. In spite of it, I could see the lightness in the sky where the sun must be hiding, and felt the slight creep of a smile at the corner of my lips as I trod across the salted sidewalks, back to the dormitory I was calling home.

Chapter 9

"You should try the bacon-wrapped dates." Zack wore a smile as he extended the plate toward me. I looked at it with hesitation born of my confusion at the word date (again) but I grabbed one of the little delicacies from the plate and tentatively put it in my mouth. I was rewarded with a lovely tang followed by a sweetness. I felt like it was a little symphony being played on my tongue, and I couldn't have been happier about it, although I did have a brief vision of Zack wrapped in bacon that I shook out of my head to the sound of Wolfe's laughter.

We were in a restaurant at the mall; an Italian place with an Italian-sounding name, lots of warm wood finishes, smooth tableclothes, and the smell of the freshly baked bread lingered in the air, enticing me. I picked up a slice from the table and dipped it into the plate of olive oil and parmesan cheese our waitress had made before I took a bite. Heavenly.

"I take it this isn't how you ate at home?" Zack's smile had morphed into a full-blown grin. Outside, the last light of day was shining in through the external windows of the restaurant. It was built into the side of the mall, which I hadn't walked through yet. I felt a buzz of excitement to be able to explore when I finished eating. It was one of the best dinners I'd ever had and we weren't yet past the appetizers and bread. Hell, I'd never even had a meal with an appetizer course before. Fancy.

"Lots of ramen noodles, some TV dinners, occasionally hamburgers made in a skillet," I said. "I think Mom attempted turkey once, with tragic consequences for the bird and us."

He made a face. "Sounds tiring, eating the same thing over

and over." He grabbed a bacon-wrapped date by the skewer and popped it into his mouth as I devoured another. "Pace yourself. You'll want to leave room for dessert."

"I don't know where I'll find room for that."

But I did. After my steak, I had some of the chocolate cake. It was richer than any Mom had ever brought home (on the rare occasions she brought one home). When I was done, I felt fuller than maybe I ever had. "I think you're glowing a little bit," Zack said.

I smiled back at him, a long, lazy one. "I'm surprised I don't feel sick after all that food." I paused for a beat. "And I'm not surprised I feel better."

"Yeah, Doc Zollers does wonders for people." He looked around. "Want to go for a walk? You probably have a meta-strength metabolism to keep you thin but I promise you, my physique doesn't come without a ridiculous amount of work."

I tried not to stare at his body because I already knew it was good. Instead I focused on his eyes. "A walk sounds like a good idea."

He paid for the meal and we left, walking outside until we reached the "official" entrance to the mall. A massive bookstore was to my left, and shops were clustered on my right down either side of a long hallway. We walked along, oddly silent, though I kept looking at him out of the corner of my eye. Every once in a while, I'd catch him looking back, and like a chicken, would pretend I was looking past him at something else.

It wasn't hard to pretend that, actually. The stores were a barrage of colors, lights, and products that I'd seen advertised on TV but had never laid eyes on in real life. I stopped at the first of the clothing boutiques; there was a plastic figure, life sized, with no features, wearing clothing in the window. I frowned at it. The dress it was wearing was black and sheer with a low cut neckline and a high hemline.

"Nice dress." Zack's voice had a far-off quality to it.

"I agree. But what's that it's on?" I studied the plastic creation, as though I could discern what it was just by staring.

"Haven't you ever seen a mannequin before?"

"No. What is it?"

"You know," he said. "Fake people."

"Like Southern Californians?"

He laughed and I gave up. I'd heard of mannequins before, but I couldn't recall ever seeing one on TV. We walked past a store filled with mobile phones and I had to curb an impulse to run inside and snatch one up to fiddle with it. Sure, I'd seen people in the Directorate use them, but to me they were still something out of fantasy. We hadn't even had a regular phone at home.

We rode an escalator up to the second floor where the movie theater was. The box office had a short line in front of it, and movie posters were plastered into frames on the walls on either side of us. Behind us was an opening that looked down on the first level of the mall and across the wide space to the walkway opposite. Intriguing smells wafted over to me: popcorn from the movie theaters, and from the food court behind us the scent of burgers, Chinese food, and maybe hot dogs; I wasn't sure.

We'd decided in advance what to see, and I heard Zack buy two tickets as I continued to look around, mesmerized by the sights, sounds, and smells that were all around me.

I was staring at an ice cream stand when a flash of dark hair across the gap caught my attention. A woman had been standing at the railing, and I hadn't noticed her until she moved. Her hair was long, like mine, dark and stretching down around her shoulder blades, and for some reason it looked wild and unkempt to me. She was close to middle age, wore a red dress, shorter than the black one I'd seen before and cut lower at the neck. She turned and I saw her profile. My heart jackhammered at the sight of her, the realization.

It was Mom.

Chapter 10

I was moving the moment it hit me, my feet pounding along the floor. I jumped to the railing and leapt across the wide gulf that separated one side of the second floor from the other. I landed, feeling the pressure of the impact run through my knees and ankles, but I felt no pain in spite of having cracked my foot earlier in the day. The woman in red turned, only a few feet in front of me, and her eyebrow raised when she saw me breathing heavily from the exertion of my running leap.

It wasn't Mom.

"I'm sorry," I said. "I didn't mean to scare you." My mind was racing. From a distance, she had seemed like a dead ringer. Up close, it was obvious that it wasn't Mom. "I thought you were...someone else." Mom never wore makeup; this woman's eyes and cheeks were covered in it, giving me the impression that she was fighting the clock with everything she had, even though she was still pretty. Also, I was a little surprised by her lack of a coat given the weather—even more so by the dress.

Her eyes were cool, and she looked around, as though she were trying to decide where I had come from. They froze on my cheek as Zack ran up behind me. She stared at him, then back at me, with eyes that were filled with a sort of concern. "Did he do that?" She pointed at my cheek and I remembered that I had a bruise from my fight earlier.

"What? No," I said with a little laugh. "He didn't hurt me. He couldn't."

"Oh," she said. "Sorry I'm not who you thought I was." She turned to walk away. I watched her go, noticed the sway of her hips, and wondered what kind of a man would be attracted to a woman so obviously starved for attention.

There was a hum from the crowd gathered around me; people were talking, those that had seen my jump, low, muttered voices of incredulity. I think I heard someone mutter, "PCP."

"Way to stay nonchalant." Zack eased up beside me. He watched her go, his eyes never moving off her backside and answering my internal question about what kind of man would be attracted to her. The looks of others as she moved through the crowd provided more clarity; apparently, any man with a heartbeat. I looked down at my simple turtleneck and jeans with my new heavy coat. Practical, I supposed, especially for the girl who kills with a touch—but not likely to generate the kind of attention she was getting. "What is she wearing?" I said it mostly to myself.

Zack answered anyway, watching her as she walked away. "Damned near nothing."

"In this weather? It's winter. Isn't she cold?"

She turned and Zack's eyes alighted on her chest. "Looks like it from here."

I looked back at him, and I tried not to make it a glare, but I failed. "What?" He looked at me with slight alarm, as though he had no idea why I was irritated with him. I looked to the store that the woman had exited, and sure enough, on one of the mannequins in the window was the exact same dress I had just seen on her.

I drew closer to it, but this time not to look at the mannequin that wore it. I felt my gloved hand touch the glass, as though I could connect with the dress behind it, feel the silk between my fingers. It was a symbol of all I could never be. All I could never have. "Nothing," I said after another moment. "Can we go to the movie now?"

"Sure." He stepped out of the way and held out an arm as if indicating I should go first.

Most of the movie I spent buried in my own head, frustrated. I mean, hadn't it been obvious that I wasn't destined to be able to touch anyone, anytime? I cursed myself for my foolishness; Zack didn't want to die, and a relationship with me was just that, a death sentence. At least, if it was to involve anything other than conversations. And if there was absolutely no physical component to a relationship, was it anything other than a friendship?

A guy like Zack had friends. I was fairly certain he could have his pick of any number of women, too. Why wouldn't he look past me at some devil woman in a red dress? Even if she was twenty years older and taller and more shapely and knew how to apply cosmetics and bleh. Was it possible to hate someone you didn't know and hadn't exchanged more than a few words with? I even envisioned walking up behind her, taking off a glove and giving her a little touch to the arm. Not enough to kill her, just enough to zap some of the prettiness away

Then I cursed myself for being petty and tried to watch the movie. It wasn't easy; it had no plot and a lot of explosions. I felt my mind wandering for minutes at a time and when it came back, I found I hadn't missed much.

Afterward Zack offered to walk around the mall for a little while longer but I declined. I suspect he saw through my terse answer, but he didn't say anything as we walked to the car.

It was a quiet ride back to the Directorate. Even though I could have sworn it was only about twenty minutes, it felt like an hour. We pulled into the parking garage and he stopped the car. I started to turn to him to say good night, but he preempted me.

"Did I...say something or do something that pissed you off?" He was staring at me, earnest, for all his faults.

"No. I'm sorry," I said. "I thought that woman in red—I thought she was my mom, from a distance. She looked like..." My words trailed off.

"Ah," Zack said with a nod. "I wondered what would possess you to jump across the mall like that, in public and in full view of a hundred people. It all makes sense now."

"Why didn't you ask me before?" I stared straight ahead, looking hard at the concrete wall that was just in front of the hood of the parked car.

"In my experience, if a woman seems upset, it's better to wait a little while before you probe to get to the bottom of it," he said. A sage, he was. "You know," he said with confidence, "in case it was something I did, I didn't want to make it worse by seeming like I didn't have a clue."

I heard Wolfe's laughter ringing in my ears and I saw red. "Of course it wasn't you," I said, calm. How did I manage that calm? No idea. "Well," I said with an urgency I couldn't define, but that welled up along with a hundred other emotions I didn't want to give voice to, "good night." I grabbed the handle to the car door and forced it open, rushing to get out before he could say anything else. My hand gripped it tighter than I intended, and I heard a squeaking noise as I stood up, and I looked down to find the door hanging free of the car, loose in my hand.

I stared at it with incredulity for a moment before a torrent of bitter anger burst loose somewhere within and I screamed a curse. I hurled the car door as I stomped away from the vehicle toward the nearest exit. I heard it crash, the window breaking when it hit the wall, and I heard it bounce into something else. The earsplitting sound of a car alarm going off echoed through the whole place as I pushed my way out of the garage's exit door and blissfully found myself out of the garage and on the snowy grounds of the Directorate.

Chapter 11

You should let your anger out to play more often, Wolfe said a little while later, as I was about to get into bed. *It's quite becoming, little doll.*

"You're a hobo who's living rent-free in my brain," I said out loud as I turned down the covers. Someone had snuck in and made the bed and cleaned the room while I was out. At another time, I might have been impressed with the turndown service. As it was, it was added to the pile of things annoying me, the lack of privacy I felt in this place.

No need to get so hostile. Wolfe's tone (in my head, the bastard still has a tone) was leering, taunting. *Wolfe was paying you a compliment.*

"I need your compliments like I need another mysterious enemy trying to kick my ass," I said, flopping down. "Since I already acquired another of those today, I'll pass on your 'kind' words."

Poor little doll, whose life is aught but mysteries and lies, he said, almost soothing. *So troubled, so sad, so...delicious. And how you feel about the agent is even more tasty.*

"Go screw yourself." I buried my head in the pillow.

There, there. What if Wolfe could make some of the mystery go away?

"Like you did with my mother? Thanks, but that turned out to be more mystery."

Such a shame, Wolfe was going to tell you all about the man in the metal suit...

I raised my head up. "You don't know anything about him."

Wolfe snickered at my uncertainty. *David Henderschott, age*

*58. He doesn't look it, of course. He ages well, like powerful metas tend to. He was pretty too, before someone...*He paused in his narrative and I could almost hear a squeal of excitement in my head...*cut him up. Now he's not so pretty anymore. Very strong, though.*

"Why is he wearing armor?" I clutched my pillow in my hand. "To hide what you did to him?"

Wolfe laughed, a shallow, short bark. *His skin can stick to whatever it touches. He used to use it to rip the flesh off his foes, but Wolfe taught him the error of his ways, oh yes he did. Now Wolfe would guess he's scared to come out and play.*

"Who does he work for?"

Tsk, tsk, little doll. What will you do for the Wolfe?

I smiled, but it wasn't one of deep satisfaction. "I'm not doing a damned thing for you." I flipped the switch by the bed that triggered the lights. "Night night."

Oh, little doll...you'll be sorry. Without another word, it was like he picked up and went to another corner of my mind and lay down. I had a vision of him, like the proverbial dog licking himself, and I got disgusted and tried to put it out of my mind.

Sleep was horrible, filled with a hazy nightmare. I walked over snowy fields into a building with brick sides and down long, yellowed corridors. I saw fire, blazing, hot, heard words spoken that I couldn't understand, and then felt the wind at my face as I ran.

I awoke as an explosion flipped me into a snow bank.

I blinked in shock as I felt the damp cold slide down the back of my shirt for not even the first time today. I got my bearings and vaulted to my feet. There was noise behind me and I turned. I was standing in the middle of the campus, somewhere between the Headquarters and where the science building, where Dr. Sessions had kept his lab, had been only moments before.

There was still some of it left, but what there was happened to be covered in flames, the fire stretching up to the heavens. I ran toward the building and felt the heat wash over me the closer I got. The brick building had once been three stories; now only a few spots remained where more than a few feet of brick stood at a stretch. I wondered if anyone could have survived just as I saw a shadow moving around behind one of the walls.

I heard screaming, shrieks everywhere around me. The heat from the burning building was intense, the smell of smoke pungent and overpowering. I looked and saw others had come, flooding across the campus toward the site of the calamity. One of the screaming voices caught my attention; it came from within the burning building.

I moved toward the wreckage and jumped over the nearest wall. I felt my flesh start to char, smelled the flames and the tang of what I suspected was the first degree burns that were already causing my skin to redden. I saw a lone figure on the ground, scorched from head to foot and I reached out, grabbing hold of him and lifting him into my arms. I vaulted back over the wall and tried to carry him away from the building. A pitched squeal stopped me long enough to look down.

It was Dr. Sessions. I was carrying him like a baby in my arms, and I hurried away, not wanting to look at him, just trying to get away from the fire. The smell of burning meat was everywhere, in my nose, in my eyes, in my throat and it was threatening to make me gag, cry or throw up. Maybe some combination of the three. The heat was steadily getting weaker until I ran into something and fire burst around me.

I fell on my backside, Sessions still in my arms. I looked up and saw the same eyes I'd seen only a day before, behind the glass of a containment cell as Clary carried it away from me.

Gavrikov.

I drew a sharp breath as I looked at him. He was wreathed in flame from head to toe, not an inch of flesh visible. The fire stood

out, reaching a few inches from his arms, his head, from everywhere. His eyes were something else entirely, just a shadow and a
shape, with no hint of a pupil or an iris, as though they were nothing but spheres surrounded by a living, breathing fire.

He drew up in front of me and I remembered what Zack had
said about him, about his power to control flame; he could start an
inferno right here with me at the heart and there wasn't a thing I
could do about it other than chuck a charred lab rat at him and run.
And that was iffy.

He stared down at me with those burning, empty eyes and
raised his hand. I scooted Dr. Sessions off me, laid him on the
snow with only a murmur of pain from him and stood, wary and
ready to dodge, for whatever that might have been worth. I stared
at him, he stared back at me.

"Thank you," he said, his voice no more than a whisper.
"Thank you." I looked at him, confused but still tense. I braced for
whatever he might do. He seemed as though he might take another
step, lifting a leg off the ground, but instead his other leg joined
him and he hovered a few feet above me. "Your kindness will not
go unrepaid."

I felt a clutch of unnerving suspicion inside, but before I
could question him, he shot into the sky in a blur, and he was
gone.

Dr. Perugini was beside me in the next moment, bending low
over the body of Dr. Sessions, barking commands to others around
her. I turned to look at him and realized that his flesh was charred,
hideous. His lab coat was burned perversely, his glasses fused into
his flesh. His clothing was blackened, what was left of it. I
couldn't see a single place where he wasn't burned, and I wondered how he could still be alive.

"Sienna," Ariadne cut through the chaos and I realized with a
shock that she was wearing a robe, a red one, silken and utterly out
of character for what I would have suspected of her. "What did

you see? What did he say to you?"

I couldn't take my eyes off Dr. Sessions. "I don't know," I lied, far too nimbly. "Is...is he going to be okay?"

"Does he LOOK like he's going to be okay?" Dr. Perugini nearly screamed the reply, her distress increasing the potency of her accent. "I need..." Her head spun around until it alighted on Kat Forrest, who was standing in a nearby knot of metas in nothing but a tank top and briefs. "You."

The delicate, gushing girl who I had met earlier in the cafeteria stepped forward, tentative. She shook from the cold, and her breath came out in great clouds as she walked in halting steps toward where Dr. Perugini waited for her. "He doesn't have all night!" Perugini snapped and Kat quickened her pace, dropping to her knees in the snow. She reached out, her hands curled up tight to ward against the cold. She unfurled them, bringing them to Sessions' face. I may have imagined it, but it seemed like the snow was melting around her legs.

Her hands were on his face, the soft light of the overhead lamps illuminating the nighttime scene. He moaned when she first brushed his cheek, then again when her fingers anchored around his cheeks. The charred and blackened flesh seemed to grow redder around where her hands rested and Sessions grunted in pain. Then he started to scream.

I made a move forward, shrugging off Ariadne as she grasped at me. I felt a hand land on my shoulder and I started to turn and attack, but as I moved to do so, the hands released me and I was left staring at Scott Byerly, his hands raised as he took a step back. "Watch," he said.

I did. Sessions was still crying out—in pain, I thought—until I looked back and saw that around her hands, fresh skin was springing up on his face, replacing the cracked and blackened with new, pink flesh. It spread out in an effect that rippled over his visible skin. New hairs sprang from his once bald head and his shrieks became a low moan then ceased. His head dropped to the ground and he let out a long, deep exhalation.

"Pulse returning to normal," Dr. Perugini said, her stethoscope on his chest. "He's in stable condition." She snapped her fingers and someone slid a stretcher and a backboard into the snow next to Sessions and they started to load him onto it.

"How did she do that?" I asked, low, but loud enough to be heard.

Scott Byerly was the one who answered. "She's a Persephone-type. She can give life with a touch."

"Give life?" I stared at the girl, still on her knees in the snow, which had indeed melted around her legs, brown grass visible against the tan skin of her thighs. I looked closer; blades of grass were turning green and waving against her sun-kissed skin, and it wasn't my imagination. It was almost as if they were trying to touch her. "Persephone was the Greek goddess of seasons. She couldn't give life to people, just to plants."

He shrugged. "I said Persephone-type, not Persephone herself. It's based on myth and legend, after all." He stared me down, and I saw a hint of a smile poke at the corners of his lips. "What are you?"

I looked away, back to Kat, who was sitting on the ground, resting, her eyes closed, gold hair flowing around her face, which was red from exertion. She looked at peace, and she sank back, laying flat on the ground, embraced by the patch of green in the midst of all the snow. Her breath was still coming in and out with regular certainty, the steaming heat of it boldly visible against the bright lights surrounding us. I saw the calm around her, watched the grass play at her fingers, touching it, tickling it, and I felt a surge of envy.

They were carrying Dr. Sessions away now, away from her, the girl who had given him life, returned it to him with her very hands. I looked back at Scott Byerly, and his eyebrow was raised in expectation. "Me?" I asked, and I felt hollow inside, empty of everything, even Wolfe. "I'm her opposite—everything that she isn't." My jaw hardened. "I'm death."

Chapter 12

I didn't sleep for the rest of the night. I'd left Scott Byerly and his stupid question behind with my cryptic answer, not even bothering to gauge his reaction. Well, maybe just a little. His face scrunched up as I was turning from him. I can't say that was satisfying, but it was better than stopping to explain the literal truth I had told him.

I am death. My touch brings it. Where Kat Forrest was a tanned, lovely, blond-haired princess of life, I was a dark-haired, pale-skinned angel of death. Her green eyes represented life; my bluer ones represented winter and the end of that life.

Worse than the nasty comparisons that witnessing Kat's power had spawned in me were the questions. What was I doing outside when the building had exploded? Why couldn't I remember it? Why was the flaming lunatic so thankful to me?

When I returned to my dorm room, I had to take another shower. The fall and the fire had done a number on me. No one had asked, probably because they hadn't seen, but my leather gloves had burned to my skin on the back of my hands. I ripped them off, the leather shredding and pulling the flesh in patches. I let them bleed out in the shower, the diluted red standing out against the cream-colored tiles that surrounded the drain. I watched the little stream of maroon as it came in streaks, circling the inevitable.

My hands still itched by the time I was done, along with a few places on my chest and legs where the same thing had happened. Good thing the Directorate seemed to have their finances in order, I reflected as I tossed my previously new outfit in the garbage. I was going to cost them a lot of money if I kept ruining clothes at the pace I was going.

The bruise on my cheek from earlier was gone, I saw as I looked in the mirror. One plus was that since I had awoken in the field, Wolfe hadn't made a peep. I wondered if he was sleeping. Or maybe the explosion scared him into a kennel in my mind.

I returned to my room and stared out the window for the rest of the night. I had a very, very nasty suspicion about how things had unfolded the night before, based partially on my dreams and partially on the fact that Wolfe had very much wanted to get Gavrikov out of his cage. He should have been overjoyed, swinging from the metaphorical rafters in my head at the fact that it happened, but he was dead quiet instead.

Not good.

The sun rose without me seeing it, once more hidden behind the clouds. I was disgusted enough that if I could have somehow wished myself to Tahiti and left this awful city behind, I would have. Actually, that might not have entirely been because of the sun.

A note was slid under my door shortly after sunrise, suggesting I attend a meeting with Ariadne and Old Man Winter in his office at 9 A.M. I shrugged when I saw it, trying to play cool in case there were cameras watching, but inwardly I trembled. Did he know? Could he know? What had I done?

I skipped breakfast. My stomach was tied in knots anyway; why bother to give it something else to bitch about? I walked to the HQ building when it got close to time. The air was crisp— actually, I'm romanticizing, it was still brutally cold, just like every day since I left my house. Tahiti was sounding better and better. There was still a smell of burning in the air and when I passed in sight of the science building, my suspicions were confirmed—it was still smoking. The smell it gave off was acrid and awful and stuck in my nose, tormenting me even once I was inside Headquarters.

I knocked somewhat tepidly on Old Man Winter's door. I was early, and a sizable part of me (all of me, if we're being honest) hoped he wasn't around. It opened to reveal Ariadne, her usual smile forced across her face. "You'll have to forgive us," she said as she ushered me to a seat, "It's been a busy night and we haven't had much time to prepare for this meeting."

"'Busy'?" I looked out the window behind Old Man Winter, who was sitting placidly behind his desk as always. His eyes had yet to remove themselves from me since I walked in, but I was used to it. It wasn't like he was undressing me mentally—at least I didn't think he was—it was more like he was always assessing, testing me, my willpower. I could swear he read the lies in how I moved, my reluctance to even be here. I worried that if he stared long enough, he'd be able to root out that I was carrying my own worst enemy inside my head, and that wasn't figurative speaking. "I'd hate to see what you'd be talking about if you started pulling out the really descriptive adjectives—you know, like calamitous, explosive, apocalyptic—"

"Yes, well." She cut me off, her politeness for once infused with iron. "It's not as though this is the usual for us."

"Sure, sure," I said in what sounded to me a very Midwestern way. "Last week, near-invincible psychos, this week, men who explode into flames and girls who touch the dead and bring them back to life."

"Even for us," she said, "that's not normal."

"When you're dealing with people who have powers like ours, what is?" I said it airily, but the word stuck in my head. Normal. What was normal? Everything I wasn't, at this point. "Is this about the history lesson I asked for?"

"Yes." Ariadne seated herself next to me. "It's also a briefing on the state of meta affairs in the modern age."

"Ooh, a briefing," I said. "I feel like I should be wearing a colorless pantsuit." I blinked at Ariadne, dressed once more in monochromatic businesswear. "Like that." I blanched inside and Wolfe howled with laughter, the first sound he'd made since last night. The sad part was I couldn't blame that one on him; there was something built into my relationship with Ariadne that made me want to insult her more than anything.

Her face was drawn, her eyes lowered. I wondered, far in the back of my mind where I hoped Wolfe couldn't see it, if my constant slings and arrows at her were actually hurting her feelings. *If so, she should get thicker skin*, Wolfe said, shattering my illusory idea of having private thoughts. I rolled my eyes, possibly insulting Ariadne further. Unfortunately, I couldn't tell her that I wasn't rolling them at her, but at the asshole brainclinger.

Old Man Winter stood, drawing my attention from Ariadne. He pulled himself up to his full height, towering over the two of us, and walked to the window, looking out on the campus. He seemed to focus on the remains of the science building in the distance. I waited for him to say something, and after a minute of silence I spoke. "How can you manage to keep this place secret after an explosion like that?" I looked from him to Ariadne. "It's not like that was quiet; it had to be audible for miles around."

"There is nobody around for miles," Ariadne said. "But you're right, it was heard in the next town over. Fortunately, the local law enforcement are in our back pocket, which means it won't be investigated, and it seems the media is still too focused on Wolfe's reign of terror to give this any thought."

"Got your own little cover up going on," I said with grudging admiration. "I suppose you guys have it all figured out, keeping things secret and hidden from the normal world."

"It has not always been so," Old Man Winter spoke finally, his low timbre crackling with a surprising amount of energy. "But the modern history of metahumans has been one of hiding our existence from the rest of the world, of letting ourselves fade into myth and legend and cloaking our activities so that humanity does not become suspicious of those of us who have abilities beyond theirs."

"You were around when metas walked tall and proud," I said. I couldn't see his reaction, not even in his reflection, but I suspected it was insubstantial. "Why the change?"

"Why, indeed?" His hand reached out and touched the window. "Metahumans did not just walk among humans in the days you speak of, they ruled mankind. We were gods among men. A thousand humans with spears and swords could not defeat a single strong metahuman. Entire armies tried and were wiped out in battles so bloody that they became the stuff of legend—and we became the bane of human existence and the single greatest obstacle to the freedom of men.

"Imagine a meta possessed of the will to become a conqueror, someone with the strength of a man like Wolfe, but more cunning and less psychotic." I heard a grumble in my head from Wolfe at Old Man Winter's assessment of him. "That was the story of a hundred dictators who threw their will onto the huddled masses of humankind, over and over again through the millennia, from the Greek gods of old to later, more subtle attempts of men like Rasputin to assert their influence over world powers."

"Why were the later ones less obvious?" I asked him out of genuine curiosity.

"Your experience in fighting metahumans is colored by your encounter with Wolfe." He was calm, dead calm. "Most metas are not immune to bullets. Technology has been the greatest equalizer for mankind. Whereas a superpowered metahuman might defeat an entire army in the old days, now he must contend with rifles and machine guns, bombs and explosives. Against the might of a modern army, with training, discipline, and handheld weapons with more ability to kill than entire armies of the ancient world, all but the most powerful among us would fall. Take yourself for example." He turned to me, those ice blue eyes seeming to glow against the backdrop of the gloomy sky.

"In the days of old, one with your power and strength, the ability to kill with a touch, to move faster than any human foe, with power enough to kill in a single blow and drain them with agonizing pain should they touch you—you would have been a goddess. Because of your speed, your dexterity, your strength, with a sword in your hand, you could have killed a thousand men and watched the rest flee in fear. Even the arrows of archers would have to have been lucky indeed to bring you down.

"But now, a man with a single gun could end your life with a well-placed shot." His finger traced a line ending at his forehead. "Certainly, you are more resilient than a human, and a wound to anything but your head would not kill you, but if one knows what they are facing...well," his voice trailed off for a moment, "it's not as though bullets and bombs are a commodity that mankind is soon to run out of."

"So metas have spent a good portion of history trying to conquer people." I shrugged. "Not a huge surprise. I've studied history. Why should we be any different than the rest of mankind?"

"Because we can be better," he said with a low intonation. "The story of mankind is one fraught with struggle, true enough. But it is also the tale of a people reaching for more, desiring more than to be static, immovable, and mired in the mistakes of the past. If we are to be nothing more than a warlike people, forever locked in a struggle for dominance, then the metahumans are of no more purpose than any other weapon or person of power in the modern age.

"The need for secrecy has become a paramount concern, especially as governments possess more and more means to control metahumans." His eyes were dull, almost sad. "We dare not challenge them openly, and thus far America has been content to let us rest in the shadows so long as we are not an open threat. I have worked with those in charge of the country's response to metahuman incidents. They have little to no desire to round up a small minority of people for internment or worse so long as we keep a low profile. Other governments..." His words drifted off, along with his gaze, "...are not so reticent."

Ariadne leaned forward. "Approximately three hundred and fifty metahumans were killed at a Chinese government facility less than a week ago."

"That's..." I let my mind run with the numbers I knew and came back with an answer. "That's over ten percent of the meta-human population, based on the number you gave me.""

"It is." She sat back and drew a deep breath. "We don't know what happened; reports are somewhat sketchy. The facility was supposed to be a training center for the People's Liberation Army's metahuman development program. Either they destroyed it after deciding that it wasn't worth the risk or someone else did it for them. Either way, the meta population took a steep dive last week."

"Ten percent?" My words were almost a croak, no more than a whisper. "I believe the literal term for that is 'decimated'." I had never met even one of the people killed, but somehow I felt a con-nection to them because somehow we were the same.

"True enough." Ariadne's hands landed in her lap. "These are the sort of things that happen every once in a while. We live in a world where metahumans keep their powers secret—unless they're—"

"Troublemakers? Ne'er-do-wells?" My hands found the pad-ded armrests of my chair, felt the cool metal where the leather padding ended and squeezed it, more out of a desire to feel some pressure than anything else. "Like Wolfe." I felt him stir in um-brage within me and ignored him.

"Similar." It was Ariadne who answered, again. "Usually a meta doesn't openly declare, committing crimes, harming people, unless they've decided to start shirking societal conventions and live by their own rules. At that point they've become a threat, both to human society and the collective metahuman secret." She shrugged. "After all, it's not as though we have something that can make a person forget when they see something crazy—"

"Like some beast rips through a dozen cops in a mall parking lot?" I saw a brief reflection of Wolfe's grin, like a Cheshire cat, in the window as I turned from Ariadne to Old Man Winter.

"That's not one we can explain our way out of," she said. "We had to leave it to the media and the government to spin it." She smiled. "Did you hear what they finally landed on?" I shook my head. "A biker on PCP and cocaine that was wearing multiple Kevlar vests under his clothes."

"I suppose he was rather scruffy looking." I ignored the shout of outrage that echoed through my head alone.

"But it's at those points that someone has to get involved, for the good of society. Once someone crosses that line, if there's no one there to stop them, they spin out of control, as though the taste of power over people and freedom from consequence is a narcotic that takes them over."

"That's where the Directorate comes in," I finished for her. "But what about the other groups? They don't do the same?"

Ariadne looked uncomfortable very suddenly. "Keep in mind our primary mission is policing the metahuman population, not spying on other groups that have metahuman interests—"

"Which is a fancy way of saying what?" I looked at her evenly. "That you don't pay attention to them? Don't know who they are?"

"We don't," she said. "We're aware that there are other factions out there, but none of them have strong roots in the U.S. yet, and we've been more focused on small scale threats and awakenings than some dread conspiracy—"

"You don't have a clue about any of them, do you?" I shook my head in near disbelief.

"Not so," Old Man Winter said from the window. "The boy you have had dealings with—his name is Reed Treston, and he works with an outfit based in Rome. They appear to be a group concerned about government interventions against metahumans but most of their operations are in Europe."

"What about Wolfe?" I sat up in interest, and I could feel him rattling around inside, almost as though he were holding his breath to find out what they knew about his employer.

"We know less," Ariadne shared a look with Old Man Winter. "Almost nothing, actually. They're a group possessed of incredibly strong metas, like Wolfe."

"And this new guy," I told her. She looked at me quizzically. "You know, the guy with the metallic complexion? He's with Wolfe's outfit."

She looked to Old Man Winter, then back to me with a furrowed brow. "How do you know that?"

"Well if he's not with the same group Reed is, then it stands to reason he's with Wolfe's group, unless there's another power out there that wants a piece of me?"

"There are several others," Old Man Winter said in his low rumble. "None of which we know much about."

"How is it you guys can be so well informed that you found me but you have no idea who your enemies are?" I sighed more out of disbelief than despair. "You don't want to know anything about your competition?"

"There's been a proliferation of metahuman groups in the last few years," Ariadne said, twisting a lock of her hair around her finger. "It's something we've recently begun to pivot to address, but it takes time to put an intelligence network in place and develop useable intel. We are working on it. But that's not why we asked you here." She took a deep breath. "Did this answer your questions about the larger history of metahumans and the role they play in society?"

I hesitated. "Yes," I said after a moment. "It's far from complete, but I get the gist. I'm still wondering about a few things—like the Agency, what my mom did for them and how they were destroyed," I said when she looked at me with a curious expression, "but that's not something I expect to know the answer to right now, today."

"It's something we could cover soon, perhaps in our next conversation." Ariadne's hands left her lap and went to a folder on the desk, sliding it across in front of me. "But all that is ancillary, unrelated to the real mission—which is why we wanted to talk to you."

"I see." I felt a nervous tension run through me. Did they suspect my involvement in the destruction of the science building? I felt an involuntary shudder inside and couldn't dispense with the idea that somewhere inside me. Wolfe was suddenly very cagey.

She opened the folder and pulled out four photographs, arranging them neatly in front of me. One was a picture of a family of four, another of a police officer, the next of a young woman not much older than me, and the last of a mother and young daughter. "This is why we're here. Last year a metahuman named Darrell Seidell went on a crime spree. He was nineteen and already had three felonies to his name before his power manifested."

She pointed to the family of four, all blond, with two girls. "He staged a daylight break-in at this couple's home—Rick and Susan Ormann of Champaign, Illinois. Rick was a lawyer, Susan worked for a local bank. They had a nice house, so nice, in fact, that Darrell chose it out of dozens of others to break into. He went there to steal from them—maybe a TV, some jewelry—and he ended up killing both of them, then their kids." She moved her finger to the picture of the police officer. But not before Melanie, the Ormann's eight year old daughter, called 911 and this man, Officer Lance Nealey, responded."

She picked up the picture of the cop, and I couldn't look

away. He was young too, probably in his twenties, around Zack's age. He had cocoa skin, big brown eyes, a warm smile, and his head was shaved. He was the perfect picture of a cop, the kind of image that was everything my skewed perspective thought a cop should be. He just...looked like a nice guy, there to help. "Seidell killed him and stole his cruiser, escaping the scene. That night he stopped at a convenience store outside Ottumwa, Iowa and ran across this girl, the clerk, Jeannie Sabourin." She handed me the picture of the young woman and I took it, even though I really didn't want to and forced myself to look into the girl's face.

"She was a high school senior who worked at the store at night to help make ends meet for her family." Ariadne shook her head, a kind of muted rage present on her face that made her pause. When she went on, her voice cracked. "She had been through one robbery already and knew to give him whatever he wanted. She went with him into the back where he assaulted her and once he was done, he killed her."

Ariadne paused, and I watched her face twitch as she struggled to maintain her composure. When she began again, her words came out strained. "Afterward he went behind the convenience store to the low-rent housing complex where he found Karina Hartsfield smoking a cigarette outside her patio door." She moved to the last photograph. "He killed her and stole her car, leaving behind her four-year-old daughter alone in the apartment." She pointed to the child in the photograph with Karina Hartsfield. "Odds are good that if he'd known she was there, he would have killed her too."

"Seven people dead." She reached back into the sheaf of photos and pulled out a half-dozen more, scattering them in front of me and causing me to hold my hand in front of my mouth as I heard a small gasp escape. They were photos of bodies, burned around the torso, the hands, the legs, burned so their insides showed and I nearly gagged from seeing them. "See, Darrell

Seidell is what we'd call a fire jotnar—a fire giant, from the same Norse myths as," she looked to Old Man Winter, "well, you know. Not nearly as potent as our friend Mr. Gavrikov, but up close, he's the breath of hell brought to earth. Without anyone to stop him, he was free to keep driving west, leaving burned corpses and sundered families in his wake."

She pulled newspaper clippings out of the stack. "Want to read his press reports?" They were emblazoned with headlines, "Killer Burns Family to Death One by One, then Kills Police Officer" and "Arson Killer Claims Two in Iowa."

"What..." I felt myself speak in a hoarse whisper. "What happened to him?"

"That part isn't in the clippings." She reached into the file and pulled out another page, handing it to me.

It was a report, signed by Roberto Bastian, the head of M-Squad. I skimmed it then looked up to Ariadne. "Your people caught up with him halfway to Des Moines."

"They wrecked his car, beat him to a bloody pulp," she said with a haunted look, "and dragged him back here where we slapped him in restraints and sent him to Arizona to spend the rest of his life in a deep, dark hole in the middle of the desert." Her eyes found mine, and I looked away first. "This is why we're here. To protect people from this sort of monster." She picked up another file from a stack to her left, slapping it onto the table in front of me, followed by another, and another. They weren't loud, but the sound of the paper hitting the rock of the desk made me flinch each time. Finally she grabbed the rest of the pile and let them fall in front of me with a thud.

I stared at it, then pulled a file from the middle of the stack, opened it, and thumbed through. It was a series of reports from an incident in Birmingham, Alabama, that was handled by their Atlanta campus. A murder committed by a kid who was no older than me. Then another, and another. They caught him on his sixth victim. They were all committed in the course of robberies; three in the same incident. Every last one of them had been beaten to death.

The next file was from Chicago and detailed a rapist working the South Side that was putting every victim in the hospital and a few in the morgue by what the victims described as "one horrific punch." And only one. Impossibly strong, the report concluded. The rest of the file laid out the evidence against the creep: the witness statements, the agent investigation. The final report was signed by Zack Davis.

I flipped through about fifty of them, not reading every detail but taking them all in. Every crime was like something you'd see in a movie or maybe a police blotter. Some of them were a decade old or more; some were very, very recent. They were from all over the country, and each one had a trail of evidence cataloged, indicating why the agent or meta investigating believed the person they caught was the guilty party. And almost all of them were slam-dunk obvious.

I closed the last file, a robbery/murder, and put it on the stack with the rest. I swallowed hard, wishing somehow I could scrub all that I had just read out of my brain, along with all the things Wolfe did to me and the things he'd shown me in flashes through his memories earlier. I felt a desire to run far, far away to a place where people didn't do things to other people like I saw in those files and in Wolfe's memories...and in my own. Too bad there wasn't a place far enough I could run to find that. "Why did you show me this?"

"Because this is the 'solved' stack." She reached behind Old Man Winter's desk and pulled out another stack, almost as big as the first and lay it in front of me. The solved stack's folders where manila; these were red. "These are unsolved, crimes where meta involvement was suspected but the perpetrator couldn't be located because they didn't make a big enough noise and we only have so many agents and resources." She raised an eyebrow at me and opened the first folder. "Take this one, for instance...thirty-eight-year-old man dies in an attempted robbery. A witness said that the perpetrator seemed to have extra arms growing out of his sides that restrained the victim while the robber beat him to death."

"That's...horrible." I was suddenly hyperaware of Old Man Winter looking at me. I felt like he was sifting me, trying to filter through to my core, and I suddenly didn't care for what he might find there. The anger made me bite back at Ariadne, hard. "I'm sorry he died, but I don't see how anything I do is going to matter. I have my own problems, and I'm only—"

"A little girl?" There was no accusation in her words, but they slapped me just the same. "A teenager with more strength than twenty men and a power that could keep any physical assailant at bay."

"This isn't my problem." I wanted to be firm. I needed to find Mom.

"So it doesn't matter if it doesn't involve you?" That time there was accusation, and it stung. I wondered if my verbal lashings hit her half so hard as hers hit me.

I reddened. "I'm a teenager; I'm pretty sure it's a biological imperative to think that way."

"I guess you're pretty normal, then," Ariadne said, staring me down.

"But you can be better." Old Man Winter said it from behind his desk, leaning forward on his knuckles to look close at me. I didn't cower from his stare, but I felt a bit of withering. Wolfe was nowhere to be heard, not that I felt like I could count on him for moral support. "You are not some schoolgirl whose blissful ignorance of the harsh realities of the world cloud her eyes with starry dreams of happy endings. Are you?"

"I'd like a happy ending," I said. "But I don't ignore the fact that the world can be cold and brutal and that there are people out there who exist solely to hurt others."

"Then you know that someone has to protect ordinary people." Ariadne leaned forward again and her red hair flared against the dull background of Old Man Winter's office. "They can't protect themselves against what waits for them out there. They have no defense because they don't know what they have to defend against. Metahumans move too fast, hit too hard, for an unprepared person to fend them off. Only someone who's well prepared—and armed, actually—stands a chance against them, and then only if they don't get taken by surprise."

"Same old story," I said, swallowing hard again. "Why are you telling me this? What do you want me to do?"

"Even when you find your mother," Old Man Winter spoke, his quiet voice devastating for some reason, "at some point you will have to decide what to do with your own life, how you wish to spend it. You are nearly a woman grown, and you need to find—"

"A job?" I licked my lips.

"A path. A career. Maybe even...a purpose," Ariadne said. "Something you can do that you can believe in, that will challenge you, that won't leave you hating your life and questioning why you're even doing what you're doing." She laughed, a low, quiet laugh that had no real mirth behind it. "Unless you'd like to get to age forty and wake up to wonder where your life went."

"Forty is a long ways off for me." I looked at my boots. Most eighteen-year-old girls wear shoes; I'm in boots. Most girls my age wear dresses sometimes, go to school, look forward to prom and graduation. I'm stuck in outfits that cover me head to toe, I've been home every day, week, and year for over a decade, and all I have to look forward to is finding my missing mother so...what? I can go back to living like that?

"It'll be here before you know it." Ariadne snapped her fingers in front of her face. "It goes fast. And the question you'll be left with is if you just got by or if you actually made a difference." She slid the stack of files away from me. "We don't expect you to make a decision right now." She pulled out a lone piece of paper and placed it in front of me. "Working for us as a meta will have its rewards—more money per year than most eighteen-year-olds make, along with other benefits—"

"I'm not super concerned with a 401(k) right now." I glanced at the sheet. Money meant almost nothing to me, largely because I'd never had any opportunity to use it. I truly didn't know the value of a dollar, nor what it bought. "What do you want me to do? What would happen if I said yes?"

"You would enter training with M-Squad and agent trainers, learn how agents operate, field procedure, all that. After some basics, you'd be assigned a more experienced partner and learn how to be a 'retriever'—someone who tracks down rogue or awakening metas and brings them back to the Directorate either through peaceful means, or, if necessary—"

"Cracking skulls?" I glanced at the compensation sheet and wondered if $100,000 per year was a lot or a little for a girl just starting out.

"You never seemed like you had a problem with physical violence before." Ariadne was unrelenting. "Like, say, when you battered Zack and Kurt, or when you went looking for a fight with Wolfe—"

"I don't." I looked up from the sheet to her. "I don't have a problem breaking the teeth out of anyone who does the things that you've showed me in the files." I felt my jaw clench as a little surge of pleasure from Wolfe ran through me at the thought of inflicting pain on others. "But I don't know that I want to be a retriever for a living, always chasing down some fugitive meta who might kill me if I screw up. And I don't know that I could..." I struggled with the words. "I mean, killing Wolfe was an accident. I don't know if I could...do that...to someone else. "

"It rarely comes to that, " she said. "And retriever's not necessarily the end of the line. You could move up, join M-Squad, move to another branch, work into one of our training positions to teach and guide the metas here at the Minneapolis branch—"

"Because that's the place for me, guiding the next generation."

"—or you could move into administration." She shrugged. "There are a lot of places you could go. We're a big operation. You could see the world, help us expand overseas if you wanted. You'd have the satisfaction of knowing you're doing some good."

"I hear you say it," I picked up the compensation sheet between my thumb and forefinger, "but how do I really know it's true?"

"Trust is a two-way street," she said, standing. "It won't happen overnight, but if you're out chasing these people down and you see what they do, you'll eventually come to realize that we're the good guys. We don't expect a decision right now."

"You have a great deal to think about," Old Man Winter said. "You stand at the edge of the rest of your life. The decisions you make now affect everything from here on. Gone are the times when simple and inconsequential matters governed your life. It is now the time for you to choose who you want to be, what you want to stand for, and what you want your life to reflect." He walked around the desk, buttoning his suit coat as he walked to the door and opened it for me. "So few people get to truly steer their course the way you have the chance to now. And the question before you is—will you strive to be normal and live an ordinary life? Or will you do what no one else can do—and be more?"

Chapter 13

I carried the compensation sheet with me, crumpled in my fist, when I left the meeting. I had read through it, though I confess I was in a haze as I left them. One item stuck out, though—a $10,000 bonus to be paid when I signed on for the training program. I still didn't have a great concept of how much that would buy me, nor what I would do with it. The sheet indicated I could continue to stay on the campus free of charge with all meals provided.

The meeting had taken longer than I expected and I'd skipped breakfast. I had a lot on my mind—after all, the question of how Gavrikov got out of his box was a pretty good one, and I hoped my theory was wrong. We hadn't discussed Full Metal Jackass in much detail; not that there was much to discuss. Why did I doubt he was the sort to just give up and go home after one encounter that went awry?

Probably because he dressed himself like a submarine and paraded himself into town in hopes of capturing me. You doesn't dress like that unless you're a hopelessly delusional loser who will continue to swing for the fences long past the time you should have returned to the dugout.

I entered the cafeteria at half past eleven. It was crowded already. I made my way through the line, again ignoring the animosity of the workers as I gathered my food. I was picking my way over to the far wall, prepared to eat by myself (again) when I caught sight of Zack, sitting with his back to me. I took one step toward him and halted. He was at a table for four and it was filled. Kurt Hannegan sat next to him and Scott Byerly and Kat Forrest sat opposite.

I began to slink back toward the window when Kat waved at me, her big eyes and a wide smile visible even from across the cafeteria. An inward feeling of desperation enveloped me as she tried to wave me over. I sighed and closed my eyes, and when I opened them, Zack was also gesturing for me to join them. He got up and pulled another chair over. With greatest reluctance, I made my way across the room and endured the enthusiastic greetings of Kat and Zack and the muted one from Scott. Hannegan ignored me, I ignored him, and we were both the happier for it.

"Scott has something he wants to tell you," Zack said as I sat down. I could feel my motions reduced to a severe stiffness, as though all my joints were locked together and it was only through acts of absolute will I could bend them to seat myself. I looked at Scott, who was at my left, and had his head bowed.

"I wanted to apologize," the young man said, his face angled toward the table. Kat and Zack watched him while Hannegan continued to shovel a burrito into his face. "I didn't really know you when I wrote that note and it was wrong and inappropriate." He managed to look up and I got the impression that he was rather like a child caught doing something he shouldn't. "I'm sorry."

"All right," Zack said. "Now we can put all that unpleasantness behind us." He looked at me, the satisfaction disappearing from his face. "Right?"

I thought about arguing, but what was the point? Byerly couldn't have hated me any more than I had hated myself when he'd written it. "Sure," I said. "Bygones and forgetting and all that." I picked up the burrito from my plate. The smell of beans, rice and chicken wafted up to me, tempered with the tang of the salsa and guacamole.

"What did you talk with Old Man Winter and Ariadne about?" Zack asked just as I was taking my first bite.

I finished chewing before I answered. "How did you know

about that?"

"I went to see Ariadne this morning and the secretary told me she was in a meeting with the two of you and couldn't be disturbed." He took a sip of the water sitting in front of him.

"History of metas, remember?" The burrito was slippery in my gloves and Byerly was giving me a funny look as the salsa dribbled down the leather and onto my sleeve. I dropped the burrito and wiped at it with a napkin.

"Uh huh." He chewed as he answered, kind of skeptical. Hannegan still hadn't looked at me and Kat hadn't taken her eyes off me yet. I wanted to knock her chair over with her still in it. Or maybe Wolfe did. No, it was probably me. "You guys talk about anything else?"

I remembered the compensation sheet, tucked away in my coat pocket. "Yeah," I said. "A couple things."

"They offered you a job, didn't they?" This came from Hannegan, who had stopped eating and was frozen with a taco halfway to his mouth.

"Yeah." I felt myself flush. "So?"

"Doing what?" Scott Byerly did a flush of his own, his ruddy complexion suddenly redder.

"As an agent?" Zack was looking at me in wonderment. "A retriever?" He looked down at my side and my eyes followed him a moment later. His hand was already in motion and he snatched the compensation sheet from where it was dangling out of my pocket. I didn't try to stop him, and he stared at it, eyes narrowed as he focused, Hannegan leaning over his shoulder. "Wait, this isn't an organizational chart...this is...this is...whoa." Zack's jaw dropped and he looked at Hannegan in near-astonishment. "I don't get paid that much. Do you?"

"Hell, no," Kurt said, scowling. "And I'm near the top of the pay scale!"

"But at the bottom of their estimation, apparently," I said and ripped the paper out of Zack's hands.

There was an eerie quiet around the table that lasted almost five seconds before Scott Byerly spoke. "Can I see that?"

I let out a small noise of exasperation and thrust it at him. "Sure. Why not?"

Kat Forrest looked over his shoulder as he looked down the page. "Wow," she said. "They must think you're really powerful to offer you so much."

"I'd offer you more to leave," Hannegan said under his breath.

"This is..." Byerly blinked a few times in rapid succession and then handed the page back to me. "A very nice offer. I wish I'd gotten one." I saw his jaw tighten as he said it.

"The day will come, my friend," Zack said. "Probably soon, in fact—" A low buzzing filled the air and he reached down, pulling out his cell phone and studying the screen. He looked to Kurt. "Ariadne wants to see us."

Kurt paused in eating, his mouth full. "Now?" Flecks of half-chewed food rained onto the table and I looked away.

"When was the last time she made an appointment to see the low-paid help?" Zack stood and pulled his coat off the back of his chair. "Yes, now." He looked back at the three of us still seated. "You guys take it easy." Hannegan followed him out, a taco clenched in his chubby fists.

"Congratulations on your offer," Kat said, her eyes shining. "That's really amazing. Not too many metas get asked to go through the training program. You should be proud."

"Why?" I took a bite of my burrito and then wiped my glove on a napkin. "I didn't do anything except be born a meta."

"Well, you killed that psychopath." Her smile glittered like a spotlight shining directly in my eyes, annoying me.

"Yeah, you did," Byerly said, then leaned closer. "How did you do that, by the way?"

I felt still, as though a great slab of ice had frozen everything inside me. "I told you—I'm death."

"What does that mean?" He leaned even closer, almost whispering. "You're an efficient killer? You're super strong?"

I felt an ugly thread tug at me inside, felt Wolfe doing something, though I couldn't tell what. I ignored him. "It's none of your business."

"Are you a human time bomb? Like the guy that blew up the science labs?" Byerly kept pressing, and I could feel the warmth of his breath on my cheek, he was so close—too close. "Can you throw energy or maybe—"

"What I can do—" I started to scoot my chair away from him but he landed his hand on my arm, stopping me. "If you really want to see, just keep your hand where it is. If you don't, move it."

"Maybe I want to know." His eyes were focused, boring in on me and I saw something else in them, an intensity.

"Scott, let her go—" Kat's plea went ignored.

My glove was already off. Wolfe had moved my hand without me even knowing it and it was on Scott's cheek. He started to recoil, but I anchored my thumb and forefinger, gripping him on the neck. Not hard enough to choke him, but enough to let him know I had a good hold on him. His eyes widened in surprise, then narrowed in anger, and he brought a hand around, maybe instinctively, to hit me. I knocked it aside and jerked him to his feet.

I saw the anger vanish, replaced with creases in his forehead from the first stirrings of pain. "Ouch," he breathed, consternation knitting his brows together. "Ow...oh..." He sucked in a sharp breath and grunted. After another second he let out a squeal that drew even more attention from those around us and then he let out an earsplitting, agonized scream that started a scramble for the cafeteria door, people falling over each other to get the hell out of there.

"Put him down!" Kat was on her feet, shouting at me. I

strained, trying to regain control of my hand, but Wolfe was in charge, holding the rest of me still. I lifted Scott Byerly off his feet and he shuddered in the air, convulsing, his eyes rolling back in his head. I looked on, horrified, unable to stop it.

I felt a blow land on the back of my head and I flew forward, releasing my grasp on Byerly. I plowed through three tables, heard some things break that sounded like it could have been me or the furniture, I wasn't sure which. I came to rest twenty feet away from where I had started, a medley of other peoples' lunches smeared on my clothes. Kat was already at Scott's side and Clyde Clary stood not far away, his lips twisted in an amused smile. "Clyde," I said, using my sleeve to mop some blood from the back of my head where he'd hit me.

"Girl, ain't no one calls me Clyde," his pudgy face went angry quickly.

"I think I just did." I stood up. "But if you'd prefer, I could just call you fatass prick—"

He charged at me, broad shoulders flashing underneath his shirt, the skin around his neck rippling, turning into something different. It looked like metal in the brief glimpse I got before he put his shoulder down and stormed at me. He moved fast, especially for such a big guy.

I grabbed the nearest table, heavy and metal, and heaved it at him. It spun, hit him in the face and ricocheted off at high velocity, flying through one of the upper windows of the cafeteria. He moved off his course not even a millimeter, his head now the same dull metal that I had seen beneath his shirt. I dodged out of the way just in time as he shredded the tables behind me, shards of them flying through the air.

"You're dangerous. I like it." He smiled and grabbed a table of his own as I rolled to my feet and he chucked it at me. It skipped off the floor, a hubcap of spinning death that grazed my shoulder as I dropped below it and heard the shattering of glass behind me. He threw another, then another, and I dodged them, executing some gymnastic evasions I wouldn't have been capable of even a month ago—before my powers manifested. I looked around for a weapon—any kind of weapon—that might be effective against a hulking slab of metal.

He stomped toward me, malice in his eyes. I met his attack, ducking his punch and grabbing his arm with my ungloved hand as he started to pull it back. I gripped onto the slick metal and held tight, waiting for a reaction; it was cool in my grasp. The big jackass looked at me, then down to my hand, then back at me and split into a broad grin. "Your succubus trick only works on flesh." He pulled his arm back, yanking me off balance and lifting me from the ground. I managed to hold onto him, but only just.

A second later I realized what he was doing. As soon as he pulled me toward him, he set me up for a punch with his other hand. His fist made contact with my midsection and I felt all the air leave my lungs in a rush, worse than any physical pain I'd felt since Wolfe had near-gutted me. I flew through the air, landing with a crash on a metal chair that promptly upended. I heard more things break when I landed and this time I knew it was me, not the furniture.

I sat up, clutching at my ribs. There was blood in my mouth, the metallic taste unpleasant enough that I spit it out. Clary stalked toward me from across the room; his punch had thrown me almost a hundred feet, from the middle of the cafeteria to near the kitchen.

"Any suggestions to keep us from getting pummeled?" I muttered the words under my breath, but Wolfe was silent. If ever there had been a time when I could have used the help of the world's most brutal infighter, this would have been it. I looked around and my eyes widened as I remembered something, a possibility. I made for the kitchen, hobbling as fast as my wounded frame could carry me, Clary not far behind.

I jumped over the cafeteria line and the serving stations with one good leap. As I reached the kitchen doors I heard Clary crash through them behind me. "You can run girl, but you can't hide!"

"You can spout cliches," I said, "but you can't find a woman who'll enjoy your company."

I plunged into the kitchen and heard the screams of the serving ladies, who had all run inside to hide after the altercation started in the dining area. There were a half dozen of them, all wide-eyed. "Get out!" I said as I pushed past them. I stopped next to the freezer and swung the heavy door open, then checked my placement. He would have to charge through a preparation station in order to get to me, with an obstructed view, and if he wasn't paying much attention (which I assumed was his usual state) he'd go charging into the freezer where with any luck I could shut the door behind him.

Clary stopped at the entrance to the kitchen. "Come on, now, girl."

"I'm not going anywhere with you," I said, holding my arm. It was actually the least of my pains, but the others weren't easily reached and pulling it closer seemed to ease the torment in my chest.

"Have it your way, then." He lowered his head. "I'll let Old Man Winter decide what he wants done with you once you're good and out." He barreled toward me, not bothering to use the aisles, charging right through the prep station, tearing the vent hoods out of the stove, destroying a cook top and counters, metal flying in every direction.

I watched him for as long as I could, but once the debris started flying my way I dodged sideways, behind the heavy door of the freezer. I hit the ground and my chest and side screamed at me. I watched him run past me into the freezer, hit the wall and bounce off, then heard the crashing of a side of beef and cartons of God knows what hitting the floor. I kicked the freezer door and it swung closed. I wrenched myself up and yanked the pin off a shelf nearby and plunged it into the lock.

I took two steps back and fell down, breathing a sigh of relief. Everything still hurt, but at least that idiot was contained where he couldn't do any harm—

That thought lasted less than the second it took for the door to the freezer to come exploding off its hinges. It flew through the air above me, skipping across my left shoulder and leaving a gash over an inch deep. I was pretty sure it broke my collarbone, but it was hard to tell among all the other agonies.

"Nice try." Clary sauntered over to me as I squirmed on the floor. I heard a hissing that I thought was in my head until I realized that the idiot had severed the gas line to the stove when he charged through. "Ain't nothin' can hold me."

"I think you've confused 'can' with 'want'," I said through gritted teeth. "For example, a woman 'can' hold you, but none of them 'want' to—"

He grabbed me in a clawlike hold around the neck and picked me up in a manner that reminded me of the way Wolfe had manhandled me, beaten me, abused me. Clary's piggy eyes leered at me from behind his smug smile and I hated him, wanted to crush him, but now I couldn't breathe.

The eyes.

I stared down at him. Sure enough, Wolfe's voice was right— his skin was metal but his eyes were the same white as always, the blood vessels visible on the sides.

My fingers lanced out and I stabbed him with my thumb right in the socket. I did not hesitate nor pull my strike and he screamed in uncontrolled misery. I fell to the ground, unable to catch myself. A lancing pain ran up my entire upper body after the impact, and I floundered on the floor, holding onto my sides.

"YOU BITCH!" Clary stomped and I bounced a few inches into the air before landing again. It hurt more. "YOU TOOK OUT MY EYE!"

"Honestly, it wasn't one of your best attributes," I muttered. "Not that you have any good ones." I managed to get to my hands and knees and looked for something to use as a weapon since it had become obvious that he was unlikely to present me with an opportunity to stab out his other eye. There was a ringing in my ears that went along with the hissing. I saw a fire extinguisher and it dawned on me that it was probably a better choice than anything else. I grabbed it and crawled along on my hands and knees, trying to avoid his blind rage behind me.

I had reached the door when he finally realized I wasn't near him anymore. "Hey! Where do you think you're going?"

I used a countertop to pull myself up and turn back to him. "Me? I think I'll go for a quiet drink somewhere. Care to join me?"

He had started towards me but stopped, his head snapping back, his jaw opening slightly. "Really?"

I grimaced. "No. Not really. I'm going to get medical treatment. You? You can burn in hell. Literally."

He stomped his foot again and his jaw made a scraping noise as he ground his teeth together. "Damn you, girl! What am I supposed to do with one eye?"

"You could be huge in the kingdom of the blind." I reached back and flung the fire extinguisher with all my much-vaunted metahuman strength.

And it missed him.

He smiled as it sailed by. "You missed—"

It hit the side of the metal countertop, hard, and sparked. I had the intense satisfaction of seeing him look back, confused, before the fireball blew me out of the room.

Chapter 14

"You!" I awoke to the sound of Dr. Perugini's less-than-dulcet tones. I stared up at her when my eyes opened. Her dark complexion was flushed, her eyes on fire as she glared down at me in the hospital bed. I took in the medical bay around me and saw Clary in the bed next to me, a bandage over his eye. Scott Byerly was across the way, Kat at his side, casting the occasional furtive glance at me.

The doctor poked her thin index finger in my face. "You keep causing me so many problems!" She let out a string of curses in her native Italian. "I used to have a nice, peaceful life! Since you get here I have nothing but bodies all the time! Before, I work on my novel and clean my instruments. Since you show up, all I do is fix hurt people!"

I coughed and tried to sit up. "Your job description includes that, I believe." Her eyes blazed and she pulled her finger out of my face and grabbed a tongue depressor out of her jacket pocket. Without a word she poked me in the side. "OW!" She did it again. "OW OW! What the hell?! Were you absent the day you were supposed to take the Hippocratic Oath?" My fingers found my wounded side where she had poked me. "Pretty sure it includes something about not doing harm."

"Not doing harm?" She thrust the tongue depressor in my face and wagged it at me. "You are a fine one to talk! All you do is harm—to yourself and others! All I do is clean up your messes! You are a menace!" The way she said it made me chuckle, which did not improve her mood. She whirled and marched away from me, back to her office. She slammed the door and dropped the blinds, giving me one last glower before her face disappeared.

"You awake, girl?" Clary's stupid drawl drew my attention to him. He was laying on his back one bed over, a bandage over his eye.

"No, I'm talking in my sleep." I tilted my head to look at him. "What do you want?"

"That was a cheap shot, blowing me out the back of the building. Hurt a lot too, when I woke up." He blinked with his one good eye.

"Oh, yeah?" I adopted a disinterested tone. "I'm so *not* sorry." It took a minute for him to register what I'd said.

"Yeah, well, I'm not sorry I busted your guts." He guffawed. "That was the best tussle I've had in a long time. Cojones. Girl, you got 'em."

"Actually, I don't." I turned away from him and stared straight up. "But it doesn't surprise me that you wouldn't know that about women."

He looked at me, blank. "That was a good fight, you hear me? That was good." He put his hands behind his head and leaned back and smiled like he'd just won a prize.

I was about to tell him just how dumb I thought he was when the door clicked open. "I can assure both of you that what you did in the cafeteria was *not* good." Ariadne stood silhouetted in the entry to the medical bay, a paper in her hand and a fury in her eyes that was only a couple degrees shy of what I'd seen from Dr. Perugini. "Thirteen people with minor injuries, Byerly—" she seemed to be flustered, searching for a word, "—soul drained or death touched or whatever, Clary lost an eye, Sienna with a host of broken bones and severe blood loss, and OH, let's not forget! Over a million dollars in damage to the cafeteria!"

She made it across the medical bay and slapped the folder in her hand down on Clary's tray. "She's not even eighteen, Clary! Did it not even occur to you that she might have made a rash decision—a mistake—in attacking Byerly?"

"Well, no," the big man said. "She was draining him pretty hard. I just wanted to put her down, you know—"

"Rhetorical question, Clary!" She thumped her hand on the tray, stunning him into silence. "Try to pretend you've never assaulted anyone before! It's not your job to break up a cafeteria altercation by bludgeoning the offender to death; it's your job to pursue the dangerous metahumans we send you after." She pulled back after delivering the last directly to his face, causing him to flinch. "Get it straight. You're not a four-year-old. Keep your damned hands to yourself and stop looking for a fight everywhere you go."

"But—"

"If the next words out of your mouth are anything besides 'Yes ma'am, I'll never do anything like it again' then I will personally have Bastian come down here and deal with you." She faded. "He wanted to, desperately." Clary shrank away, almost seeming to recede into the bed.

I snorted and instantly regretted it. Ariadne turned her withering stare on me. "Don't get me started on you."

I coughed and tried to look contrite. "I'm sorry. I...overreacted when Scott put his hand on me."

She continued to stare for a second longer then shook her head in disbelief. "Overreacted? You nearly killed him. How is that an overreaction?"

I thought about it for a moment and shrugged. "Because it sounds better than the way you put it. He wanted to see what I could do in the worst way. So I showed him. In the worst—"

She let out a noise of disgust. "Is that how you're going to operate if we train you to be an agent?"

Clary looked up in surprise. "You're gonna make her an agent?"

"Shut up," Ariadne spat at him and whipped her head back

around to me. "You wrecked the cafeteria and blew up the kitchen. You could have killed somebody."

"Um," I shook my head, "I believe that the persons most likely to have gotten killed today were myself and Byerly, in that order."

"What about me?" Clary's face was puckered, as though he were insulted by what I said.

"You don't count." I looked to Ariadne, who was steaming. "He was trying to kill me! I just repaid the favor." I looked down. "If it's going to be a...um...an insurmountable obstacle—"

"It's not an insurmountable anything." Ariadne's withering stare turned to a simmer. "But if this is what we can expect from you as an employee—"

"I didn't mean to." I said it low, almost under my breath. "It just got out of hand, I'm sorry." An ugly thought occurred to me. "Oh, God. If I take the job, does that mean you'll be my boss?"

She folded her arms in front of her. "Yes. Why?"

"I think that might be a dealbreaker." I tried to sit up. "There's no way I'm going to be able to not make insubordinate wisecracks about you."

"Tell me about it," Clary said, nodding his head.

"I said wisecracks, not dumbasscracks."

"I think we can typically overlook incidents of..." she paused, "...over-exuberant verbal witticisms. However, failure to follow orders is looked down on, as is destroying campus property." She frowned. "Or in your cases, the whole damned campus."

I stiffened and wondered if she was accusing me of blowing up the science building. It didn't seem fair, since I was being held responsible now for two incidents which were started by the houseguest in my skull, that mongrel that still needed to be house-broken and taught not to play with other people's bodies.

"Be that as it may," she looked daggers at Clary and then turned back to me, "we can overlook this, but any further incidents would provoke our full displeasure."

Clary looked at me. "They're gonna let you skate!"

I looked over at him. "Yeah. Awesome." I turned back to Ariadne. "Anything on my mother's stuff yet?"

"What?" She took a step back. "Oh. That. Our forensics lab was in the science building."

I took a deep breath and let it out slowly. "So it's gone."

"Yes." She wavered, looking as though she wanted to offer me some sympathy, but thought the better of it. "I'm sorry."

"Bummer." Clary was nodding his head, then he brightened. "When do you start training? Cuz that'll be fun."

Chapter 15

I walked out of the medical unit under my own power shortly before nightfall. My broken bones were knitted, though my skin still had scabs in numerous places that would take until the next day to heal.

"Get out and don't come back!" Dr. Perugini shouted as the door swung closed behind me. Clary walked out along with me and I kept an eye on him, though he was whistling a pretty happy tune the whole way out. Turned out that Kat Forrest had given him his eye back with her healing power after I blew up the kitchen. It took a little while before Perugini was sure it was fine, but when she ripped the bandage off I almost fell off the bed in shock. No wonder he wasn't holding a grudge.

Byerly had left a few hours earlier. It was awkward after he woke up. Clary leavened the moment with a few choice jokes that were fairly graphic and involved my powers and how they'd affect someone in an intimate setting. Needless to say, Byerly didn't laugh and neither did I, and when Perugini pronounced that he was in fine form after Forrest's ministrations, no one was more relieved to see him gather his clothes and dart out than me.

"You wanna get something to eat?" Clary asked me as we cleared the Headquarters building. "I'm starving. I didn't get my lunch before we got into it, y'know." His earnestness would have been endearing if he hadn't been trying to beat the daylights out of me only a few hours earlier.

"I'll pass." I left him behind, walking back toward the dorm. I was hungry too, but I doubted I'd be welcomed in the cafeteria for a while—assuming it was even operable at this point. I had a feeling that the below-zero temperatures I'd encounter would make any sort of meal eaten there a chilling experience. And that was just from the pissed-off people. We'd broken a lot of windows, which meant it'd also be literally cold in there.

I went back to my room, closed the door, and dug into the stash of food I'd gotten from my apparent burglary of the cafeteria a few days earlier. There was no doubt in my mind that Wolfe had done it, taking my body for a joyride while I slept. Now that he'd taken control during my waking hours, that was even more worrisome. I could tell Ariadne and Old Man Winter, I suppose, but only at the risk of being locked away and never allowed out again. I didn't enjoy the thought of a cell of my own in Arizona, so I'd decided to play the whole incident off as me being reckless. I assumed it worked. It was hard to say.

"How do I get you out of my head?" I asked the question aloud, but no answer was forthcoming from inside or out. I chewed on a piece of beef jerky and sat down on my bed. No one but another succubus could answer my question, and the only one I knew of was Mom.

It occurred to me that I had a few powers to go along with the fatal touch of my skin, one of which was something Wolfe had called "Dreamwalking"—the ability to touch the minds of others while sleeping. I'd had conversations with Reed and Wolfe by doing that, and all it took was a willingness to fall asleep while concentrating on the person I wanted to talk to.

I was a little afraid to sleep after the control Wolfe had exerted on me, but I was more afraid of having to admit to Old Man Winter and Ariadne that I had him in me and that he was taking control. I finished my beef jerky, chewing slower and taking more time than was necessary even for that tough stuff.

When I was done, I lay my head down on the pillow and clicked off the lights. I thought of Mom, of the house, of the old days when we were a family. I could feel the tug of fatigue on my eyelids, but I lay with them wide open in the dark, worrying over what might happen when I closed them. Wolfe was a monster, a beast that I had once hoped I could put down like a rabid animal. Instead he was cohabitating with me in my own body.

It was bad enough when I only heard his voice. Now he'd set free a crazed man who could explode with the force of a bomb and turned even more of the Directorate against me. If I took the job they offered me, there would be no doubt it was going to be a hostile working environment. Most of the metas I encountered in the halls had done a swift direction change when they saw me coming as I walked back to my room.

I lay there in silence, the only noise coming from the warm air rushing through the vents above me. I could hear a tap-tap-tap of metal in the ventilation system somewhere as the ductwork vibrated from the furnace-heated wind that pushed through it. I could smell that clean, sterile scent that lacked the authentic aroma of a house. The whole room felt less lived-in and more generic, as though it was a room made for anyone. My room at home was mine, made for me. I looked at the blank walls, lit by the glow of lights outside, and thought that maybe I should get a painting or something.

The sheets were cool against my skin. It was comfortable, neither warm nor hot. The spice of the beef jerky lingered on my tongue and I thought about getting up to brush my teeth, but now I was drifting and it was too late. I tried to bring my thoughts back to Mom but things were hazy.

I woke to an insistent knocking on the door. The drowsiness was overwhelming, a fog hanging around my head. I tried to ignore the sound, but the thumping grew louder and the interval between it shorter and shorter until I finally shook off my covers, pulled on a pair of long gym pants and a t-shirt and threw it open. "What?" I wasn't kind about asking.

Zack was waiting outside, Kurt behind him, leaning against

the wall. "Get dressed. We're going."

"Going where?" I was so bleary eyed at that point that my thoughts were coming in fits and starts. For a fraction of a second I wondered if they were there to try and dispose of me.

"We got a vague report of a meta causing some trouble at Eden Prairie Center—the mall we were at the other night, you remember? Ariadne wants you to come along."

"What?" I blinked twice and rubbed my eyes, still trying to shake off the sleepiness. "I don't work for you guys." I shook my head and added, "Yet."

"She still wants you to come along. She said to call it a ride along, and if you didn't like that, to call it penance for the cafeteria because M-Squad is busy chasing down a lead on Gavrikov a hundred miles south of here." He chucked his thumb back at Hannegan, who waited, staring out the window in the hallway. "We'll wait for you out here. Think you can be ready in five minutes?"

I looked at him with great pity. "You don't know many girls, do you?"

He cracked a smile. "Ten minutes?"

I shut the door on him. Thirty minutes later and after some insistent knocking at one point, I joined them in the hall, wearing what was probably my eight hundredth black turtleneck and jeans since coming to this place. I'd pulled my hair back in a ponytail and someone had left another coat for me in the closet, the same kind of black, heavy wool that I'd been wearing all along. I was growing a little tired of the flimsy boots they'd been giving me and made a mental note to ask Ariadne for some with a steel toe if I was going to keep fighting people bigger than I was.

"I don't get it," Hannegan said as we walked toward the garage. "What took you so long? It's not like you're wearing any makeup."

I blushed. "Shut up." I had actually been trying to get my hair to lay flat, but after sleeping it was a mess, which is why it ended up in a ponytail. Again. "What are we going to investigate?"

Zack frowned as he opened the door to the garage and held it for me. Hannegan darted his bulk through first, drawing a look of acrimony from me. "There was some sort of altercation earlier today, some local youths tried to get tough with a guy and he smeared them all over the pavement." Zack looked over at me as he let the door swing shut behind us. "Literally. Two of the youths died, and the others said the guy moved so fast that it was like he was blurry."

"Why are we doing this now? Isn't it Saturday night?" I opened my own door to the car and got in the backseat as usual. "I thought people only worked 9 to 5 on Monday through Friday?"

"Most people do," Zack said. "But you don't wanna be normal, do you?" He winked at me and put the car in reverse, backing out of the parking spot.

I ignored the leering grin from Hannegan. "Perish the thought."

When we got to the mall we circled, passing a department store with a roll of police tape staked out in a circle on the sidewalk. "That must be where it happened," Kurt said.

"You catch on quick," I said. "Was it the 'POLICE LINE DO NOT CROSS' written in big letters that tipped you off or the fact that there's a smear of blood on the sidewalk that looks like someone slaughtered...well...you?" He shot me an acid look that brought a big grin to my face. "What's the matter? Am I annoying you?"

"Annoying is the Facebook statuses my twelve-year old niece posts. You are a hazard," he said, shaking his head. "'Like for a rate'—what does that even mean?"

I frowned. "A rate? Like an hourly rate? Like a hooker?"

"It's for photos," Zack said. "They 'Like' your status and you tell them how you think their profile picture looks."

Kurt nodded his head as though a mystery of the universe had been revealed. I looked at the two of them and asked the dumb question. "What's Facebook?"

"You don't need it," Hannegan said. "You have no friends."

His barb hit home and I tried to ignore it, not bothering to come up with a reply. It's not like he was wrong.

We parked and walked to an entrance after passing the police line for a quick look. "Without a chance to look over the forensics, checking out the scene won't do us much good," Zack said as we entered.

The mall was much more crowded than it had been the last time we were there. It felt like there were people packed from wall to wall in the place, a throng that was moving, bustling. There was a hum as we passed the food court and the smell of all sorts of goodness reached my nose. I stopped and sniffed, feeling a little bit of salivation in my mouth.

"Come on, shut-in," Hannegan said, passing me. "We've got work to do."

"I'm hungry," I said. "I don't know if you heard about it, but someone got into this big fight that destroyed the cafeteria and so I haven't had anything to eat since lunch."

Zack shook his head, stifling a laugh. "Let's sweep the place once and we'll grab you a burger as we come back through."

"But I want a burger now." I looked plaintively at the restaurants and took another deep breath through my nose. "What are the odds some meta killed two people earlier and decided to hang around the scene of the crime?" My gaze drifted to a couple cops, standing off to the side, watching the crowd pass by.

There was the sound of breaking glass behind us and I turned as people started screaming and someone went flying through the air toward us, tossed like a child would throw a toy. "Good odds, apparently," Zack said, reaching into his coat and drawing his gun. "I'd take 'em."

The crowd started pouring past us, women and men alike

shouting and crying out. I jumped onto a nearby planter to get a better vantage point. I made it up in time to see two policemen go down hard under the assault of a familiar figure—a guy with metal plates on his body. "Damn," I breathed. I used the planter to vault over the retreating crowd, leaving Zack and Kurt far behind.

Full Metal Jackass held one of the police officers by the arm. The guy was screaming and crying, probably because he was on his knees and his arm was twisted in a way that would not be comfortable at all. After a moment, Henderschott yanked him up in the air and brought him down with sudden, violent force. I heard the snapping of bones and sinews and the officer went still. I stared at Henderschott, he stared back at me, those eyes glaring at me from tiny slits in the metal helmet. "I feel like we haven't been formally introduced," I said. "I'm Sienna, but you probably know that. And you're David, right? David Henderschott?"

He froze, then nodded once, slowly. He had yet to make an offensive move toward me. "So, David—hope you don't mind if I go on a first name basis with you, since you're trying to kick my ass—you're all alone in the big city, you're supposed to hunt down a girl, and so you decide to murder a couple of locals to draw out the group she's hiding with, get a bead on them and follow them back to where they work, am I right?" He nodded. "But something happens you couldn't possibly suspect—they actually bring the girl with them! What fortuitous luck! You must be having the best day." I stared him down. "What a contrast with your life thus far." He was frozen in place. "What's the matter, David? Wolfe got your tongue?" I smiled at him wickedly.

That lasted about two seconds before he grabbed at his belt and threw something at me. It was small and circular, and I flipped back as it sailed only an inch over my nose. I hit my back and sprung to my feet like Mom taught me, already in a fighting stance. I heard a strangled cry from behind and chanced a look.

Kurt and Zack had made it through the crowd and were standing behind me. While I had dodged what he threw, Hannegan hadn't. It was a collar of some sort and it had caught him perfectly, locking around his neck. He was shaking like a cartoon character caught in an electrical current, screaming, and I could have sworn I smelled urine and worse. Zack took a step toward him, but stopped, afraid to touch him as the big man fell to his knees.

I turned back and dodged another thrown collar. I watched it sail by and as I got back up, Henderschott charged at me. I jumped on top of the planter closest to me, vaulting up and running down the side of it toward him. I came off in a running jump side kick, the kind I used to break boards with Mom. I hoped the heavy sole of my boot would protect me from hurting myself on his helmet.

It mostly did. I hit him where his face would be and I felt the shock of the impact up my leg. It hurt, but not too badly. My knee was locked into place and it held. He had been barreling toward me full steam when we hit and the strength of my kick lifted him off his feet, delivering him on his back as I landed just past him. My leg buckled when I hit the ground, but I managed to stagger and recover, keeping my footing as I swung around to deal with him.

He was flat on his back, legs and arms in the air as he tried to rock to his side. "So, who are you really, David?" I said as I took a couple steps toward him. I reached down before he could roll over and grabbed him by the bottom edge of his helmet. I hoped two things—one, that Wolfe hadn't lied to me, that his skin wasn't going to unstick to his helmet while I was doing this; and two, that I was strong enough to pull off what I thought I could. "Just some asshole working for the same people as Wolfe, hunting down innocent metas who don't stand a chance against your superior experience?" I heaved him up and swung him by the head like a hammer at a track and field tournament (thank you, Olympics).

He flew twenty feet through the air and made solid contact

with the wall, crashing through the plaster and leaving a massive hole. I knew I had to press the attack now, while he was dazed, or risk getting stomped when he got his bearings again. I didn't know if he was stronger than I was, but he certainly didn't take damage like I did, not with his armor on. I stepped through the hole and saw him on the ground against a concrete wall. We were in a passageway only a few feet wide, with lights overhead.

"Or are you just some sick douchebag who got a hard-on reading Iron Man comics as a kid?" I grabbed him by the leg, dodged the kick he aimed at me, heaved him into the air a few feet and brought him down on his forehead. "Were you the kind of guy who got way too excited at the thought of being Tony Stark? You know he's not a real person, right?" I repeated the process twice more, producing a satisfying clang of his face meeting the concrete before he managed to twist and kick, sending me flying back.

I blasted through the drywall and hit the floor out in the mall. With a cringe, I rolled to my feet.

"You okay?" Zack appeared at my side.

"I'll be fine once I mash this comic book geek into paste in his own suit." I rubbed my chest where the kick had landed. "How's fatboy slim?"

"He'll live," Zack replied as I walked to a nearby wall and opened a box containing a fire extinguisher and pulled it out. "What are you doing?"

"I'm on a roll with these things. Shhh." I held a finger up to my mouth and positioned myself next to the hole in the wall after I pulled the pin out of the spray mechanism. I waited and sure enough, Henderschott didn't disappoint, sticking his head out of the opening. I jumped out and yelled "BOO!" mostly for effect, and depressed the trigger. Foam shot out, covering his face, the slit for his mouth and the eye holes—which was the point. He staggered back, clawing at his face. I ducked through the hole and went beneath his flailing arm to get behind him. Once I was, I put my back against the wall and jumped as he edged backward toward me, using the strength in both my legs to give him a hearty shove.

He went sprawling back through the wall and landed face-down with a clang, his metal chestpiece landing on the tile floor. He ripped at his mask and I smiled; he couldn't see a thing because I had covered his eyes with foam. "Looks like you need some glass coverings on your helmet with some little windshield wipers." I grabbed him by the helmet again and lifted him over my head, slamming him to the ground. Fragments of tile shattered and flew everywhere; I saw Zack dodging away from us. I lifted him again and started to bring him down but I felt him slip out of his helmet on the downward arc.

Henderschott bounced and landed on his hands and knees, his head exposed. His hand came up to his face and wiped the powdery film of the fire extinguisher away from his eyes as he rose to his feet and his hands dropped to his side. His face was scarred, hideous, with scars from his forehead to his chin. One of his cheeks was sunken in, like the flesh had been stolen from it. His teeth were jagged, what of them were left, and his jaw hung at a funny angle.

I cocked my head and looked at him, pretending to appraise. "You know, I liked you better with the helmet. Here." Without telegraphing I threw it at him, as hard as I could. He didn't dodge in time, didn't even get a hand up. The helmet hit him in the nose and a geyser of blood erupted as his head snapped back. He staggered, moaned and his hand came up to his face. After a second of trying to clench his nose with his metal encased fingers I saw him drop one of his gauntlets to the ground. He held his hand over his nose, but it didn't do much good. He was bleeding badly; it was slick down the front of his armor.

He looked to be unsteady on his feet and I pulled my gloves off one by one, tucking them into my pocket. He looked at me, his eyes watering. In the distance I could hear police sirens. Hender-schott heard them too, his eyes flicked around and he turned and ran into the department store to the side of us. I took off after him in spite of a shout from Zack. "Get Kurt out of here!" I yelled back to him. "Pick me up outside!"

I saw Henderschott running through racks of clothing, fling-ing them aside, metal and fabric all around me. There were shouts and screams as people tried to get out of his way. He was slower than I was but he made good use of the obstacles in the store to slow me down. He heaved a circular rack that was five feet in di-ameter at me and I was forced to dodge to the side, pulling a stroller with a kid in it along with me.

I landed on all fours, staring at the face of a very scared baby before jumping back to my feet and returning to the chase. I heard a scream of gratitude from the kid's mom and the beginning of a serious cry from the kid as Henderschott blasted through the glass exit doors feet first. I wondered why he had jumped through them that way until it occurred to me that with his head unprotected he'd get sliced like lettuce if he had plowed through the glass in a shoulder charge.

The window shattered as he broke through it. He landed on his back just outside the door and grabbed a trash can from the sidewalk. I had just rounded the corner and was about to follow him through when he whipped the trash can at me. It was big, looked to be encased in concrete, and it blasted through the win-dows that hadn't already been broken between us. I was forced to throw myself out of the way to avoid a shower of broken glass that cut through the air where I had been standing only a moment be-fore, shredding the clothing on the rack behind me.

I picked myself up from the floor and looked up to find Henderschott gone. I ran outside through the glass he had broken, my hands ready to seize him by the face and drown him in uncon-sciousness, but as the biting chill of the outside air prickled my hands and face, I looked to either side. He was gone. Just in case, I looked up the side of the building. No sign of him.

What there was a very clear sign of, however, was police presence. Red and blue lights were flashing at the entrances and more were lighting up the night at all corners of the parking lot. A car screeched to a halt in front of me, Zack at the wheel and Kurt sprawled out in the back. Zack made a frantic gesture for me to get in, which I did, and the tires squealed as we made our getaway.

Chapter 16

"What happened to the armored guy?" Zack's hands were clenched tight on the wheel as he steered us through the parking lot and to an exit that didn't have red and blue lights swarming along the road it led to.

"I don't know." I pulled my gloves out of my pocket and slipped them back on. "He threw a trash can at me and when I got back up, he was gone. I guess he hid in the parking lot."

"Doesn't matter now," Zack said, sending me a tense smile. "With that many police officers on the ground, we would have had a hell of a time apprehending him."

"Not as tough as you think," I said. "All I needed was another minute without the cops and I think I could have put him down."

He looked from the road to my hands, now back in their black leather sheaths. "You really would have done it?"

"I would have knocked him out." I looked at Zack's earnest eyes. "I think I can do that without killing someone. I mean, I don't really want to...you know."

"Yeah." He turned back to the road. "I know."

I looked to Kurt in the back seat. He still wore the collar but seemed to be unconscious and presumably no longer electrified. Zack pulled out his cell phone and made a call to Ariadne, filling her in on the encounter at the mall.

When we returned to the campus, we did not head to the garage but instead to the small underground parking area under Headquarters. When we pulled up in front of the door, Dr. Perugini was waiting along with Ariadne and Kat Forrest. When she saw me, the doctor began wagging her finger before the vehicle had even stopped. "You! I knew it was you!"

"I didn't do it," I said, shutting the door behind me and opening the one to the backseat.

Perugini's eyes narrowed. "Why is it that I do not believe you?"

"Isabella," Ariadne said with excess gentleness. "Perhaps you could make sure Hannegan is all right?"

"I will treat him," she snapped. "What is this?" She leaned down and pointed at the collar around his neck.

"Some sort of electricity-based capture collar," Zack said. "It was meant for her," he inclined his head toward me, "so it's probably pretty damned strong."

She poked at it, and Hannegan jerked and screamed, electricity running through his body. I jumped back from the door, leaving him plenty of space to writhe about. He fell out of the backseat, landing on his shoulder and coming to rest in a heap on the curb. Everyone else kept their distance except Dr. Perugini, who stood only a few inches away. "I need to get this off of him." She whirled to Ariadne. "I need the lab rat.

Ariadne looked taken aback. "Dr. Sessions? Perhaps you remember he was flambéed last night? He's on leave."

"Unless you want Hannegan to leave the planet, get me the lab rat so he can get this *maledetto* collar off of him!" She spun back to me. "You! Make yourself useful and pick him up!"

I did. Zack stared at me as I set Kurt down on the gurney and Dr. Perugini strapped him in across the midsection and legs. She jerked her head toward Kat, who had been watching the whole exchange so far without saying a word, looking like someone in far, far over her head. "Can you tell me how hurt he is?"

Kat blinked a few times then stepped forward, laying her hands on his face. She didn't look quite as tanned as she usually did; in fact, her face had a kind of pallor about it and she looked almost gray. I started to ask if she was okay but I remembered that when last I had seen her she was trying to undo my handiwork on Scott, so I shut up. Her hands hovered over his face. When she withdrew them she appeared to be unsteady on her feet. "He's hurt, but not too bad," she said. "Some nerve damage, I think. Maybe some tissue damage to the heart, I can't tell." She looked up at us, weary sadness filling her face. "I'm sorry. I can't do anything to help him, I'm too exhausted."

"That's all right, sweetie," Perugini said, soothing. "That tells me most of what I need to know." She looked back to Ariadne. "Sessions. I need him now."

Ariadne nodded and pulled out her phone. "I'll have him meet you at the medical unit." We watched as Perugini pushed Kurt inside on the gurney, Kat trailing behind her. Ariadne was on the phone for less than thirty seconds and when she got off, she gave Zack and I a wan smile. "So, it was a trap?"

"I think so." I answered before Zack did, causing him to blink in surprise. "This guy wanted to stir up enough meta trouble to get the Directorate involved and tail your agents back here so he could find me."

"How did you know who he was?" Zack stared me down, drawing Ariadne's attention to me as well.

I almost panicked, then realized that there was an easy answer. "Reed told me this guy was looking for me but he didn't know when he was gonna show up."

Ariadne let out a sigh of exasperation. "You could have mentioned this before."

I smiled weakly. "Trust."

Ariadne crossed her arms in front of her. "Fine. Give me his name and I'll see if we have anything on him." She looked me over. "How are you feeling?"

I thought about it before I answered. "I'm fine. It felt...really good to win a fight for once." I frowned. "Without getting pummeled to a near-death state."

"Try and make a habit of that, will you?" She looked back to the door where Dr. Perugini had gone only moments before. "I don't think *il dottore* is very pleased with you at present."

"I'll add her to a list that's growing by the day," I said. "I don't know what it is that makes people so angry with me."

"Perhaps you insulted her," Ariadne said with only a touch of irony. I let it pass. I actually did feel good. She turned to Zack. "I'll expect your report tomorrow morning." With a nod at me she went back into Headquarters, leaving the two of us alone.

"Anything else you want to tell me about the man in the iron lung?" Zack looked at me with hard eyes as soon as she was gone.

"Umm." I pretended to think about it. "His name is David Henderschott, he's a Pisces, he likes long walks on the beach at night, and his favorite drink is a fuzzy navel. He's also a fan of Streisand movies, and he listens to Nickelback when he's alone and in the shower." I snickered. "I might have made a few of those up."

Zack did not appear to be amused. "I'm not surprised.

"Well, seriously, I mean I don't know anything else about him except that his skin is what binds those metal plates to him." I shrugged, my arms expansive. "I only have the basics."

"And you didn't mention this before, when we first encountered him?" Dark suspicion glassed over his eyes.

"Like I told Ariadne, we're not to the full-trust stage yet." I stared him down. "Give it a little more time, maybe."

"Time," he said with a shake of the head. "I don't know what it's going to take, but I doubt it's just time. I'm gonna go check on Kurt."

He left, and I felt a stab of guilt for lying to him. I exited the garage through a side door, stepping out into the winter night. It was starting to snow, the flakes landing delicately on my shoulders. Had I been less preoccupied, I might have tried to catch one on my tongue. Yeah, I'd just dealt a hell of a beat-down to Henderschott, but he wasn't dead, and for some reason, I suspected he'd be back. Wolfe was still somehow able to take control of my body at unfortunate moments (not that there would ever really be a fortunate moment for him to assume control) and because of him, I suspected I'd let loose an extremely dangerous meta to wreak untold havoc upon the world.

Did that mean anyone Gavrikov killed was another death on my conscience? I already had 254 that I blamed myself for. I'd kept a very careful accounting, sadly enough, and that was the tally. Sure, I hadn't physically killed any of them myself (except Wolfe) but I regretted them all (except Wolfe).

I entered my room, shutting the door behind me. I had been tired hours ago; now I was exhausted. I threw down my coat, noting white powder spots from the drywall all over the exterior and a nice rip along the back, presumably from the fight with Henderschott, and I wondered if I should be worried. Did most seventeen-year-old girls get into as many fights as I did? I doubted this was normal for anyone but the worst delinquents.

A knock at the door jerked me out of my thoughts. I looked at myself in the bathroom mirror. Drywall dust was speckled through my hair and I had three visible rips in my shirt. I sighed and went to the door.

When I opened it, I was faced with a man I'd never seen before. He had a deeply pale face, his hair was brown and short, and his eyes were bright blue, in a shade that glittered even in the dim light.

"Yes?" I looked at him as I spoke. He was older, probably in his thirties or later. "Can I help you?"

"May I come in?" He spoke with a heavy accent that sounded Russian or Slavic.

"Umm...do I know you?" I looked at him, trying to determine if I'd seen him before. He wasn't Henderschott, I knew that much. His face was normal, handsome even, though pale.

"Can I please come in?" He looked back down the hall, furtive, and lowered his voice to a whisper. "I saw you outside and followed you back here so we could talk."

"Saw me outside?" I drew the door a little closer to shut. "There wasn't anyone outside just now. The campus was deserted." I straightened, trying to project the image that I was strong by drawing myself up to my full height. I doubt it worked. At 5 foot 4 inches, I was shorter than almost everyone. Including him. "By the way, telling a girl you followed her back to her room? Not exactly a turn on. Kinda makes you sound like a stalker."

He brought his hand up to his eyes as though he were frustrated, massaging his temples. He looked out at me from behind his fingers. "I need to talk with you." He pulled his hand away from his face and held it up. I stared at it, wondering what he was going to do next when the tip of his finger burst into flames. I yelped in surprise and the flame spread across his entire hand, stopping at the wrist. With an abrupt flick of his fingers, the fire died and his flesh returned.

"Aleksandr Gavrikov," I whispered.

He stared down at me with those intense, blue eyes, and I swore I could see a hint of fire deep within them. "Yes. Now can I come in?"

Chapter 17

I took a few steps back trying to get away from him, but Gavrikov took it as a sign to enter. He closed the door after checking the hallway again. He pressed his back to the door after shutting it. He was haggard, his face pale, the coloring washed out. Big beads of sweat ran down his forehead and he was breathing heavily.

I didn't want to ask, but I did it anyway. "Are you all right?" The backs of my thighs felt the soft impact of the edge of the bed; I could not retreat any farther without making it obvious.

"What?" His accent was more pronounced and he blinked a few times, as though his eyes were hurting him. "Oh. I have not been..." He stared down at his hands, as if seeing them for the first time. "It has been very long since I last quenched the fire." He took another deep breath. "I don't think I've done it since..." He looked up, concentrating as if trying to recall. "Not for over a hundred years."

"Uh...how do you eat?" My brain screamed at me for my stupidity, asking him dumb questions when I should be jumping out the window, running far, far away from the man who blew up an entire building last night.

"I don't," he said with a grim smile. "When I am afire, I don't need to eat, I subsist on air—it keeps the flames burning."

"Oh." I pondered that. "You don't like being human?"

He looked down at his hands again. "Flesh is easily hurt. Not so with flame; it can be elusive, unquenchable—and it feels no pain."

"Ah," I said, still feeling dumb. "So...what do you want to talk about?"

"Have a seat," he offered. I don't know why, but I sat down on the bed. If he burst into flames, it wasn't likely to matter whether I was standing or not. He walked past me to the window and looked out. "I have to thank you again for freeing me." He looked out through the glass, then to either side as if he were trying to find curtains.

I shook my head when he turned back to me. "The glass is mirrored. No one outside can see us."

His hand touched the window and he looked at it, curious. "So many differences since I was a child. We did not even have windows in the house I grew up in."

"Yeah, me neither, for all intents and purposes," I said, drawing a surprised look from him. "I had a somewhat unconventional childhood."

"Unconventional." He nodded and half-smiled. "I like that. I had an unconventional childhood as well."

"So." I felt a little awkward, and I still wondered why he was here. "Mr. Gavrikov—

"Please," he said with a wince. "Call me Aleksandr."

"Well, I was trying to be a little more formal—"

"I hate that name. " His mouth was a thin line. "I am only Aleksandr."

"Okay." The awkwardness did not abate. "Why are you here?"

He kept his distance, walking over to the desk and the computer that I had yet to use. He pulled out the chair and tentatively sat down in it. He was still sweating profusely and I wondered if he was suffering some sort of withdrawal from not using his power or if he was simply nervous. "Your Directorate—"

"Let me stop you right there," I said, drawing a look of curiosity from him. "They're not mine. I've only been here a couple weeks, and mostly because I have nowhere else to go since that psychotic Wolfe," I felt him stir inside but he kept blissfully silent, "was chasing me down."

"Wolfe?" He squinted at me. "You drew the ire of the beast and yet live?"

"Drew his ire?" I snorted. "I drew more than that."

"No matter," he said with a wave of his hand. "I have heard the legend of this beast. Help me and I will kill him for you."

"Too late. I already killed him."

I watched Aleksandr's face drop, a hint of disbelief permeating his clenched expression. "You killed him?" He pointed his finger at me. "You? You did this...by yourself?"

"I—" I tried to find an easy way to explain but failed. "Yes, I did."

"Very impressive." He nodded. "It explains why you were able to help me escape the lab. But I still need your help to free another."

"Um...free them from what?" I tried not to overly worry about it, but I suspected that my potential new bosses here at the Directorate would be less than pleased that I had helped Gavrikov escape. I suspected they'd be even more peeved if I helped him break someone else out. As if having Wolfe running through my head wasn't a bad enough mark on an employment application.

"The Directorate has imprisoned someone at their Arizona facility." He took a deep breath. "Someone I must help."

"Umm, I don't think I'd be able to help you with that," I said. "First of all, I don't know where that is; second, I have zero pull with this organization." I laughed under my breath, but it died after a second when I caught sight of his face. "Truth is, I've done a few things here that would be likely to land me in their jail before too much longer."

"I need help," he said again, this time almost pleading. "I don't care if it costs my life, I must get this person out of their hands."

"I can sorta understand that. Who is it?"

"My sister, Klementina." He took a deep breath. "Only...it is not her."

I let the air hang with silence while I tried to digest that. "I'm sorry...what? It's your sister...but it's not?"

He stood suddenly and his breathing was heavier. His eyes moved left and right, and he twitched. "My sister died in 1908."

I started to wonder if I was dreaming, because of the surreal nature of the conversation. Then I remembered that I could talk to people in my dreams, and wondered if me being dead was a simpler explanation. My head hurt, mostly from being confused. "So they imprisoned her corpse?"

"No." He stood and started to pace, his agitation becoming greater as he went. I could have sworn I saw thin drifts of smoke waft from him. "She died...but somehow they brought her back. Except it is not her, because she does not remember anything."

"Like a clone?" I know my eyes were wide, and I was trying not to do anything to set him off, but by this point I was fairly sure he was crazier than I was. And with a psycho nutter in my head, I was probably pretty crazy by any objective measure.

He snapped his finger at me. "Yes! A clone. I worked for...an organization. After a time, I heard rumors that they were working on something. Something for me, as a gift—they wanted my loyalty, to buy it forever. But the facility at which they were working on this gift was lost to an attack by your Directorate. So I went there. I found the scientists that have taken over, but they have no answers for me. All the research was moved when the Directorate took over the facility, and now all that is left are files, some videos. I see her in the records, her face, Klementina's. Somehow they brought her back, but the Directorate took her away with the other research subjects and sent her to Arizona."

I had a sudden, annoying suspicion that sent my skin to tingling. "Describe her for me."

"She was tall, with long blond hair, and green eyes. When I

saw her last, her skin was tanned from working our farm. In the pictures I saw, she is still so." He halted in his description and anguish flowed across his features. "Please. You must help me. I have to tell her—" He choked on the words. "I have to make it right."

"Hrm." I thought of Kat Forrest, our new arrival from Arizona, and wondered about the likelihood that Old Man Winter would have had her brought up here, thinking that he was about to capture Gavrikov. "Did she have any powers? You know, like you?"

"No," he said with a shake of his head. "She was kind, and gentle. When father would—" He looked away. "She would come to me, try to soothe my injuries."

"Uh huh. So would you say she had a," I swallowed, "healing touch?"

"I suppose you could say that." He paced back to the window. "I owe her...an apology. I failed the Klementina that was my sister." He whirled to face me and all I could see was the resolve on his face. "I owe her—this shade of her, at least—freedom. I must get her free."

"I can appreciate that you have," I scoured my mind, "unfinished business or a debt or whatever. But, um...when I said healing touch, I meant literally." He looked at me in confusion. "Can her hands heal wounds, grow flowers, stuff like that?"

His brow was furrowed. "I—"

For the second time since I'd been here, the giant window that ran across the entire wall behind my bed exploded inward. I dropped, using the bed for cover as glass flew over my head and I felt a blast of heat from where Aleksandr had been standing. I poked my head back up and found Clary, skin turned into some dark rock, stepping through the window. Behind him I saw the outlines of Parks, Bastian and Kappler, lurking about a hundred feet away. Gavrikov was already covered in flame again, hovering about a foot off the ground. The influx of outside air had turned the room a frigid cold in seconds.

"We went all the way down to Fairmont tracking you," Clary said as he dropped onto the floor, shaking the room. "Found your handiwork. Blowing up a propane truck, Gavrikov? Not cool." Clary hesitated and his voice turned gleeful. "Actually, I bet it was cool to watch when it happened, but now it's just a big damned smoking crater and a hell of a lot of lanes of I-90 that ain't gonna be open again for a longass while. And that poor trucker's family—"

Aleksandr didn't let him finish his sentence. He heaved two enormous fireballs at Clary, one of which burned the big man's clothing off, exposing a chest of blackened stone. "I liked that shirt," he said, staring down. "You better not—" Gavrikov fired two more blasts at him, each worse than the last. I felt the air turn superheated around me and closed my eyes to protect them from the intensity of it. Every single bit of the flame that Aleksandr had thrown at him had bounced off, hitting the walls of my dormitory room. The drywall had begun to blaze in four places and the carpet was beginning to catch fire.

"You're gonna burn the girl's stuff up, Gavrikov!" Clary shouted at him.

I was coughing, but I managed to get out, "I don't own much of anything."

"Well you're gonna burn the girl up, and she's already hot enough without your help!"

I was crawling toward the exit to keep that from happening, although I did blanch at Clary's comment. I heard a fire alarm klaxon start wailing and then the sprinklers activated, and suddenly I was no longer hot but now cold again as the chill water soaked me through my already damaged clothing. I stopped at the door and used the wall as an aide to pull myself up. There was smoke billowed at the ceiling, but Gavrikov and Clary were already outside. Kappler, Bastian and Parks were circling them, but keeping their distance.

I watched them out the window. Gavrikov was throwing fire at Clary ineffectually. Clary advanced on Aleksandr but every time he would get close, Gavrikov would fly away and hurl another burst at him, with an occasional shot toward the other three to keep them at bay.

"Aleksandr," I called, staggering to the window. By now, the sprinkler system had almost extinguished the flames in my room and the carpet was sodden, squishing underfoot with every step. "He's invulnerable to your attacks! Get out of here before they capture you!"

With that, Parks, Kappler and Bastian, all three of their heads swiveled toward me, as if seeing a new threat for the first time. "I'm not getting involved in this," I told them, hands raised, as I stepped over the window ledge and into the snow. "Just hate to see him get overmatched and pummeled."

As I stepped out, I saw a ring of black-clad agents in the distance, along with Old Man Winter and Ariadne. They were far enough away that I could only distinguish them by Ariadne's red hair and Old Man Winter's staggering height. It occurred to me that they either saw Gavrikov enter my room through a security camera and figured out who he was or else they were listening and/or watching my room.

Gavrikov floated away, drawing Clary charging after him. He reached a distance away from me and then with a flash of heat and light he shot back toward me, stopping a foot or so away. "Will you help me?" His voice was different now, laced with a kind of crackling heat, something that sounded far different from human.

"I..." I stopped and looked around, the agents closing in, ringing us. Gavrikov turned and saw them and he burned brighter, as though ready to explode. "No! Wait!" He turned back to me, his head whipping around, the fire burning brighter. I held out my hand. "I'll help you, but you can't hurt them! Please! Just go for now, come find me when things have calmed down, I'll..." I looked at the agents charging closer, Old Man Winter with them.

The air grew colder; I could feel it because I was soaked from the sprinklers and I felt ice start to form on the outside layer of my clothing. "Go!" I said. "Get out of here!"

He looked around once more and the heat blazed hotter around him. A short blast of fire filled the air in front of me, knocking me backward over the window frame. I landed on my back with a wet splash in my room, a stinging pain in the hand I had held out which quickly moved down my wrist and stayed there. My head ached from the landing. I saw a streak of fire trace across the sky like an angry star, flaring in the night until it disappeared.

Faces appeared above me, and I didn't feel like I could fight my way through all of them or adequately run, so I just lay there. Clary was the first to climb into my room, followed by the rest of M-Squad, then a few agents, all wearing their tactical gear and black masks. One of them pulled his off; it was Zack. He shook his head at me in deep disappointment.

"Yeah, I know. Save it," I said, feeling surprisingly weak. His disappointment changed in an instant, into something more approaching horror. His mouth was open, his normally handsome face twisted in disgust. "What?"

"Sienna," he gasped as Old Man Winter appeared in view above me with the others. "Your hand."

I looked down at my hand, the one I had extended toward Gavrikov, but it had nearly vanished, all the way to the wrist. There was no flesh, no muscle, no connective tissue left—only bone, scorched, blackened and bare.

Chapter 18

They took me to the medical unit, where no one spoke to me, not even Dr. Perugini. The rest of them were just quiet, but Perugini was irritable and glared at me constantly, in addition to giving me the silent treatment. She injected something into my other arm and I didn't stop her, mostly because M-Squad was standing around watching me. Before my eyelids fluttered and I drifted off, I reflected that I wouldn't be surprised if I woke up in a confinement cell. Whenever they allowed me to wake up.

I came to still in a bed in the medical unit. The room was dark, and there was not a sign of anyone else, even in the dim light. A machine to my right was beeping every few seconds. My hand hurt, which was funny because it wasn't there the last time I checked. My mouth was dry and my arms were restrained, a large steel bar locked into place across my upper body and another at my waist. My hands were pinned beneath them so that I couldn't even get enough leverage to move them a half inch. My right hand, the one that was missing, was encased in a box of some kind, but it was difficult to see with the bar across my abdomen.

Also, I had an itch on my nose and had to pee worse than I've ever had to before.

I didn't want to say anything, but those two urgent needs brought words to my lips faster than anything else could have. "Hello?" I was hesitant, almost as if I was afraid of who would answer.

The door to Dr. Perugini's office opened and she stepped out, her hair pulled back. I heard the click of her high heeled shoes on the floor and when she got close enough, saw the weariness in her eyes as she stifled a yawn. "I've grown so tired of you I can't help but fall asleep in your presence."

"I've grown tired of being here, Doc." I chafed under the bands keeping me in the bed. "When can I leave?" I felt tension as I waited for her answer.

I was surprised when it was hysterical laughter. She bent double, hand over her face, clutching at her sides. After a few minutes, she stopped, letting out one last chuckle (that I suspected was fake) and turned serious, looking daggers at me. "Oh, I'm sorry," she said, her voice rising, "it takes a while to REGROW AN EN-TIRE HAND!" She shook her head self-righteously and took a needle out of her pocket.

"Hold up," came a voice from the door. I looked past her as she turned and saw Dr. Zollers standing there, hands folded over his sweater vest. "Don't administer that just yet." He walked over to the bed and looked me over. "Living a little rough, Sienna?"

"What can I say? I live a hard-knock life." There was a steady, thrumming pain coming from my missing hand. I had a suspicion that I was getting some new nerve growth.

Zollers chuckled. "I wasn't even talking about that. I was talking about the personality conflict you've got going on inside. You know, you versus the beast within?" He leaned closer. "It'd be a hard thing, living your life when you've got Wolfe in your head."

I blinked at him in disbelief, and I felt all the blood drain from my face. "How did you know?"

"Old Man Winter told me," he said, straightening back up. Perugini watched him with a glare and he smiled at her. "He's suspected for a while now. But thanks for confirming it."

"I didn't want to tell anyone," I said. I felt the slow gut-wrench of fear settle over me. If they weren't going to lock me away before for aiding Gavrikov, this would surely do it. "I figured you'd all think I was crazy—or worse. And when he started taking over my body—"

"You should have said something." He pulled out a needle of his own and pulled the cap off it with his teeth. "We might be able to control him with medication. Or some dog treats." He smiled.

"So that's what makes a good headshrinker," Dr. Perugini said with a roll of her eyes, "an overdeveloped sense of irony and a willingness to engage in psychopharmacology.

"That and a bitchin' sweater vest collection." He tugged on the front of his outfit. "You like?"

Dr. Perugini snorted in disgust. "She's in a lot of pain. She needs something to help with that."

He raised an eyebrow at her then looked down at me in the bed. "Pain she can deal with, I think. Crazy is a whole different problem, and typically more serious. Make no mistake, having Wolfe as a mental hitchiker means you are opened up to all sorts of crazy."

I gulped. "Will this make him go away?"

"I doubt it," Zollers said. "This is just gonna take the edge off a little. It's called Chloridamide. It's a low-grade antipsychotic; it hasn't quite passed the FDA yet, but I think it'll be just the thing to keep you calm for a bit while we work out what to do."

I smiled weakly. "Any side effects?"

He shrugged. "Nausea, vomiting, burning while urinating, blood loss, diarrhea, liver failure, renal failure, heart failure, cancer, tumors, paralysis-"

"Nice." I faked a smile. "You're joking, right?"

He laughed. "Wouldn't matter if I was serious. You're a meta, you shrug off all that stuff." He took a sterile swab from Dr. Perugini and rubbed it along my arm where my sleeve was rolled up. "Except the burning while urinating. That would probably still sting."

"There's a cautionary tale in there somewhere," I said, sarcasm tingeing my words. "How did Old Man Winter know I was carrying around Wolfe with me?"

Zollers smiled again as he injected the needle in my arm. "You're not the first succubus to cross his path. I think he's playing things a little close to the vest, though. Big surprise, coming from him, right?" The last words were delivered with unrepentant sarcasm. "But as he is the boss, that's his prerogative, I suppose."

"Yeah," I said, my head starting to grow hazy. "I get the feeling it's not the first time."

"You're probably going to sleep for a while," Dr. Zollers said. "This is something new for your system, and one of the genuine side effects is drowsiness, which is working along with the fact that you're tired because your body is healing. You'll build up some resistance after the next few doses and pretty soon it won't affect you at all, okay?" He took care rolling my sleeve back down, making certain he didn't touch my skin, even with the latex gloves he was wearing. "When you get out of here, you'll go talk to Ariadne and Winter first, but they'll tell you I'm next on your list after them. Doesn't matter if it's day or night, you come see me."

I stared up at him. His chocolate skin was blurring, running into the white ceilings in the most bizarre mixture. "Why?"

My eyes were already closed when he answered. "Because together, we're going to find a way to put Wolfe in a cage."

Chapter 19

I awoke again to the beeping of the machines, this time with Dr. Perugini standing over me. "Oh, good, you're awake," she said without enthusiasm.

"I had to pee before I fell asleep," I said. "Did I..."

"You got a catheter after Zollers injected you." She delivered the news with a little snippiness. The restraints were gone, though my hand was elevated. The flesh on it looked to be an angry red, with blisters standing out like little white bubbles against a torch red background. Also, now it itched.

I rubbed my eyes with my good hand. "I'm hungry." My stomach growled as if to emphasize the truth of my statement.

"I'll send for the cafeteria to bring you something in a few minutes."

"Poison?" I asked with a smile.

She ignored my wisecrack and used her stethoscope to take my pulse, avoiding touching my skin even with her gloves. "You are nearly back to normal, which is good because I want you out of here as soon as possible."

"Oh, I don't know about that, Doc." I said trying to be coy, but I think it came off sneering. "After all, I can't do any more damage when I'm here. Once I'm out in the world, it'll be no time at all before you've got the medical unit full again."

She let out a hiss that startled me, it was so violent. "You," she said, spitting it at me with the same vehemence as the Italian curses she so frequently used.

"Me what?" I shot back. "I didn't ask for any of this—not my powers, not my mom to disappear, not Wolfe to come after me, nor this Armored Assclown. I wasn't looking for Scott Byerly to grab at me when Wolfe was so close to the surface of my mind, and I damned sure wasn't spoiling for a fight with Clary! I didn't ask Gavrikov to vaporize my hand, I never wanted a single person to die—but they all happened, and I can't do anything about them now."

"*Porca miseria*!" She withdrew her hands and took a step back, and for a moment I thought she was going to spit on me. "Oh, yes, you have had such a miserable time. So many bad things have happened to you, poor you, nobody else has it as bad as Sienna." Her voice came slow, mocking me.

It smarted. Enough to bring that curious burning to my eyes, the one I wished I could disavow. I hate crying, and I wasn't going to do it in front of an enemy. Not that I had many friends at this point. Or ever. "Yes, I have had a miserable time. And you don't hear me griping about it."

"No, not griping," she said, almost as if she were agreeing. "Moping. Sulking. Stewing, I think they call it also? You are a girl, about to be a woman, yet you act like a child."

"Act like a child?" I almost choked on it. "I've had all these things—"

"Happen to you, yes, such miseries, I already acknowledged." She folded her arms. "So sad, no one in the history of the world has ever been through any worse."

"Been through?" I almost choked on my own words. "How about 'still going through'. They're still after me, the people who sent Wolfe—I still have him hanging around in my brain—"

"You are not the first to go through that, either." She shrugged, as though it was a matter of little consequence. "You're hardly the first succubus. They made it through somehow, so will you muddle through—if you ever decide to stop moping."

"You know, I think after all I've been through, I'm entitled to a little— "

"No, you're not." She cut me off. "You're not entitled to a damned thing. This is where Ariadne and Old Man Winter make their mistake with you. Yes, you have had a hard life up to when you left your house, being locked in, boxed up, crated, whatever you want to call it. You leave your house, all hell breaks loose and worse. All this is true. You have had very bad things happen to you, no denying. But you take responsibility for the things you shouldn't and take no responsibility for the things you should." She threw her arms up in the air. "You will be a bitter, pathetic shell of a person if you continue down this path."

"Well, awesome." My words were acid. "Because I've always aspired to be like you."

A self-satisfied smile made its way across her face. "I hurt your little fragile ego, so you lash out. Very mature."

"Yeah." I tasted bile in the back of my mouth. "Well, I'd call you old school but you're really just old. Die already."

Her hand came down and slammed the bed and I jerked back, reacting to the idea that she might actually hit me. "At some point you have to accept some responsibility for your actions. Not Wolfe's. He killed all those people, not you. If you blame yourself for those, you are stupid. But now you want to blame Wolfe for some things you control. It's not always him that lands you in trouble. Bad things happen to all of us. You cannot control bad things that happen to you any more than you can control the weather. It's less about the things that happen and more about how you react to them."

She turned away and stalked back to her office. "Or you can sit here in your little pity party and let whatever life you could have pass you by—be a vegetable of sorriness, feeling bad for yourself, curl up in a little ball and waste away, waiting for momma to come find you and hoping those people you didn't even see die will somehow vanish from your conscience."

"Why do you care?" I snapped it at her, trying to find some

way past her infuriating facade. "I'm just another patient, another pound of flesh for you to minister to. Why does it matter?"

She stopped at the door to her office, put her hand on the frame and rested on it for a split second before turning back to me. There was emotion peeking through from behind a wall, some reservoir of feeling that I couldn't see the depth of. "Me? I don't care what you do, whether it's waste away in a little ball of sadness or become a useful, productive, happy member of society. Neither one matters to me." She pointed at me. "But if you're going to do the former, at least leave so I don't have to watch you throw your life away?" She smiled all too sweetly. "Okay? You can go now." She turned and I heard her office door shut softly and her blinds closed a minute later.

Chapter 20

I pulled the IV out my arm and slapped some gauze on it, along with some medical tape. I didn't see Dr. Perugini, but the blinds in her office moved a few times. She was watching, I knew it. I stormed out in my outfit, burnt and haggard once more. I didn't even want to know how much of a mess my hair was, but I saw it anyway in my reflection on the metal wall.

I rode the elevator to the top floor and found the offices abandoned. I could see out the windows that darkness had fallen. A clock nearby told me it was the middle of the night. Old Man Winter and Ariadne were not in their offices, which were both were locked.

I walked out the door to the Headquarters building and found myself in the middle of a light snowstorm. Again. I kicked a trash can savagely, sending it hurtling across a snowfield. I started back toward the dormitory building at a brisk walk, as though I could exorcise the demons of Perugini's words by walking them off.

I was already in the building and almost to my door when I remembered that Gavrikov had burned my room. I stopped outside the door, which had caution tape across it and gave it a gentle push. It swung open and I found the space covered from the outside by several tarps. The broken glass was gone from the floor, as were the carpets, leaving bare concrete.

The room was frigid and the furniture was all gone—desk, bed, everything. The walls had already been replaced, the scorch marks gone, vanished with the addition of fresh drywall. It hadn't been painted yet, giving the place the smell of a construction site.

I walked into the closet and found the clothes were missing. I smiled as I wondered if the Directorate had finally run out of jeans and turtlenecks in my size. My smile vanished when I realized that would bode ill for me; my current outfit was scorched, stunk of acrid smoke and was missing a sleeve.

I heard the scrape of a footstep on the concrete and all my amusement vanished as I sprung to attention. I stood in the darkness of the closet and heard someone walk to the door, opening it wide to let light from the hallways outside my room filter in. "You were supposed to come see me." Dr. Zollers stood in the doorway, leaning against the frame in the way of a man who'd been awakened from a deep slumber and might return to it while standing there.

"Dr. Perugini called you?" I took a step toward him and he nodded. "I thought maybe it could wait until tomorrow."

"Well, that was dumb," he said and turned, then gestured for me to follow him. "Let's go."

I went with him, out of the dormitory building, back to his office. He didn't talk the whole way there and I started to wonder why, but when we got to his office, he poured a cup of coffee and gestured for me to sit. He yawned, took a big swig of his mug and cracked a smile. "Much better." He pointed to his cup. "Want some?"

"No, I had a bad experience with coffee." He looked at me quizzically. "I tried to drink it with meatloaf. It was my first time with both of those things, so..." I shrugged.

"All right, so let's talk." He put his mug down and picked up his notebook, all business. "You've got a maniac in your head."

"Plus Wolfe," I said with a smile.

"Clever. How's it feel?"

"Being clever? Damned good. It's my only vice." I grinned, then turned more serious when he didn't smile back. "He mostly just talked, until recently. Smarted off and whatnot. Told me a couple things—like where his lair was, who the man behind the armor was."

"When did you figure out that he could hijack your body?" He was already writing feverishly, but paused to look up when he asked the question.

I looked away, uncomfortable. "Um...probably when the Science Building exploded and I woke up in the snow with no idea how I got there." I hesitated. "But I had a suspicion before that. Ariadne said they had footage of me breaking into the cafeteria and I didn't remember doing it."

"Sleepwalking is not usually a good sign, even if it's just to get something to eat." He put down the pen and looked up to me. "We have no scientific idea how you drain a soul. Sessions is mystified." Zollers stopped to smile. "He's always a little confused, but this one started him on all the possibilities of other mythological powers that might hold some truth. For example, the ability of a succubus to influence dreams?" He waited, eyebrow raised, as though he were expecting an answer.

"Yeah." I nodded. "I can contact people in my dreams. It's a kind of weird, two-way communication dream. Like a video conference, but entirely in my head." I frowned. "Like a hallucinatory video conference."

"Anything else you haven't been telling us?" he asked with a cocked eyebrow and a half smile. It could have come off as an accusation, if anyone else had done it. Zollers pulled it off like a pro. I think I smiled when I shook my head. "All right. So...how are we going to get the Wolfe under control?"

I shrugged expansively. "I dunno. You're the doc."

"Yeah, and you're the patient and the one that has to live with him in your head." He leaned forward in his seat. "Which means you stand to lose a lot more than I do if we can't. The good news is, Old Man Winter assures me that succubi have been living with this particular quirk for thousands of years, so I assume it's manageable somehow." His face squeezed into a look of concentration. "Obviously it'd be easier if we had some firsthand experience from someone who'd been through it, but..."

"Since I'm the only succubus currently available to talk to..." I shrugged. "On my own again. Big shock."

"Is that a note of self-pity I hear? Cuz' that's not an attractive quality."

I rolled my eyes. "Because being attractive is my biggest concern." I tugged on the shredded turtleneck and stared down at it. "Actually, even if it was, it'd be near impossible given the crap I've gone through lately."

"There it is again!" He pointed the end of the pen at me. "That little quavering of self-pity in your voice."

"Oh, who cares?" I threw my hands up in the air. "So I feel a little sorry for myself sometimes. So what?"

"Because it doesn't do a damned thing to make you feel better." His dark eyes were locked on mine. "Yeah, you had some stuff go wrong in your life. Real wrong, in fact. I feel bad for you. But wallowing in it won't make you feel better."

"This conversation is getting repetitive." I drummed my hand on the arm of the chair to emphasize my point. "Perugini gave me the same line. Couldn't quite figure out her angle, though. She doesn't like me, after all."

"She doesn't hate you. That's important to realize."

"Why is that important?" I was close to beyond caring. "Whether she loves me, hates me, or wants to kill me, the message is the same. You guys think I'm being self-indulgent, I think I'm justified—at least a little bit. It's not like I'm whining to anybody but you about how much my life sucks."

"Got a question for you." He looked me in the eyes. "If you're thinking about yourself and how bad things are for you, how much time and thought are you devoting to other people?"

I glared at him but didn't argue his point. "Go on."

He shrugged. "Seems to me if you're that worried about being alone—enough that you've mentioned it both times we've talked, you'd look at what you could be doing that's causing that situation. Self-involved people don't tend to make the best friends because they're too busy thinking of their problems. Ones that are bitter and hurting tend to be the ones that push others away, sometimes with their actions, sometimes with their barbed tongues.

"So congrats." He clapped twice for me. "You had a bad past. You've got stuff going on right now that I wouldn't want to have happen to me. But everything you're doing that's alienating people around you is because you're so busy worrying about who to trust that you're missing how trust gets built. You're missing how to connect with people on a basic level and get to know them—and you're giving up the possibility of a future because you're stuck in your past. Your mom, the abuse—yeah, she abused you, get it straight in your head."

"How can I have a future? How can I connect with anyone?" My words came out in a rage, but I felt the burning of curiosity at what he might say. "I can't touch anyone—ever! Without causing them pain or death. And there are a ton of people no longer walking this earth because of me, because of what I didn't do, because I hid while Wolfe was on the rampage, trying to draw me out."

"Yeah, that happened," he said. "But you went into the basement to face him knowing you were going to die, didn't you?" I nodded. "That was your penance, kid." I didn't take umbrage at him calling me kid, surprisingly. "Yeah, a lot of people died at the hands of that maniac, but you didn't wrap your fingers around any of their throats, didn't kill a single soul up to that point and hey—news flash, you haven't killed anyone since! You are not a killer, Sienna. You went in there to die, knowing he was going to eat you alive and do God-knows-what to you. You knew and you went anyway. You faced the fire and you walked out the other side. Yeah, it's not all spun out yet, and there's the little complication of him mind-jacking you, but past examples say that that can be settled. So my question is—are you gonna blame yourself forever for stuff you didn't even do?"

"I..." My voice was ash. "I don't know. They're all dead, and I'm alive."

"Mm-hm. Got a way to fix that?" I shook my head. "Did you do it? Really do it? Go out there and kill a swath of people?" I shook my head again, this time tears welling up. "Forgive yourself. Explain it however will get you through the day—that you couldn't have stopped Wolfe then anyway, that it wouldn't have made a difference, he would have killed just as many people over the next hundred and thousand years he lived—whatever it takes to reconcile in your head that it was not your fault. Anyone who calls you weak for not wanting to die is an idiot. If that includes you, then stop being an idiot."

"I could have gone sooner." My voice was even hollower now. "I don't have a future." I looked up at him and the lump in my throat was big, enough that it was choking me, enough that a little sob escaped and I wanted to hit myself in the chest for letting it out. "I lost my future in the moment I killed Wolfe—when I found out what I was. Even if I got past all the rest, I still have no future, not a normal one anyway. I can't touch anyone. Ever."

"Can't touch anyone? Your mother was a succubus, yes?" He waited for me to nod. "You're familiar with human biology, how we breed? Explain your existence, please."

"I don't know. She could have," I faltered, "artificially, you know. I never asked her the finer details because I didn't know what she was at the time. There are ways it could have happened without touch, real touch—but none of that changes anything. I can't lead a normal life. I can't have a normal relationship. I'm a smoking crater with nothing around for miles." I bowed my head. "I am death."

"Wolfe was death," Zollers said, stern, "and you're nothing like him. You're like...like a fragile package. 'Handle with care'."

He stood up and grabbed a blanket from the back of his couch. He threw it around me and hauled me up, wrapping his arms around me in a hug. I started to struggle but something stopped me.

"I just..." I choked out, "I just...want to be normal."

I could hear the Cheshire Cat-like smile in his voice. "You're seventeen years old and you feel like the world is ending around you." He pulled me tighter, and the gentle pressure was reassuring in a way that I had never known. "Sienna...this *is* normal."

Chapter 21

"Gavrikov wants Kat Forrest." I stared across the desk at Old Man Winter, a few hours later. I felt better after talking to Zollers, more determined. I had some clarity. Old Man Winter watched me the same as always, but next to him, Ariadne seemed to study me with more suspicion, more wariness. "But you probably knew that, because you know her name's not Kat, not originally."

Ariadne's facade of wariness broke and she looked at Old Man Winter, then back to me. "What do you mean? What's her name?"

"Klementina Gavrikov," I said, forcing myself not to smile. It wasn't funny that Old Man Winter hadn't told his top lieutenant, who I liked to snark at, something of vital importance. Or at least that's what I told myself as I mashed my toe into my shoe and against the floor. Nope, didn't smile.

"She's his..." Ariadne blinked three times, then looked to Old Man Winter for confirmation.

"Clone," I said, "or at least that's what he thinks."

"He is incorrect," Old Man Winter said, his hands steepled in front of his face.

"Don't tell him that," I said. "I don't want to see what happens when a human bomb gets told he's wrong."

"She is his sister," Old Man Winter said, as though I had not interrupted. "Not a clone."

"Oh?" I cocked an eyebrow at him. "Gavrikov...Aleksandr," I said, softening my tone, "seemed to think she had died in 1908."

"She did not." He stared back coolly. He did everything coolly, dammit...I wished I had his glacial reserve. Half the time I was trembling beneath my badass exterior, just a scared kid. "She is as long-lived as any other powerful meta and as adaptable at healing. Whatever happened to her, she recovered." He hesitated. "Though there is a...cost to her power."

"There's a cost to any power, it seems." I breezed it out, way more than I really felt. "After all, if I used my power constantly, I'd end up with the mental equivalent of a clown car."

Ariadne didn't seem to find that amusing. "Her power, when used to excess, triggers almost the opposite."

"Personalities leave her?" I shrugged. "Explains a lot."

Old Man Winter spoke. "She loses her memory. If a Persephone-type reaches the end of their strength and continues to heal or grow a life, it is at the cost of their own faculties. They become a blank slate, new, fresh. Young again, as well, but at the cost of all they remember."

"Tabula rasa," I said with a breath.

"Indeed." Ariadne took her usual place by the window. "If Gavrikov is after her, it would be best if we hid her for a while."

Old Man Winter gave her a subtle nod. "You know where."

"The basement? You're gonna send her to the basement, right? Where you stuck me when I was hiding from Wolfe?" I shook my head. "Bet the flower girl will love that. Couldn't you send her to another campus?"

Old Man Winter's reaction was subtle, but not so subtle I missed it. "It would be best to have her close at hand."

"Why?" I was curious. "Because you can protect her better here?"

His answer was lacking in any kind of subtlety, and it rattled me. "Because it is not wise to deprive a man who can explode with the force of a nuclear bomb of the only thing he desires—the thing he would be willing to do anything to get."

I felt a pressure deep in my throat, this time less raw emotion and more...unsettling. "Yeah...that doesn't sound too wise."

Chapter 22

I found myself in the cafeteria. The glass had been repaired from when Clary and I had our epic battle, but the kitchen looked as though it were closed. The options for meals appeared to have been carted in by caterers; the serving buffet (which we had destroyed) was gone, replaced by long tables, heating elements and silver devices designed to keep the food warm. Most of the cafeteria ladies were gone, but the few that were left gave me glares as I passed. Nothing new there.

Until I got to the end. I picked up a croissant and put it on my plate, ready to face the inevitable crowd to see if there was a place for me to sit by myself. "Excuse me?" The light voice jarred me and I looked up to see one of the cafeteria workers. She was young, a little older than me, but round of face and with big brown eyes. She smiled at me and I looked back at her. "Thank you. For warning us to get out of the kitchen before it happened."

I stared at her. "What?"

"When you and the big man fought into the kitchen?" She indicated with her eyes to the corner where M-Squad sat, Clary laughing his way through three plates piled high in front of him. "You warned us to get out right before it exploded." Her eyes were sincere and her smile was sad. "I just wanted to say thank you."

"I wouldn't have let you get caught in the middle of what was going to happen." I managed to croak the words out. In truth, I didn't even remember saying anything to them. If I had, it was an offhand comment, no more worthy of recognition than anything else you do without thinking about it.

Yet somewhere, deep inside, I felt Wolfe, almost buried, stir in revulsion. Zollers had given me a second dose of the drug after our session in his office, and the drowsy effects were considerably less (though I was still tired). I could feel him though, in there somewhere, upset at what I had done.

Naturally, it caused me to smile back at the girl. "You're welcome."

I walked across the cafeteria to where a guy sat at a table for two, all by his lonesome. He looked, honestly, like someone had stolen all his happy. I stopped in front of him. "Is this seat taken?"

"What do you want?" Scott Byerly's voice was worn resignation, all shot through with deadness.

"I want..." I took a deep breath. "I want to apologize." I swallowed my pride and went on as he looked up in surprise. "There may have been some other influences pushing me toward what I did to you, but it was still wrong and ultimately it was on me. I...I'm sorry."

He seemed to awaken, his glazed-over eyes darting back to life. His leg slid the chair out across from him and a nod of the head was all it took to convince me to sit down. "You know where Kat is?" He looked at me with a little hope.

I froze, mouth full of Swedish meatballs (they were awesome, way better than anything Mom made). "Yes," I said at last. "She's in the basement at Headquarters."

He leaned across the table and whispered to me. "Why is she there?"

"It's kind of a long story."

His eyes narrowed. "Maybe you'd prefer to talk about something else? Like, say, damned near killing me?"

I swallowed hard. "You didn't accept my apology, did you?"

"Not yet. Why is she down there?"

I looked around on all sides of us. Nobody seemed to be very interested, and no one was in earshot. "She didn't tell you?" I waited until he nodded before I looked around one final time. "The exploding guy, the one that trashed the Science Building—he's after her. Wants her released from here."

His face flushed. "She's not a prisoner. She's here because she wants to be."

"That's not how he sees it."

His hand slammed the metal table and left an indentation. "It doesn't matter how he sees it; she's not going anywhere with him!"

"Take it easy. I'm not arguing with you, just telling you the why."

He stared off into space and then his eyes came back to me. "You're a succubus?"

I chewed on the next Swedish meatball, almost afraid to answer. "Yeah."

"They don't have the greatest rep among metas."

I laughed. "Hard to see why that could be; we touch people and they die."

"'I'm death'." He shook his head. "That's what you meant when you said you were Kat's opposite."

"She can give life," I speared another meatball with particular violence, "all I can do is take it away."

"Hm." His eyes were sad. "You haven't asked me about my power yet."

"Huh?" I looked back at him. "Oh, yeah. Well, can you blame me? Until now, I was afraid a mutual discussion of powers might out me for the weirdo I am." I turned my gaze back to my plate. "Besides, I didn't really want to...um..."

"Be civil?"

I didn't glare, but it was close. "Connect...with others until now. I didn't want to be disappointed or burned or let down." I gritted my teeth. "In case I had to leave abruptly."

"Leave, huh?" He picked at his food. "I could see that, if I was in your shoes. So why weren't you more pissed when you found out I wrote that note?"

I flicked my eyes away from him but allowed a slight smile. "With as many real, legit, scary enemies as I've got, it seemed like a waste of time to worry about one more person trying to take a shot at me for something I already blamed myself for."

"Yeah, well, that's kinda dumb as far as reasons go, but I'll take it, I guess. I took a cheap shot at you, you took one at me, we're square."

I frowned. "Yours helped drive me into a confrontation with a maniac that nearly killed me."

"Yeah, well yours almost ended up taking my soul."

"Touche."

"It's all a wash—" He stopped, looking past me then nodded slightly. "Here come Zack and Kurt."

They stopped at our table, Zack looking a little haggard and Kurt looking like a blowfish ready to explode (I saw a nature documentary once). "Hey, guys." Zack started talking, a little wan and more pale than usual.

"What's the matter?" I leaned back in my chair, arm draped over the back as I looked up at them. "You look like you've had a rough day," I nodded to Zack, "and you look like you were forced to skip breakfast, lunch and dinner." I smiled at Kurt.

"Byerly," Zack said as Kurt glared at me, "Old Man Winter and Ariadne want to see you."

"Oh?" Scott pushed his tray away. "Might as well go see what that's about."

He stood and left, with a nod to Kurt. Zack watched his receding back for a minute then turned to Kurt. "Can you give us a few minutes?"

Kurt didn't look amused. "Keep your hands to yourself," he said to me.

"You sure?" I shot him a dazzling smile. "I could goose him a little bit, then maybe you'd look smart and commanding by comparison." Kurt emitted a grunt and stomped off toward the serving line. "Don't eat too much! You don't want to mess up your girlish figure!" I turned back to Zack with a smile. "I just love antagonizing him. It's like having a little piggy whose tail I can twist any time I want."

He looked at me warily. "You feel better after making him feel worse?"

I ate another Swedish meatball. "Always."

"Did Dr. Zollers give you a psychological explanation for why you do that?"

"Don't need one. It's because I have time and wit to spare."

He sighed, his body uncomfortable. "There's things you haven't been telling me."

I put my fork down. "In fairness, there are things I haven't been telling anyone. It's not like I've been looking forward to admitting I have Wolfe rattling 'round up here." I pointed to my head.

"And that you can touch other people's dreams," he said, quiet. He wouldn't meet my eyes, but I thought I recognized his posture. He looked like he'd been betrayed.

"Not something I really wanted to brag about; first because I didn't know I could trust you guys, then later, because I forgot."

His eyes were accusatory. "You should have told us."

"I did." I felt a little guilt burning at me. "It just took me a little while."

He stood. "That's not fair, Sienna. We've been square with you since the word go and you've been holding out." He shook his head. "I guess I expected more."

"More what?" I snapped the words back at him. "You broke into my house, remember? I didn't come looking for you guys, you stepped into my room with a tranquilizer gun, not vice versa. You talk about trust but you act all surprised that it's been two weeks and I'm not ready to sign on and be a member of the team. Forgive me for not jumping in and telling you all my dirty little secrets yet."

He stared at me evenly. "Feel better?"

"A little." I sighed. "Seriously, though. I've been through the ringer with Perugini, Zollers, and now you. Can we just...talk about his later?"

"Yeah." He looked down at his feet. "Ariadne wanted me to tell you that they assigned you a different room and moved your stuff."

I took a slip of paper from his proffered hand. "Good timing, actually. This drug Zollers has me on to suppress Wolfe really takes it out of me."

"Sleep tight," he said. "I gotta get back to guard duty."

"Zack," I called after him when he started to leave. "I'm sorry."

He nodded his head, just slightly, causing it to bob as he looked back to his shoes. "I know."

"But it's all out there now." I looked at him hopefully. "I don't think there's anything else. No more secrets." I smiled. "Now it's just decisions to make."

He smiled. "Get to making 'em, will you? Kinda curious if I'm gonna be working with you or not."

"You think you could handle that?" I smiled at him impishly. "You might have to partner with me someday."

He looked up as though he were thinking about it, then slowly nodded, only a hint of a smile visible, arching his lips up. "I think I could handle that. You know, for the good of the team."

I flung my napkin at him in mock outrage. "For the good of the team, eh?" He laughed, retreating. "Keep yourself out of trouble, will you? Watch out for men on fire." I looked at my hand, now covered in a glove and felt the itching that was coming from the last layer of skin returning. "They tend to leave a mark."

He nodded and gave me a playful salute as he left the cafeteria, Kurt trailing behind him. I rubbed my eyes. Zollers' drug was putting me down. I looked out one of the windows; it was probably midday, the cloud cover overhead still masking the sun from my sight. I walked back to my room across the grounds, the white blankets of snow still covering to the horizon. It wasn't quite as oppressive today, for some reason.

I followed room numbers in the dormitory to the one on the paper Zack had given me. I opened the door, feeling like I was ready to collapse. I found a room inside that was the same as the one I'd had before, which gave me a moment's pause. I unlaced and then kicked off my boots, pulled off my shirt, throwing it straight to the garbage, then stripped off my jeans.

I fell on the bed, on my back, not bothering with the covers. The cool air tickled my exposed skin and below me I felt the silky smoothness of the bedspread. The slight smell of construction was in the air; my old room was just down the hall, after all. I still had the faint aftertaste of Swedish meatballs lingering in my mouth and I hoped that when I woke up there would be more in the cafeteria. If there weren't, maybe I could order them directly from the caterer. Or that nice girl in the cafeteria who thanked me. Saving her life had to be worth a few Swedish meatballs.

I stared up at the lightbulb above me as my eyes started to shut. They squinted as I tried to force them open one last time, but it didn't work. I saw the light and it distorted and glared, reminding me of the rising flame in the darkness that was Aleksandr Gavrikov, hovering above me like what the sun must look like, lighting up everything around.

I closed my eyes, and he was there, on fire, just like all the times I had seen him but one. The flames flickered where his skin should have been, an inferno in place of flesh. I could almost smell the burning, taste the ash that should have been in the air. He edged closer to me but there was no heat, and for a bare moment I couldn't figure it out, then I did. "Dreamwalking," I whispered.

He floated closer, and I watched the fire recede from his hands, from his face. His dark hair appeared, then his nose and eyes. He looked less pallid than he had when I'd seen him in real life, and the world around us coalesced into my old room. Fire crawled up the walls, slowly burning around us as his feet touched the ground. The silence consumed me like the flames, surrounded me. He stood in front of me, staring into my eyes. "You said you would help me."

I felt the burn of his almost accusatory stare. "I was trying to save your life." I looked away, walked a few feet in the other direction, as though placing distance between us could absolve me of my promise. "Not to mention the lives of the others."

His voice came back to me, cold and empty. "Did you tell them? Do they know what I want?"

"I did." I turned back to him. "They're not going to release her. They think you're a dire threat."

I saw the haunting in his eyes, the guilt in his face. "I am a dire threat. I am more than that. I am death; more death than they can handle."

I didn't blink away from him as he said it, but a part of it hit home. "Sounds familiar. I don't think they're going to just give her up on your say so, though."

He took a deep breath, in and out, closed his eyes and smiled. "Then I'll convince them. I'm in Glencoe. It's only about fifteen minutes west of you. Tell them to come and see me and we'll talk."

Something about how he said it raised the little hairs on the back of my neck. "You just want to talk? Why do I doubt that?"

"I have a message for them," he said with an icy calm. "Tell them. I'll be waiting in the middle of town. Bring as many of their men as they'd like."

I felt a chill of fear. "I don't love the way you're saying that."

He burst into flames again, his brown eyes replaced by soulless, dancing fire. "Tell them. Tell them to come to me. I'll be waiting." He remained afire, but dimmed in my sight until he was gone, replaced by the light over my bed.

Chapter 23

Less than an hour later I was cruising west along a highway with Zack and Kurt. In front and behind us were vans, one filled with agents and the other carrying M-Squad. It was early evening, the sun was already down and a bitter cold had followed with the darkness. The thermometer on the rearview mirror said that it was already -4 degrees and I had to guess it was falling. We had streaked through a small town already and now there were snowy fields to either side as we chugged along the highway. I could see the lights of another town in the distance, and as we drew closer the car slowed.

"He said he's waiting there for us?" Kurt looked back at me, nerves plain on the older man's pudgy face.

"Yeah. You scared?" I didn't put much venom into it, but I didn't need to. His gave me a nasty look anyway.

"If you're not, you're stupid." He turned forward again. "In case you missed it, he burned your damned hand off."

"I can see why you're worried; that'd be a fatal blow to your sex life."

I heard the seething noise he made in the front seat, but he didn't turn back around. Zack let out a soft chuckle and when Kurt turned on him, he said, "What? It was funny."

We turned off the main highway at an intersection. After passing a few cross streets, we turned left onto the main street of the town. There was a bank across from a flower shop and a jewelry store. It looked idyllic as we pulled into the empty parallel parking spaces. I stepped out onto the curb, over the small mountain of accumulated snow, onto the sidewalk.

I felt my breath catch in my throat. My coat was buttoned, my hands were covered with gloves, but I could still feel the frigid air creeping in. I felt like I was going to turn to ice. I looked down the sidewalk, but it was empty, the streetlights shedding the only illumination. There was not another running car in sight. Agents exited the van behind us, their weapons concealed under heavy coats. Clary stretched as he got out of the vehicle in front of us, Parks and Kappler joining him as Bastian walked around from the driver's side.

The agents huddled around Bastian, who didn't order anyone to come over to him; they just did it automatically. I watched and nudged my way into the circle next to Zack as Roberto started to speak. "We're gonna sweep Main Street. If you find him, do not engage. Keep eyes on target and maintain a healthy distance." I watched him touch his ear and realized he had some kind of miniature microphone in it. I looked around the circle and saw the others with the same and felt a little irritation that I hadn't been offered one. "We're sticking with the same strategy. This guy can kill any of you faster than you can pull a trigger, so Clary is our point man when we find the target."

They were all so focused, they didn't notice a familiar (to me, anyway) figure step out of an alley across the street. "Uh, guys?" I felt the pressure of so many sets of eyeballs lock onto me, but I kept watching Gavrikov as he stepped onto the road, heading toward us. "I have eyes on target," I said, prompting them all to swivel.

"Scatter!" Bastian's words echoed through the night as Gavrikov burst into flames in the middle of the street and shot twenty feet into the air. Three fireballs lanced out from his hand and destroyed the front van in an explosion that sent me to my knees. He sent another blast at the jewelry store behind us, a bigger one that caused the storefront to burst into flames.

Zack was huddled behind the car, along with Kurt. One agent

was down after the explosion of the van and I couldn't tell from where I was whether he was hurt badly or not. Disregarding most of my good sense, I stuck my head up over the top of the car and yelled to Aleksandr. "Is this the message you wanted to send?"

"Hardly," came back his reply. "That was to get your attention. You have two minutes to get back in your cars and leave this town. After that, you have until tomorrow morning at six A.M. to bring Klementina to me at the top of the IDS tower in Minneapolis. After that..." He let his voice trail off and even from where I was behind the car, I could see a smile. "Well...you'll see in two minutes. Let us call this town...a warning. For what will happen if you don't deliver."

I heard Bastian scream behind me. "Back in the cars! Move out!"

I ignored the frenzied action around me and focused on Gavrikov. "Aleksandr...this isn't the way."

He drifted to the ground as the first van shot out of its parking place. Agents were hanging from the side and I looked back to see the one still left on the sidewalk. He was not moving. I heard Zack shout my name from the car. His hand extended toward me, fingers dangling in the air between us. Kurt was struggling with him, trying to pull him into the vehicle. One of the agents in the back punched Zack in the back of the head and he crumpled forward, slumping against the dashboard as the car pulled away, slinging snow and mud.

"They left you behind." His words were calm, icy even, as his burning eyes continued to stare at me.

"Yeah," I said. "They didn't try to shoot you, either. I'm guessing they took your threat seriously."

"They should." The flames around his hand died, revealing his fingers, then his arm. He took hold of my hand, and I let him. "These are men who understand nothing but force. They are weapons, turned loose when necessary, meant only for destruction." He sounded weary, bitter even. "I know these men. I was one of them, but on a grander scale."

"Should I be afraid?" I said it without fear, but I had the beginnings deep inside, the smallest well of concern.

"You have nothing to fear from me; you are not one of them." He pulled the glove from my hand as he said it, twisting the leather in his grasp. The cold in my hand didn't bother me. "There is only one thing that matters to me now. I want her; she is my penance. Freeing her is all I have left. Everything else..." He grasped the glove and it burned in his hand, turning to cinders and slipping from his fingers into the wind. "...is ashes. Those who stand between us have everything to fear."

He stepped closer and I blanched. "Not to worry, little *matryushka*. You could not run fast enough to escape what is coming to this town if you had to." His hands, now flesh, reached out and enfolded me and I felt the ground lift away under my feet. "I will help you." I was flying, the wind whipping my hair, the freezing cold streaking in my eyes, drawing tears and an exclamation of joy from me. The fresh, cold air hurt my nose and lungs as I breathed it in. He held me tight, carrying me through the night, his flames gone and his body pressed against me.

I felt us slow as the ground approached, and my feet touched solid pavement. I felt his arms let loose of me and his face drifted away. My teeth chattered involuntarily, and I looked behind him to see the town of Glencoe, the faint city lights glowing against the clouds above. "Remember my words," he said, hovering in front of me. "Six in the morning—less than twelve hours, on top of the IDS Center in downtown Minneapolis. Otherwise..." He burst into flames again and streaked into the sky, headed back toward the town.

Headlights on the highway raced at me, slowing at the last possible second. A van rolled up and the passenger window came down. "Girl!" Clary opened the door before the car even came to a stop. "Get in here! Old Man Winter will have all our asses if you get left behind."

My eyes were transfixed on the distance. Glencoe sat, still shining into the winter sky, a little beacon of light in the middle of the nothingness of snowy fields. "Hey!" Clary reached out and started to grab my arm, then must have thought better of it, because he waved his hand in front of my face. "We gotta go!"

"We're fine," I said. "Just wait." The second car full of agents came to a skidding stop behind the van and Kurt popped his head out, eyes bulging in shock at the sight of me.

I couldn't take my eyes off the town. I knew there were people there; there had to be. It wasn't just some ghost town, some empty place...

A light glowed in the middle of town like a cigarette lighter sparking, then there was a flash that blotted out my vision. A wave of force came rushing toward us and the only thing that kept me on my feet was that I reached out and grabbed Clary's arm as he turned to steel, anchoring me in place as the shockwave hit. I turned my eyes back to Glencoe as a mushroom cloud of fire and smoke blossomed into the sky.

The smell was what hit me first, the awful smell of something burning. I could hear the rumble still in the distance as the cloud drifted up into the sky, mingling with those already hanging above Glencoe. Little pieces of ash began to rain down around me like a falling snow and my hands were numb, along with my nose, followed by the rest of me.

Zack opened the door to his car and staggered out, his hand clutching the back of his head, stumbling over to me. "You okay?" He asked the question while I still stood transfixed, staring at the remains of the small town where I had been only minutes before—and which was now wreathed in flame and smoke, the last resting place of its occupants. "Are you all right?"

His glove brushed my cheek, stirring me back to reality. The explosion had died down, but the light of the fires still burning in Glencoe reflected off the clouds, casting the night in the most surreal light. "I'm fine," I said, barely managing to get the words out. "How many people lived in that town?"

Zack's hand was still on the back of his head, but his gaze fell. "I don't know. Several thousand."

I spoke in a voice of awe. "He killed them all. He'll do it again, Zack, he's going to do it again in less than twelve hours if he doesn't get what he wants. He said this was his warning—his only warning."

"Even Gavrikov wouldn't be so insane as to..." He didn't finish his sentence. His eyes stared back into the distance, to the fires that still burned. "He wouldn't. He just wouldn't."

"He would," I whispered. "He will," I said, this time with firmness. "Unless we bring Kat to the tower tomorrow morning, he absolutely will.

"And you can kiss the city of Minneapolis goodbye."

Chapter 24

We stood arrayed around Old Man Winter's office, Zack glaring at Kurt, Ariadne leaning against the wall looking faint, the four members of M-Squad situated behind me and Kappler. Ostensibly because we were women, we were the ones that got the chairs. I didn't care; I was tired. Old Man Winter sat behind the desk, his usual inscrutable self.

"Why's the girl in here for this?" Clary's words came out in a kind of low whine. "She ain't an agent or one of us."

"She's here because she's got more experience dealing with the hostile than any one of us," Bastian said in a clipped tone. "He spared her life from the explosion, after all."

"He did more than that," Kappler said in a heavy, Germanic accent. "He picked her up and carried her clear." Her eyes were narrow by nature, now they were slitted, her thin face looking like nothing so much as a snake. "I think a good question would be 'Why'?"

"He perceives me as the only one who will reliably deliver his message." I was so tired, I didn't care if they thought I was in league with Gavrikov. I guess technically I had let him loose.

"I figured it was because he was sweet on you." Clary said it with a suggestiveness that made me assign him once more to the category of "idiot" in my head. Thank God Wolfe was quiet.

"He's gonna do it," I said. "You don't get Kat to the top of the IDS Center, he's going to send you another message and this one will be a hundred square blocks of flattened buildings and an inferno at the middle of it."

"He won't do it," Ariadne said, quiet.

An uneasy silence settled over the room, broken by me. "Um, yes he will. He's already done it once tonight just to prove his point. If you've already killed several thousand to make a point, why not a few hundred thousand to actually get what you want? Just because you hope he doesn't, don't think that bears any resemblance to what will actually happen."

"He will do it," Old Man Winter said, quieting the whispers I heard from M-Squad. "Let there be no doubt. But equally certain is the fact that we cannot turn Kat over to him. She is an innocent and he is...unstable to say the least."

"Sir, we'll do as you order," Bastian said, "but the girl compared to a several hundred thousand lives..."

"You will eliminate him," Winter said.

"I'm sorry," I interrupted again. "But you guys had a chance to go a few rounds with him down in South America, as I recall, and it's all well and good that you captured him, but it seems like the nuclear option wasn't on the table for him back then, for whatever reason. Now it is." I turned around to find Bastian staring at me, along with Parks, while Kappler glared and Clary looked on with a kind of cluelessness. "If you couldn't take him down then, when he wasn't up to using his full power, how are you going to do it now?"

Bastian turned to Parks, the wizened guy with his long, gray hair and goatee that looked like it was almost white. "This time," he said in a gruff voice, "we get to kill him instead of playing the capture game, ma'am."

"Oh, good," I said, "you get to try and kill the walking nuclear bomb. That won't piss him off at all."

"We'll kill him, ma'am." Bastian's voice was filled with conviction. Too bad it didn't convince me. "With the kid gloves off, my team can take him down."

"Glorious." I'm pretty sure the wearying effect of the drug I'd been taking leeched any chance of me pulling off false sincerity, so I didn't bother. "Couldn't you maybe...I don't know, lay the situation out for Kat and see what she thinks? She might consider it an acceptable risk to jump through his hoops for a bit to keep him from blasting the city into rubble."

Old Man Winter's reply was like a crack of thunder. "Placing her into that situation is unacceptably risky."

"For her? Or for the city of Minneapolis?" I leaned forward, tossing all caution aside. "You're playing a hell of a game here. You're placing the survival of an entire city on the idea that these guys—no offense," I waved vaguely at Kappler, who was still glaring at me, and the rest, sitting behind me, "can kill him before he can go critical. That's a pretty big risk considering he dropped me off in the countryside, flew back to the detonation site and I bet he wasn't there for more than ten seconds before he went off. That means if they err even slightly, a lot of people die." I saw no change in any of the faces around me, except maybe Ariadne, who had grown slightly paler. "More than I let die, that's for sure."

Old Man Winter's cold gaze burned over my head to Bastian. "You have your orders."

I bit my lip and wrenched myself to my feet. "I sense my presence is no longer needed here. If you'll excuse me, I'm going to go find a quiet place to hide until the atomic apocalypse is over." I didn't exactly storm out, but I did break the door behind me. Because of my super-strength, not because I was in a snit. Well...maybe a little bit of both.

I seethed in the hallway and all the way down to the lobby, which was quiet save for a few guards standing around. Different than agents, they wore tactical vests and held submachine guns slung across their chests. A few of them had stood guard outside my door back when they held me in the basement room where Kat was currently residing. I wondered where they recruited all these yahoos. They should have given them all red shirts.

I started toward the front doors, intent on leaving, on running far, far away, wanting to go someplace where I'd never again have to be put in a position where all I could do was sit back and watch a massacre take place. I slammed into the glass doors at the front of Headquarters, sending them rattling open on their hinges. I would have been far more satisfied if they had broken, but apparently they were designed to be abused by metas, because they started to pull shut on their own.

I stood outside, sucking in the cold air. It all came down to power—it always did. With Wolfe, I didn't think I had the power to face him, to beat him. It turned out I did, but I didn't know that at the time. Now, with Gavrikov...I was really unsure. It wouldn't take him much to vaporize me if he got pissed, that was certain after what I saw him do in Glencoe.

But what if Kat was with me? I thought about it a little harder. He wanted to save her, to keep her safe, more than anything. If I took her to the rendezvous point, I could get close to him, maybe stop him. I stared at my hands. It didn't have to be for good, just long enough to get him contained again. I cringed. In another one of those boxes. Surely I could keep him out of sorts until the Directorate could find a way to crate him up again. I didn't like that option, but I liked it better than the thought of him waltzing away with Kat, who didn't even know him, or letting M-Squad and that assclown Clary take a crack at him, or worse, letting him level Minneapolis.

To save the city, to make amends for what I had let happen with Wolfe, I was going to have to consign Aleksandr Gavrikov to a fate I was all too familiar with—confinement in a coffin-like containment chamber. A box of his very own.

I cursed the irony of the whole situation, of how it had all played out. I turned back to Headquarters, studying it and wondering how I was going to make this work, when I heard the scuff of a shoe behind me and turned, ready to strike—

Scott Byerly stood there, hands in front of him. "Whoa, I'm

just here to visit Kat," he said, circling around me toward the Headquarters building.

What was it he had said about writing me that note? "Hey," I said. "You have family in Minneapolis?"

He stopped, turned back to me. "Yeah, my whole family is from around here. Why?"

I steeled myself for what I was about to have to do. "Just thought you might want to know—the guy that blew up the science lab?"

He furrowed his brow. "Gavrikov, wasn't it? Russian guy?"

"Yeah," I said. "He just nuked Glencoe, you know, that town west of here."

Scott's face paled, his dark complexion going white. "I heard about that earlier. I didn't know it was him."

"Yeah, well..." I tried not to belabor the point, but I wanted to draw him in a little, "...I was there when it happened. He did it as a warning to us—to show us what would happen to Minneapolis if we didn't bring Kat to him by tomorrow morning at six."

"Excuse me?" The reaction was immediate. His jaw clenched, he took a step toward me, his fist balled up. "He threatened the city?"

"Said he'd nuke it to the ground," I said. "Bye-bye, City of Lakes."

He turned without saying anything else, started to stalk off. "Where are you going?" I asked.

"To stop him," he tossed back.

I ran after him. "Wait. You can't just attack the guy, he'd turn you into the stuff you find in the bottom of a microwave."

Byerly stopped, but the fury was still evident on his face. "What, then?"

"Well," I said, "M-Squad and the boys have a kill order—"

"Not good enough," he said and started to walk again. I reached out and grabbed his arm, keeping my grip firm enough to catch his attention but not enough to spin him around. He did that on his own, looking like he was ready to explode on me, his face red, his eyebrows locked into forty-five degree angles, and his mouth in a thin, downturned line.

"Whoa!" I held my hands out in a gesture of peace. "I'm with you on this one. I think M-Squad is gonna foul it, big time. I mean, if you heard about how things went for them in South America, or you've had five minutes to consider that Clary is the linchpin of their strategy, you recognize that giving them this shot means that you're basically comfortable with turning Minneapolis into a burning wasteland. Which I am not," I said, trying to reassure him and dislodge his angry face. "But you can't just charge after him without a strategy."

"I have a strategy," he said in a kind of roar. I took a step back, more out of concern for his safety than mine. "I find Gavrikov and I drown his ass."

"And a fine strategy that would be," I said, suppressing all my smartass instincts for the sake of my penance, "but may I suggest one that's got a better chance of success?"

He drew up to his full height, arms folded in front of him and said, "I'm listening." His posture said he was not, but I was desperate enough to try anyway.

"The thing you have to understand about Gavrikov is that he thinks Kat is a clone of his sister," I started.

"Why the hell would he think that?"

"Because she actually is his sister," I said, "and don't interrupt me. He feels guilty because he thinks she died or something, back in the early 1900s, and the only thing he cares about is giving her spiritual successor a chance at freedom." I paused, taking a breath. He looked at me with less rage, but also a look that told me he didn't totally understand. "Because he thinks the Directorate is keeping her imprisoned here."

He frowned. "They are."

"Yeah, but not totally," I said. "I mean, if she really wanted to, she could probably get out—speaking from personal experience."

He looked at me with skepticism. "I have my doubts. Kat doesn't strike me as much of a fighter."

"Doesn't matter. Anyway, if she's with me, he won't go nuclear because he doesn't want to hurt her. That gives me a chance to neutralize him without anyone having to get hurt. I can bring Kat back here, safe and sound, and keep Gavrikov down." I stared him in the eyes. "You know I can."

He blinked, then his eyes clouded with suspicion. "Why are you telling me this?"

I took a deep breath. "Because I don't know how to drive. And I don't exactly know where I'd be going. And Kat...well..." I hesitated. "I don't think she's going to come willingly just on my say so."

He held his hand up to his head. "So you want my help convincing her, too?"

"I do. I really, really do." I added a note of pleading to my voice. "Look, if we leave this up to the so-called pros, I don't know how it's going to turn out, but I suspect bad. Really bad. And I mean, yeah, we could hide here, we're probably safe from the blast radius, but..." I didn't know what else to say.

Scott Byerly just stared at me, with those eyes, those cool blue eyes. "One question. If you answer it honestly, I'm in."

I smacked my lips. Why did my mouth always dry out at dramatic moments? "What is it?"

He stared so hard I almost felt his gaze burn through me. "Why are you doing this?"

It felt like he'd wound up a swing with a sword and punched it straight through the middle of me. "You know why," I said, my mouth even drier than it had been a moment earlier.

He shook his head, impassive. "I really don't. Why?"

"Because..." I swallowed, trying to get the taste of ashes out of my mouth. I felt like I could taste them, like I had been on the main street in Glencoe after the detonation, and it reminded me of blood. Blood in my mouth, from fighting with Wolfe. "Because the last time someone super-powerful held people hostage I let the clock tick down and a lot of people died." My hand came up, brushing the hair out of my eyes where the wind had tossed it. "I felt helpless, weak, like I couldn't do anything. I can't ever undo the consequences of my inaction. But this..." I tightened my hand into a fist in front of me, "putting down Gavrikov...this I can do."

He looked left, then right, then back at me. "I'd shake hands with you, but I know what that would do to me. I'm in. Let's go get Kat."

Chapter 25

We took out the guards with minimal effort. We did it fast because I was afraid Old Man Winter would get wise to our idea and send M-Squad to protect Kat. Fortunately, he must have had them working on the plan to take out Gavrikov, because there was no siren, no klaxon as the last guard slipped from my grasp, unconscious. I cracked the knuckles of my right hand, the one that had been burned off just yesterday.

Scott raised an eyebrow at me. "Feeling okay?"

"Better than him." I picked up the card key looped to the guard's belt and ran it through the reader on Kat's door. It slid open and she jumped up from the bed, looking a bit haggard. Her hair was tangled, as though it hadn't been washed for a few days, and she wore a tank top and sweatpants. I started to crack wise about the way she looked but remembered a similar visit I had in this room from Zack and wisely shut my mouth. "Check out time," I said, drawing a look of surprise from her.

"What are you doing here?" She looked to Scott. "Both of you."

"He was coming to visit," I chucked a thumb to indicate him. "I was coming to give you a choice. Did they explain why you're down here?"

She nodded. "The man who blew up the science building thinks I'm his sister, and he's after me."

"I'm told you actually are his sister," I said, "but the point is, he doesn't want to hurt you. He thinks you're being imprisoned and he wants you set free."

She looked around her gilded cage, with its wide-screen TV

and luxurious private bathroom. "Um, I am being imprisoned."

"Perfect, let's escape," I said and started to turn.

"Wait!" The alarm was urgent in her voice. "I don't want to go to him, either!"

"He's going to blow up the city of Minneapolis if we don't turn you loose and bring you to him. He already blew up a town west of here to prove he'd do it." Scott delivered the news I didn't want to.

I watched Kat as she took it in. She was always pretty; enough to make me jealous, at least. She was like the cheerleader everybody loved because she was just so sweet and perky and innocent. Even despite her somewhat unwashed appearance, she was still pretty. That annoyed me.

But I watched her face crumple as Scott's news hit her. Her green eyes lost their glow immediately, turned hollow. Her face fell, her eyes dropped to the floor and her shoulders slumped. She took a step back, staggered, as if she had been punched in the stomach, and she dropped back to the bed. When her voice came, it was no more than a whisper. "He did that...? For me? Because...because of me?" She looked younger than eighteen years old, and as I watched the emotions played across her fine features like the ravages of age. I felt a tightness inside that I didn't really care to explain. It was all too familiar.

"He's going to blow up Minneapolis if we don't get you to him." Scott closed the distance between them and knelt down. "But it's okay. Sienna and I will protect you from him." He looked at me. "He doesn't want to hurt you, Kat. Sienna can take him out; you've seen what she can do." He smiled. "And you know what I can do. He's not going to try and hurt you, but even if he did, we can protect you—we can stop him."

"I...I don't want to go." Her words were choked. "I don't want anybody to die, but I...I don't want to go."

"It'll be okay," he said. I watched her eyes; the soothing

wasn't working. "We can stop it."

"It may not be okay." I said the words before I could stop myself, drawing a startled look from her and a venomous one from him. "Aleksandr Gavrikov just killed thousands of people to convince us to bring you to him." I took a deep breath, and watched the horror in her eyes. "He's a monster in his way, but I know him—or rather, I've gotten to know him. You're the only thing that matters to him. He thinks you're caged, tortured, and he wants you free. There's something in the past between the two of you that happened that he desperately wants to make amends for. I think he needs you to forgive him for something. It's all he cares about."

"Why would you tell me this?" The first hint of tears broke through onto her face, sliding down her cheeks, sparkling in the overhead light. "I don't want to face him, he's a monster!"

"He is. But if you don't, a whole city of people will die." I took two steps forward and reached out to Kat, putting my gloved hand on hers. "When Wolfe was tearing up the city, I sat back because I was afraid, because no one could fight him, no one could face him, and I didn't think there was anyone that could stop him. I was wrong. I could stop him the entire time, but it required a sacrifice that I wasn't willing to make. I sat by as more and more people died until I couldn't stomach it anymore." I saw the emotion flicker behind her eyes. "People are already dead, and it's not your fault, and there's nothing you can do about it. I don't blame you for not wanting to go. I wouldn't blame you if you wanted to run and hide, because Aleksandr is broken inside, and powerful, and that is a dangerous combination.

"But I'm going to fight him," I said. "Whether you go or not, I'm going to try and stop him. I doubt I'll be able to do much because he's fast, and could vaporize me from about a mile away before I even got a chance to take a shot at him. But I'll be there." I set my chin. "Because I know what it's like to stand by, to hide and to have people die, to have those deaths on my conscience. And I won't do it again."

She stared me down, her eyes brimming, full of emotion and the flickers of guilt and fear, and I wasn't jealous of her any more. All I felt was sorry for her, sorry that she had to experience the same hell that I had, but with even larger consequences. "But..." her voice trembled. "...you..." she looked to Scott, then back to me, "you'll be there? I won't have to go alone?"

I squeezed her hand in mine, felt the depth of her plea all the way through me, tingling my emotions and bringing me back to a morning in the basement of my house where I was forced to confront all my fears. Alone. "We'll be with you every bit of the way."

She looked ghostly, but her eyes came back to life and she stared back at me. "Okay." Her voice gained strength. "All right."

Byerly gestured toward the door as he swiped the card I'd handed him from the guard and it slid open. He and I led the way after giving Kat a minute to change into something more protective than a tank top. She came out wearing a black turtleneck, black leather gloves, jeans and a black wool coat that looked terribly familiar. I frowned at my "twin" and she shrugged. "They brought me here and didn't bring any clothes. This was all that was left in the closet." She looked down at her pants. "The jeans are kinda loose on me, though. And short."

Instead of smacking her, I started toward the stairs, the two of them in tow. I rounded a corner and a guard stood in front of me. I chopped him with a hand to his throat, causing him to gag, then slammed him in the side of the head with a punch that put out his lights. I turned to tell them to watch out for any other guards, but I found Scott letting loose of a guard of his own and Kat pummeling another with a flurry of punches that sent the man reeling, finishing him with a reverse side kick that caused him to ricochet off a wall. When she caught my surprised gaze, she smiled. "What?

Everyone always thinks I'm so delicate because my powers are healing. I'm a meta; I've got strength too."

"And moves," I said. "Where'd you learn those?"

She shook her head as we started toward the lobby doors. "I don't know. My memory is pretty fuzzy before Arizona. I don't know if you're aware of this, but Persephone-types have limits on our powers. We can only heal—"

"Until you run out of strength, then it starts leeching your memory. So you don't remember anything?"

"I still have skills, abilities," she said as we brushed out of the double doors, Scott looking skittish as he trailed behind us. "I can understand other languages, I can fight some." She frowned. "I can farm. Don't remember how I learned that."

"Memory loss isn't cool," I said, "but every time I kill someone with my power, I absorb their personality into mine."

"Eep!" She blanched. "So does that mean that the psycho you killed..." She paled.

"Yep," I said, pointing to my skull. "I've got Cujo panting in my brain. The good news is Doc Zollers seems to have found a way to keep him under wraps." I yawned. "Unfortunately, there do seem to be some adverse effects."

We ran to the garage, which was unlocked. Scott grabbed keys from a box that held a bunch of them, and I knocked out the guy in charge of watching them and stuffed him under the desk he sat behind. We made our way through the garage as Scott pressed the button on the key fob until he found the right car, a nice little SUV. I sat up front with him and Kat took the back seat. She looked nervous as we pulled out and headed for the front gate. Scott pushed a remote on the visor and the gate opened, fast.

We shot out and took a quick turn, zipping down the road at about sixty. "I'm not exactly an experienced driver," I said, "but I'm pretty sure there are speed limits."

"I'll keep that in mind," he said, mumbling.

The night was black, and up ahead there was a van pulled off to the side of the road. Scott slowed as we drove by and I caught a glimpse of the logo—a local telecommunications company—and saw, very briefly, the worker jump out of the way for us as Scott screamed by. "You know, saving the city isn't going to do us a ton of good if we end up killing a hundred people on the drive there."

He rolled his eyes, but I saw him slow the car a little. We passed through Eden Prairie as the clock on the dashboard flashed 4:30 A.M. Traffic was almost nil, a few cars as we got on the interstate. Kat was a silent hole in the backseat, and I cast frequent looks back to make sure she was still there. Scott gripped the wheel, white-knuckling it, the tension evident on his face as he steered us onto another major freeway. As he angled the vehicle onto it, I could see the lights of downtown Minneapolis in the distance.

The outline of the skyscrapers was pressed against the horizon, lighted shapes that gave form and substance to my thoughts of a city and what it should look like. A thousand windows gleamed and shone out at me, and some sort of lighted display shimmered in a rainbow of colors atop one of the buildings. They grew closer slowly as the distance between us and the city faded. We passed a few cars here and there, and soon enough the skyscrapers towered above us. "Which one is the IDS building?" I asked.

Scott craned his neck to look up and he pointed at the tallest one, made all of glass and jutting up into the sky. "That one."

I studied it. "He picked the biggest. I bet he didn't want a sniper shooting down at him."

Scott cast me a glance. "Really?"

I shrugged. "If you think about it, it's probably the only way he's vulnerable. I'd bet most low caliber rounds would melt before they hit him. Anyone attacks him physically, he can keep them at bay long enough to explode. But it's hard to concentrate enough to blow up when your brains got sent out the other side of your head."

"Good point. Wonder why they didn't do that to him in Glencoe?"

I kept my eyes on the building that dominated the skyline above us. "I think they were going to try, but they didn't get a chance to set it up. Which reminds me, M-Squad will be here in an hour or less. Best we're done by the time they show."

Scott eased the car onto a side street and found a parking garage. I heard the noise of another vehicle somewhere below us as we stepped onto the street. I watched another telecommunications truck pass us and I felt a tingle of nerves. It was the cable company for the entire Twin Cities, after all. Not unusual to see a couple of their trucks out, even at this time of morning. "Let's go," I said as we entered the glass lobby.

All around us was a dramatic promenade with trees, restaurants and shops. I was a little surprised, but I kept my focus as Scott led us up escalators to a bank of elevators. I stood looking at him and Kat, watched him take her hand and squeeze it with encouragement. I felt a pang of jealousy that turned to sadness by the time the elevator dinged and the doors opened. I shuffled in after them and watched them hold hands. I tried to feel good for them, really I did. Kat needed comfort right now. So did Scott, surely. So did I, when it all came down to it. But as per usual, there was no one there to hold me.

We reached the top floor and stepped off the elevator. I saw a sign for the stairs and headed toward them, Scott and Kat trailing behind. I looked up, and sure enough, there were steps leading up to a locked door. I broke it with ease and we stepped out onto the roof, the winter air chilling me as I led them out under the open night sky.

Snow was piled in drifts around edges and corners, but it looked as though someone had shoveled the roof to keep it mostly clear of snow. A few shacks and some ducts and machinery sat atop the flat surface, but most of it was empty space. I walked across to the far side, wondering if Aleksandr was here yet.

I heard Kat and Scott's footsteps behind me, soft and even as we padded our way across the roof. "Aleksandr," I said. The wind carried my words away. I had not bothered to shout it.

"Here." A small voice reached me and I saw him step out of the shadow of one of the boxy structures. He wasn't in flames and he wore different clothes since the last time I'd seen him. "You brought her..." He said with something approaching joy, then his eyes alighted on Scott and they narrowed. "And another."

"Precaution," I said. "I had to break her out of the Directorate myself. I needed help." I glanced back to Kat and then to Aleksandr. "There's something you should know; this isn't a clone of your sister. It's actually her."

His face wrinkled in confusion. "How is that possible?"

I shrugged at him. "How are you possible? She's a meta, like us. She's what they call a 'Persephone-type—'"

"I am familiar with them." He said it brusquely and then took a couple tentative steps closer to her. "You presume her memory is gone, then?"

I looked back at Kat and gave her as reassuring a smile as I could muster. "Ask her yourself."

He took another step and stopped, still a dozen paces from her, as if he were afraid she would disappear like a mirage when he got closer. "I was sure I lost you." He took another step, cocking his head to the side, examining her from all angles. "I watched you burn, watched your skin flake off in the fire." He swallowed and his cracked lips brushed together. "It was an accident. I am...so sorry. It was my first time...to learn my power, and you thought I was hurt, and tried to help me...and I couldn't...couldn't stop it in time—" He choked on the last bit. "I am so sorry, Klementina."

"My name is Kat," she said, her voice faint. "Katrina. Or at least that's what they've called me for as long as I can remember."

He hesitated, then stepped again, now only a couple arm's lengths away from her. "Your name was Klementina. You are my older sister."

"I don't remember." She held tight to Scott's hand, but didn't step back. "You said you last saw me when?"

"1908." Another step closer. I knew I was going to have to act soon, but I almost couldn't bring myself to break up the reunion. Gavrikov was so fixated on her, little pieces of his joy at seeing her were breaking through his normally impassive mask. "We grew up together on our father's farm outside Kirensk."

"I see." Her words were soft, contemplative. "Is he still alive, like us? Or our mother?"

Aleksandr seemed to shudder. "Mother died giving birth to me. Father..." He hesitated, looked away, then turned his face back to her but the joy was gone. "Father died on the same day I thought you did."

There was a cold silence, broken only by the howl of the wind around us. When Kat spoke, it was with more chill than the tempest around us. "Did you...kill him too?"

I cringed and waited for Aleksandr to respond. He did, but not as I expected. "I did," he said with a glint of pride. "He was not kind to you, Klementina, nor me. He...tortured us. You would come to me, to help salve my wounds after he beat me. And I would console you, after..." He broke off, unable to finish his sentence. "You remember nothing?"

Kat licked her lips and looked to Scott for reassurance. "Before the lab, I can't really remember anything concrete. I remember a light. I remember...burning. Some other things...a baby crying. But it all seems very far off, so long ago."

"But not what he..." Aleksandr shuddered, emotions tearing through the formerly seamless mask of his face. "Not the nights, not...what he did...?"

"I don't—" Kat looked away, to Scott, then to me, then stopped mid-sentence and screamed, but it was too late.

I didn't see the fist come at me, didn't sense it coming in all the air rushing past us on top of the tower and by the time I reacted to Kat's warning, it was too late. I felt my legs buckle as the fist hit the side of my head and I went flying, smashing into the metal ducting that ran across the roof. It collapsed on impact with my shoulders and back and I came to rest, blood dripping down the side of my head to my cheek. I blinked, trying to assess the damage. It hurt. A lot.

I tried to rise to my feet but before I could move, he was on me, hand around my neck, suffocating me. David Henderschott, his armor now all black, clutched me in his metal-clad hand, his cold mask blacked even to the eyeholes, not a trace of remorse or humanity visible as I started to pass out.

Chapter 26

A fireball exploded behind Henderschott, causing him to stagger and drop me. I would have been thankful, but one of his armored feet caught me as he stumbled and tread on my midsection. I felt pain in my guts like I hadn't experienced since Wolfe stuck his finger in my belly and started ripping. I tensed my abdomen and heaved, knocking him off balance and sending him clattering to the ground. I clutched at my stomach, fighting for a breath and left with a perfect view of Kat, Scott and Gavrikov.

"She's not coming with you," Scott said, holding his hand out, palm facing Gavrikov, who had already burst into flames.

"Do not stand in my way," Aleksandr said, that lifeless rumble in his voice again, the guttural horror that he sounded like when he was an inferno. His hands were out, one beckoning to Kat, the fire put out of it, the other pointed at Scott. "I will not warn you again."

From where I was, rolling in agony, cursing the day I left my house, it looked like Scott smiled. "Do you know what I am?" He seemed to be asking Gavrikov. "Ever heard of a Poseidon-type?"

I didn't have time to connect the dots before water rushed out of Scott's extended hand, a pressurized force that knocked Gavrikov back thirty feet into a radio transmitter. I heard the impact; I compared it to the blow I'd taken when Henderschott hit me and thought myself the lucky one.

I started to pull myself up, trying to ignore the pain as I hoped it would subside, but Henderschott was faster. He was on his feet and reached me as I got to one knee. His armor had been painted, all black, causing a bizarre contrast against the night sky, a shadow in the dark. He grasped at me and I lunged. My shoulder hurt as I caught him under the arm, knocking him off his feet with a tackle that I rolled out of. He landed on his back, once more looking like a turtle.

I leaned against some ductwork as I tried to stand up straight. His foot had done some damage to my insides, of that I was certain. I grunted at him as he stood up. "First you were obsessed with Iron Man. Now what?" I stared at his black armor. "You a Darth Vader wannabe? Or just a big Johnny Cash fan?"

He took a swing at me and I dodged, falling to my knees and rolling away. Not my preferred method of avoidance, but it worked. His fist caved in the ductwork I had been leaning on, burying his arm up to the elbow. His metal mask swiveled to look at me and I dodged his other hand, wrapping my arm around his neck, trying to get my upper arm between the metal plates to choke him out.

It was a stupid move on my part. He brought his helmet down and pinned my wrist between his chestplate and the metal that protected his chin. I heard the bone break and I cried out as he grabbed me by the arm and tossed me through the air like I weighed nothing. For the few seconds I was aloft, it was like flying with Aleksandr again.

I landed, skidding and bouncing until I hit a wall. My arm screamed at me where he'd broken it, and I was gritting my teeth. I caught a flash as Gavrikov flew nearby, a thick burst of fire shooting forth from his hands in a continuous stream like he was holding a flame thrower. I saw it meet a similar burst of water on the other side and saw Scott Byerly with a cocky smile on his face, pushing Gavrikov back while keeping Kat behind him. Gavrikov shifted directions and Byerly countered, a jet of water hitting Aleksandr across the chest, snuffing out the flames and revealing his bare chest beneath before it ignited again.

Full Metal Jackass came hammering across the roof at a run,

and I had only seconds to move out of the way. He clipped me with a clothesline that caught my good wrist and shoulder and flipped me. I landed on my back and all the breath rushed out of my lungs. I watched him lift a foot to stomp and I had the presence of mind to reach up and catch his foot, pushing and sending him teetering off balance as he fell again to his back. It was one of the only weaknesses I saw from him, the fact that it took him a minute or so to get up. Like a turtle.

I got to my feet, clutching my injured wrist to my side and ran away from him. It wasn't my best plan but I was hurt badly, and needed time to recover. Or formulate a strategy. Or hurl myself over the edge to end the aches and pains. Maybe the last one, actually.

I slumped behind one of the outcroppings on the roof, trying to catch my breath and assess the damage, and remembered my last fight with Henderschott. It brought a little smile to my face because it had gone so much better than this one. And it was all predicated on the fact that in both fights when he sucker punched me, I ended up dancing to his tune, to my detriment. Then the question became how to get him to dance to my tune, how to beat him, get the Full Metal Jackass out of his armor. Or kill him. I looked out over the edge of the building and realized it was a long way down. One question was answered.

I heard him behind me over the dull roar of the fight between Scott and Gavrikov, the weight of his footsteps causing the roof to tremble. He sounded like he was heading in the wrong direction, and I breathed a sigh of relief as I worked out how I could get him to the edge and fling his sorry metal ass over it. I hoped that would kill him; I thought it would. If it didn't, I'd have to find something else, but as far as strategies went, it was the best I had with the little I had to work with.

I peeked over the top of the little radio shack I was hiding behind and saw Henderschott moving parallel to me. With ease I got to my feet and stayed low, trying to creep up behind him. I had an idea, but it was based on stealth, on being able to sneak up and turn the momentum of the fight.

Making my way around one of the ducts, I slid through the snow beneath to come out a little behind him. I kept low, almost walking hunched over, creeping up behind the armored man. I took a last step and started to reach up. I planned to grab him by the helmet, drag him down with a horse-collar tackle, pull him to the edge of the roof and send him flying. I didn't want to kill him, but I had a feeling it was down to him or me, and I wanted to live. Really, truly, down to my bones, I wanted to.

My last step led me to a small patch of ice that wasn't visible. My boot found it and I went down with a loud cry as the landing jarred my already hurt innards. Henderschott swiveled and was on me before I could recover, one hand on my neck and the other on my broken wrist, pinning me against the rooftop. He wrenched hard on my hand, drawing a scream of pain from me, then another. I hit him with my free hand, right on the head, doing no damage to him but causing him to yank my wrist so hard my vision blurred and I started to black out.

I thought I was crying but I couldn't tell through the pain. All I could feel was the anguish from the damage he'd already done and the screaming of the nerves through my forearm as he bent it back. A thrumming sound in the back of my consciousness made its way through my ears, the blood rushing and making a connection for me.

The cable company truck I'd seen at the Directorate and outside the tower were the same. He'd followed us. Somehow he'd found the Directorate and watched. Sure, Scott nearly ran him over, but he'd recovered and managed to tail us all the way here, follow us up the elevator and show up when we least needed him to.

I saw Gavrikov and Scott, still facing off in the distance. I complimented myself on my knowledge of how Aleksandr would react; he hadn't exploded yet. Then I felt the squeeze of Henderschott's iron grip on my neck and wrist again and I realized that was of little consolation as he hauled me into the air and dangled my feet over the edge of the tower. I felt the brush of the freezing wind as it rushed past my face and then felt the push as his hand let go and I started to drop.

Chapter 27

My broken arm reached full extension and his grip on my wrist stopped me. I screamed again, the surge of pain down my arm dragging cries from my lips. The sound of blood in my ears had gotten worse, so bad that I could tell that Henderschott was talking to me, but I couldn't tell what he was saying, only hearing fragments. "Submit...do not resist..."

I twisted and dangled, hanging by my broken wrist and staring fifty-something floors down to the plaza below where we had entered, the atrium lit up like a light with spiderwebs of darkness running through it. There were no clouds for the first time I could remember since leaving my house, and the first strains of light on the horizon told me it was close to sun up. The noise in my ears was getting worse, and finally I realized that it wasn't the blood rushing through them, or the wind.

A Black Hawk helicopter dropped into view from above. Henderschott looked up and froze, almost as if he were shocked at its appearance. I could see the members of M-Squad inside, the door was open and someone wearing a tactical vest was hanging out as it swooped low over the rooftop. It didn't slow down and I saw the person jump out about ten feet above the roof as the helicopter started to pull up and gain altitude. I saw an M16 with an underslung grenade launcher go skittering as they landed rather badly.

Henderschott dragged me in from the edge and tossed me to the ground, then placed his boot on my chest. I felt the pressure of his weight lean onto me and I couldn't breathe. "Don't...go...anywhere." His words came out in low gutturals but I understood every one of them.

"Why...would I go anywhere?" I put my good hand on his foot. "I like this...spot," I said, fighting for breath. "It's you who...needs to move!" I lashed out at the last, rocking my hips and pushing my legs up so my heels hit him in the chest, sending him teetering off balance. I pulled in my leg again and then kicked him, knocking his feet out from underneath and sending him toppling.

I stood, ignoring the fire in my side. "You know," I said, "I used to spend hours encased in metal too. Probably wasn't as pleasant as how you're doing it." I tried to grab him by the leg but got a metal boot to the chest for my troubles. If possible, the already painful injury to my stomach multiplied and moved north. I suspected he had broken some ribs. I curled up into a little ball and tried to catch my breath, then attempted to force myself to stand. I watched as Henderschott got to his feet and I backed away from him, taking one hobbling step at a time.

"Hey!" The shout caught my attention, forcing me to look back and see Zack, holding the M16 with the barrel slightly elevated, pointed at Henderschott. I covered my ears and dived to the ground as I watched Henderschott's metal head tilt in confusion (or maybe amusement) at the sight of Zack. He didn't stay confused (or amused or whatever) for long. A low, whumping noise cut across the roof as the grenade launcher on the bottom of Zack's weapon fired and it caught Henderschott right in the armored chest and exploded, sending him backward, arms pinwheeling, over the edge of the building.

I got to my feet and lurched over to Zack, still holding my chest and side. "Big strong man, come to save me," I said, cringing from the pain.

"You looked like you needed some help." He pointed his gun in the air.

"He sucker punched me," I said. "Again."

"Yeah?" He looked at me with a little acrimony. "Maybe this wouldn't have happened if you hadn't totally disregarded what Old Man Winter told you—"

"Yeah, yeah," I said, mocking. "I don't see the city leveled, so don't count my strategy out yet."

"What was your strategy again?" He looked at me. "Get pummeled by the man in black while Scotty and Kat tried to avoid getting toasted?"

"You should talk." I took a deep breath and cringed at the pain from it. "If I'd had a helicopter, none of this would have happened. That armored assclown followed us from outside the campus." I looked back at the helicopter, which was swinging around for another pass. "Besides, what was your strategy?"

"Parks is up there with a sniper rifle," he said, pointing to the Black Hawk. "Clary's jumping down on their next pass, but if we get even a sign that Gavrikov means to explode, Parks will drop him."

"Why didn't Clary jump the first time?" I looked at him. "You know, with you?"

He looked a little hesitant, almost embarrassed. "I uh...I wasn't supposed to."

"You fell out?" I tried to hide my amusement.

"I jumped out," he said, "to save you. Clary was tasked to Gavrikov, he wouldn't have helped you in time, so I forced the issue. The crosswinds are a real bitch up here, though, and it wasn't the best moment to jump. Bastian is having a hell of a time keeping the chopper steady."

"Makes me wonder how Parks is gonna pull off his shot," I said, starting to limp toward the other side of the roof. I could see Gavrikov and Scott still going at each other, the flame versus the water.

"He'll pull it off," Zack said. "But honestly, we don't really need him to." He pulled his gun up and stared down the sights. "I can riddle him with holes if we get closer."

The helicopter swooped overhead and Clary appeared at the door. It looked like Bastian was trying to keep it level but there was serious chop and the helicopter was swaying in the wind. I watched Clyde yell out something that sounded like "Geronimo!" and jump, his skin turning to darkened steel on the fall. He was aimed perfectly, and hit the roof only a few feet to Gavrikov's left, causing the flaming man to look up from his battle with Byerly. I watched Clary land—

And disappear, falling through the roof. I turned to Zack. "Boy, am I glad we amateurs left this crack mission in the hands of you professionals. Marvelous work."

He shot me a pained look. "I'm sorry, I gotta—"

"Go," I said. "Do what you have to in order to stop him." I started to say more but a black metal glove hit Zack across the back and he went flying, his gun skittering off the roof, his body stopping just before the edge. I wheeled and threw myself back in time to dodge Henderschott's next assault. "Next time we throw you over I suppose I'll have to make sure you really fall." He swung at me again and I started to panic; I couldn't evade him like this forever.

Something stirred inside me as the fear took over. He had beaten and pummeled me, hurt me again in a way I would never get used to. Whatever it was came from deep inside, was primal, destructive, awakened by my purest survival drive. It was familiar, a feeling and a consciousness that had been suppressed by the drugs that I hadn't taken in...I glanced at the lightening sky...over 24 hours.

"You've got more lives than a cat, Henderschott." I shouted as I dodged another attack. The pain started to fade and it felt like it had in the cafeteria when I had attacked Scott; I was there, but parts of me were starting to respond to someone else's command. I vaulted over him, the pain in my side masked from my feeling it, and I grabbed hold of him before he could turn to face me, somehow gripping him with both hands. This was going to hurt tomorrow. A voice, deep and sinister, something absolutely nothing like my own, filled my ears with a hissing, lustful sound. "But not as many as Wolfe."

My good hand grabbed at his helmet and pulled, ripping at it with a strength far beyond my own. I twisted, dragging him off his feet, tearing at the metal surrounding his head, knowing it was attached to his skin and ripping as hard as I could. I could hear him screaming inside his suit and his hands reached up for me but I fended them off, turning him over, stretching out of their reach even as he hammered at my wrists and I ignored it, blind to any sort of pain at all.

With a last, wrenching tear the helmet came off, filling the world with Henderschott's scream. His face dripped blood as the helmet came off and my hands brought it down across the back of his head. I heard a sickening crunch of metal on bone. Henderschott went limp, but I wasn't the one who brought the helmet down again and again. My hands did it while I watched, dumbstruck, his head turning to little fragments of flesh and bone before my eyes.

"Wolfe," I said, whispering, "enough." But he was in control and I had none. My hands grasped Henderschott by the remains of his head and dragged him across the roof to the edge. I lifted him up in one hand, his eyes dead and rolling, but they found mine for a second and the awful, hissing voice of Wolfe came back. "Wolfe should have done this a long time ago, but Wolfe showed you mercy. Now there is only the mercy of gravity."

Henderschott spoke, but it was hard to hear. "They'll keep coming for you." His eyes were locked on mine, even as his head lolled back at a sick angle.

I wanted to ask who, and I fought, fought for control of my voice. "Who...?" I said it, and it came out as a whisper.

He blinked his eyes, the blood trickling down from the top of his head falling into the lids, turning them red, as though he were crying tears of blood. "Omega."

Before I could ask him anything else, my hands drew him back and heaved Henderschott off the side of the tower. I saw his eyes look at me as he passed, and they were haunted, horrible. He flew out in a lazy arc and started to fall. I watched him sail downward, but it took an impossibly long time for him to finally land on the street below.

When he did, a scream tore through my head and I realized it was my own. I dropped to my knees at the edge of the tower, Wolfe receding to the back of my consciousness. I cried out, again, tears freezing on my cheeks as I stared down, far below to where Henderschott had landed; the second person I had killed with my own hands.

I wanted to cry, wanted to scream, but I heard both from behind me before I could let out my own. I lurched to my feet and started back toward the far side of the roof. Gavrikov hovered, bursts of flame flying through the air, balls of fire aimed at the helicopter above, forcing it into motion.

Kat was kneeling next to Scott, whose body was burned horribly. Her hands were already on him and his skin was returning as I stepped onto the long, empty section of roof where they were. Gavrikov turned to them from where he hurled another bolt of fire at the helicopter and his face changed, even beneath the flames. "What are you *doing*?" He threw a small fireball at Kat, forcing her away from Byerly. "I save you from them and this is the thanks I get?" The Black Hawk shifted and flew off, coming around in the distance angling to approach the tower.

"I don't need saving!" Her words came out as a cry. I was still a good many paces away from them, but I could see Aleksandr's skin begin to glow brighter. "I don't even know who you are! I don't want to go anywhere with you, I want to go back to the Directorate—it's my home!"

Gavrikov was quiet for a moment, but he hovered only a foot or so off the ground. "I tried to save Klementina. My penance for failures, for crimes—for murder. For the murder I did when I was too young to know how to control myself." He edged closer to her.

She skidded away from him, sliding across the roof, almost on her back. "I didn't ask for this—not for you to help me, not for any of this!"

Gavrikov drifted closer to the ground. "I see how it has become. Things are not so different from the world we grew up in. Family betrays you at every turn, it is cold and dark and miserable and bereft of light. Everything Father did to us was nothing compared to what the world will do, with its cheap brutality and meanness." He let out a tortured howl that shook me inside. His skin glowed all the brighter, but he had stopped advancing on Kat. "You'll see soon enough."

There was a crack of gunfire and a bullet whistling through the air. I saw it hit Gavrikov and he dropped to a knee, the flames around his shoulder dissipating to show puckered flesh, blood squirting out in short intervals. He seemed like he was going to fall over but steadied himself. "Thank you," he said, "for proving my point." He heaved the largest fireball yet at the Black Hawk and I watched it sway as Bastian tried to dodge, sending the chopper into a dive beyond the edge of the rooftop and out of our view.

I was only a few feet away now and Gavrikov saw me but didn't react. I stopped, my chest heaving from the effort of crossing the roof. "And you too, *matryushka*? You are more like the sister I remember than this one is." His hand reached out, the flaming fingers extended to indicate Kat, who quailed away from him. "You know the pain she has forgotten. You have tasted the rich inequities of life." He smiled, but it was rueful. "You have fought, been hurt, been beaten down."

I stared back at him, exhausted. "What of it?"

He smiled and his chest burst back into flame. "I will give you the greatest gift I can." He rose into the air a foot. "Life doesn't get better from here, it gets worse." His hands came up at his sides, giving him the rough look of a human cross and he started to grow brighter. "I will give you the only gift I can. The same gift I will give all these people." His hand waved to indicate the city spread out before us. "Peace. True peace, lasting and final."

"You say peace," I said, drawing closer to him, "but I kinda think you mean death."

Even through the fire that engulfed his face, I could see the line that was his mouth twist into a rough smile. "Death is the only peace in this world."

The flames leapt all around him, the glow encompassing him like what I imagined the rising sun to look like. "I'm sorry, Aleksandr." I peeled off my gloves and let them fall to the ground. "I can't let you do that."

His burning eyes looked down at me and he drifted closer, the flames receding from his face so that he could look at me with his own eyes. He glowed ever brighter and I knew I had only seconds. "What will you do?"

My mouth was dry. "Give you peace," I whispered and brought my hands up to touch his face. I felt the skin singe as I touched him, the fire from his body so hot that it started to burn me. I ignored it and looked into his eyes, saw through the pain, the anger, saw the wounded soul beneath. He smiled when I touched him, and closed his eyes. His face went slack, even though I knew he hadn't felt the effects yet. He jerked for the first time a few seconds later, and the fire around his body started to gutter out.

"A metal box to spend the rest of your life in would do you no favors," I whispered as he sagged to the ground, then fell to his knees. I held his cheeks clenched in my fingers and he jerked again, the fire now out. Tears streamed down my face as I felt him heave for the last time and I let go, staggering back and falling over, my brain on fire with memories and visions, whirling in my skull. I looked over and saw his body start to blacken, then turn to ash that was carried away by the wind.

My head was pounding but I forced myself to turn over and sit up. Kat passed me and knelt next to Scott, putting her hands on him. He started to stir, a few moments later, his skin rejuvenated, coming back to life. I felt a hand land heavily on my shoulder and turned to see Zack. I tried to force words through the jumble of thoughts clogging my head as my brain made way for Gavrikov inside it. "Are you okay?"

"I feel like I just spent an intimate evening on the freeway being made love to by a Mack truck." Zack's face was bruised.

"Is that better or worse than spending the evening being made love to by a trucker named Mack?" I said it, huffing as I tried to stop the spinning in my head. I started to shake my head, but it felt impossibly heavy, like it would roll off my shoulders at any minute.

"What happened to Gavrikov?" Zack reached out and tugged at my arm, helping me to my feet.

"He wanted...peace." I stared over the edge of the roof to the east. "I gave it to him...as best I could."

"So he's..." He looked around. "Gone?"

"No," I said and pointed to my head. "He's in here, now. With the other one."

"Oh, I'm sure that'll end well," he said as I caught sight of Clary hobbling toward us from the stairs. I could hear the blades of the chopper as it hovered above us and Bastian drifted her down, using the wind to steer his approach. He brought the helicopter down to a mere foot off the roof, resting the front wheel as Kat and Clary helped Scott into the side of the chopper.

I paused as Zack pulled me toward the door and turned around. The sun was rising in the cloudless sky, a bright red disc slipping over the horizon, the sky lighting up gold around it, with the first strains of blue transitioning to a deep indigo in the west. I stared at it, trying to savor the moment. I stopped resisting Zack's tugs and let him guide me into the helicopter and I watched the roof drop away beneath us as the Black Hawk turned and we headed west. I craned my neck in my seat, trying to watch the elusive sun as it cast a light on us.

"It does get better," I whispered so low no one could hear it over the chopper noise but the one I intended it for, nestled as he was in mind. "It has to." I watched the light as we raced the sunrise back to the Directorate.

Chapter 28

Our first stop once we landed was the medical unit. I saw Dr. Perugini waiting along with Old Man Winter, Ariadne, and Dr. Zollers as the helicopter came in for a landing. I thought about bracing myself for the inevitable onslaught, but instead I just soaked up the rays of the sun, beaming down from outside. When the blades spun down and the doors opened, Scott was the first out. He looked a little discombobulated, but his skin was pink and fresh, like I suspected a newborn's would look. He caught my eye as he passed and nodded.

Roberto Bastian and Eve Kappler were in the cockpit but Parks and Clary were in the back with us. The whole way back, Clary had a look on his face like he was pissed off he missed the fight or something. Parks, on the other hand, stared out the window, like me. Zack had been on his headset pretty much the whole time, except for firing a reassuring smile at me now and again.

I waited until Clary had cleared the door and then Parks gestured that I should go next. Ariadne looked especially stiff, standing with her arms crossed, stern, head held high. Old Man Winter still dwarfed her, his hands relaxed at his sides. I felt Zack behind me as I walked across the helipad cradling my wrist. It didn't seem to hurt anymore.

Dr. Perugini looked up from where she already had Scott on a gurney, wrapped in a blanket, and gave my arm a cursory glance. "Might be fractured. Let's get it set before you do anything else."

Dr. Zollers caught my arm as I started to go by. "We're gonna have a long conversation later, I'm sure." He didn't look mad, just...knowing, or something. Like he was sharing a secret only I could know about. He pulled a needle out of his lab coat and pointed to my arm. I rolled up my sleeve and he gave me a quick shot. I felt the drug start to work in less than thirty seconds as the cacophony that had been present in the back of my head began to die down and I started to feel drowsy.

I followed Dr. Perugini as Clary pushed the gurney into the Headquarters building. We navigated the corridors to the medical unit quickly and were settled in within minutes. Dr. Zollers began monitoring Scott's condition, more as a precaution, it seemed, while Perugini found her way over to me.

She poked and prodded at my hand and wrist. She reached under the cart she had slid over with her and pulled out a brace. "No point in doing a cast since you'll be healed by tomorrow, but it will be best if we control the direction of the healing." She took the brace out of the box and began to wrap it around my wrist. "Got into trouble again, eh?"

"See it however you'd like," I said to her, inflectionless.

She didn't bite immediately, but after a moment she did. "How do you see it?"

I thought about it before answering. "I made amends for some bad decisions in my past."

She stopped and looked up from what she was doing, as though she were trying to smoke out the truth by looking in my eyes. Whatever she found, she kept to herself. "Good for you," she said, and finished tightening the brace before she turned her attention to Zack, who was talking to Scott. "You! You're next." He protested, but she didn't let him sway her. She had him take off his tactical vest and then his shirt, examining some bruising on his shoulders from where he jumped out of the helicopter. I watched.

Kat made her way over to me as I lay on the bed, trying to work up the motivation to move. "You saved my life," she said with a little smile.

"You're welcome." Her eyes clouded over and she looked

troubled, as though she were trying to find a way to say what was on her mind. "Spit it out," I said with an air of impatience.

"I was thinking about the rooftop." She fumbled with her hands, gripping the rail of the bed. "When you faced that maniac in your basement, you were the only one there."

"Yeah, and?"

"So...I mean, you faced someone as bad or worse than..." she tried to say it but it didn't come out as anything but a pronoun. "...Him. But you faced Wolfe alone, all by yourself. And on the rooftop, you didn't have to be there. You had no reason to stay, you don't know anybody in Minneapolis. Scott has family in the area and Gavrikov would have chased me around the planet...but you didn't have any reason to be there."

"I told you before." I crossed my gloveless hands in my lap. "I had my reasons."

"Well...thank you." She smiled at me, and I still felt bad for her.

She started to shuffle back to Scott's bedside but I called out to her. "Wait!" She turned, almost expectant. "Do you know if there were anymore of those turtlenecks and jeans in the closet down in the room you were being held captive in?" I fingered my shirt, which was once again tattered around the arms and shoulders and my jeans were wet and caked with dirt and blood from the rooftop battle. "I think the rest of my clothes got lost in the fire."

"Yeah, there were a few of them," she said. "Coats and gloves, too."

"Oh, good." I looked back down at my bare hands.

She walked back to Scott's bedside and I looked around the room once. Zollers and Perugini were consulting in the corner, Zack and Kat were talking to Scott. I presumed M-Squad was with Ariadne and Old Man Winter. I tried to decide if I wanted to talk to them today or tomorrow and realized I didn't really care which, so long as I got some fresh clothes.

I left the medical unit without saying anything to anyone. I didn't sneak out; I didn't have to. Everyone was occupied and no one saw me leave except Zollers, who caught me with a sly smile that told me I'd see him later. That was fine, so long as it wasn't now.

I went to the staircase and found my way to the basement. The confinement room that they'd kept Kat in was unlocked now, no key card necessary. I walked in and went to the closet, finding exactly what she had promised inside. I grabbed a change of clothes, along with some undergarments that also fit me and went into the bathroom.

I took maybe the longest shower ever known to man, taking care to keep my wounded arm out of the spray but drowning every other inch of my skin in hot water. I scrubbed off the dried blood, the caked-on grit from the roof, and afterward I combed all the tangles out of my hair. I stared at myself in the mirror. I was the same girl I had seen a thousand times before, in the mirror of my own bathroom, back home, before all this happened.

Except I wasn't. The blue-green eyes were different. Not weary, but aged. I'd aged even in the weeks since I left home.

I heard a noise outside and dressed quickly. I didn't slide my gloves on until after I opened the door to find Zack waiting. I let out a breath I didn't know I had been holding and rolled my eyes. "What are you doing here?"

He looked at me innocently. "Came to check on you. Kat told me you were coming for clothes but I didn't realize you were going to shower too." He nodded at my wet hair. "I can wait if you want to dry off first."

I shook my head. "No big deal. I'm fine. I might sleep down here; it's as good as anywhere else and I don't know if I have it in me to walk all the way back to the dormitory building tonight. Besides, I'm sure Ariadne and Old Man Winter will be looking for me tomorrow morning."

"I wouldn't worry about that." He said it with more assurance than I would have expected.

"I'm not worried." I blinked my eyes, as though I could just shed the tiredness out of them with that little effort. "Worst comes to worst, I move along on my own." I felt a strength in those words that wouldn't have been possible a week earlier. "I'm okay with that, really. Maybe for the first time."

"I don't think they're going to ask you to leave," he said. "But why the change? Not that you showed much sign you were feeling all dependent before, but what triggered the shift?"

I took a deep breath. "I don't know. I guess I've been so busy feeling sorry for myself for all that's happened, for all the tough breaks—literal, in some cases," I held up my wrist, the brace still snug around it. "I've been jonesing so hard to be normal, whatever that is, that all I could think about was myself, about how I'd have to live a life where I had walls up all the time, where I couldn't really connect with anybody." I held up my hands as I slipped the gloves on. "Where I'd live untouched by people or emotion or life."

He nodded slowly. "It's up to you whether you connect with people or not. And I hate to break it to you, but your own little world is not the center of the universe."

I cocked my head at him and shot him a "duh" look. "Thanks, Galileo. You're a little late to the party on that one. And not fashionably so, like...party's over, GTFO. I figured it out, thanks."

"How?" He took a step closer to me, reminding me for some reason of Gavrikov as he took the first steps toward Kat.

"It was Aleksandr," I said, thinking about it. "He lived over a hundred years with his flames up all the time, by choice, ever since...whatever happened with his sister. He chose to live that way, isolated, alone. I think..." I felt the loneliness creep over me, the walls start to rise, and pushed them away, "...I would give anything to be able to take the barriers down and just live. And I can do that for most of them." I held up my hands, uselessly, showing him the gloves once more, the things that separated me from everyone. "All but one, anyway. It's not normal, but it's all I can do—"

He interrupted me by taking two strides to close the distance between us and before I could say anything his arms wrapped around my back, enveloping me, and he pressed his lips to mine. My eyes closed; the touch was magnificent, warm and sweet, and he pulled away just as I felt the first stirrings of my power start to work. I took a breath and opened my eyes, and his were staring back at me, brown and big and with his smile reflected in them. He had a really nice smile.

He didn't say anything else, just pulled away, leaving me speechless, standing there with my wet hair, and walked to the door. "See you tomorrow," he said, and the door shut before I could answer.

Chapter 29

I sat across from Old Man Winter, playing the staring game. Oddly, my eyes didn't seem to burn this time, so I just kept going.

Ariadne was there, of course. "We've already gotten M-Squad's report and spoken with Scott and Kat, so we have a general idea of how everything went, for the most part. Zack said that Henderschott showed up?" She flipped through the file in her hands as if looking for confirmation.

"Yeah. He had the campus under surveillance and picked us up as we left. He must have followed us all the way to the IDS tower, because I saw the cable truck he was driving pass us as we went into the lobby. Didn't really put it together until he hit me, but that's the only way it could have happened unless someone tipped him off we were going to be there."

Ariadne closed the file. "Makes sense. Would you like to explain your actions?"

I was still locked on Old Man Winter's ice blue eyes. "Which ones?"

Ariadne coughed. "Taking two untrained metas and yourself into combat with not one, but two, extremely deadly foes, stealing a Directorate car, assaulting our guards, interfering in our efforts to contain the situation—"

"Your containment strategy sucked," I said, still not breaking my gaze away. Ariadne's jaw dropped and she took a step back. Old Man Winter didn't look away from my gaze. "It would have resulted in about a million deaths; the crosswinds on top of the tower made a clean shot against Gavrikov near impossible without a stable platform to shoot from. Hell, I'm amazed Parks even hit him."

"And your plan was better?" she said with an air of snottiness. "Byerly almost got burned to death, Forrest was cornered—"

"But I saved her," I said.

"—Zack jumped from a helicopter, injuring himself, and Clary ended up going through the roof—"

"That was his own fault, you can't blame me for Clary being stupid."

"And then there's you." She came around and sat on the edge of the desk, just to the side of my staring contest with Old Man Winter. "You disobeyed our explicit commands and substituted your own judgment for ours."

"You're right," I said, firm. "Based on my experience with Gavrikov, I handled the situation as I thought best. None of the rest of you knew him personally or knew what to expect from him. Don't put me in a position where I have to watch countless people die. Let me take the responsibility a thousand times before you hand it off to someone else who will screw it up. I won't stand by and take dumb orders. I did what I thought—what I *knew* was right. And if you expect anything less from me as an agent or a retriever or a whatever you wanted me to do, you need to find someone else for the job."

There was a freezing effect in the room, as though all particle motion had halted, and Ariadne spoke first. "I'm sorry, what?"

I still didn't look away from Old Man Winter. "The job offer you extended. If it's off the table in the wake of this incident, I understand. But I figured you ought to know that if it was still open, that I'm not some brainless shell that you get to use just for my powers."

Ariadne shifted from where she was sitting on the desk. "I...don't think we would ever expect anything less than your full opinion at any time. And..." She looked to Old Man Winter, who finally broke his gaze away from me to look to her. I mentally declared victory and pumped my fist. They pretended not to notice.

She turned back after a look was shared between them. "The offer is still on the table."

"Then you have a trainee," I said. "And I have a signing bonus, I believe." I looked at her. "Do I get paid with checks or cash? Because I don't have a bank account. Yet."

"I'll...have someone cut you a check," she said, standing. "I'm sure we can find someone to take you into town to make banking arrangements."

"I'd like to go to the mall." I stood. "I need some clothes." I pulled on the shoulder of the black turtleneck, the thousandth I'd worn since arriving at the Directorate. "Nothing personal, but I'm kind of sick of wearing black all the time. Who does that?"

She nodded. "Anything else?"

I thought for a moment and remembered something. "One last thing. Henderschott, before he died—"

"Ah, yes." Ariadne opened the file. "Rather spectacular, that. A 57-storey plunge to the street?" She looked away from the photograph I could see in the folder. "Not a pleasant way to go, especially when strapped into a tin can as he was."

"He said something before he died, about his employer." The silence in the room became oppressive in an instant. Old Man Winter seemed to perk up and Ariadne had a wide-eyed look on her face. "He said they'd keep coming after me. I asked him who, and he gave me their name—Omega." I looked at the two of them as they exchanged a look. "That mean anything to you?"

"No," Ariadne said after appearing to consider it for a moment. "So we have a name for this new threat—"

Old Man Winter cut her off. "No. Not a new threat at all. Not Omega." His blue eyes glowed, shining in the dimness of the tinted office. "An old one, rather. A very, very old one." The office was warm enough, and I was already wearing my coat. But the way he said it, the timbre of his voice, the delivery—gave me a very real shudder that was absolutely unrelated to the cold.

Chapter 30

It was a Monday, I think. I let the nice agent (he didn't sneer or get pissy at all with me, a rarity for people from the Directorate in my experience) drive me to the bank. They were very pleasant and understanding, having had a long relationship with the Directorate, and so I opened an account and the money was in it within just a few minutes. Which was fortunate, because I didn't have a driver's license. Somehow, Ariadne had gotten copies of my Social Security Card and Birth Certificate, which made things easier.

I left the bank with a temporary checkbook and a debit card, walking across the parking lot back to the car where the agent was waiting for me, the heat from the exhaust causing the tale pipe to steam in the cold. And it was cold, cold but beautiful, the sunlight streaming down from above, shining off all the ice and snow. I looked up, just to make sure the sun was still there. It was, seated in the middle of the blue sky. I smiled and got in the car.

The drive to Eden Prairie Center only took a few minutes. I entered through the same entrance by the food court that I had fairly destroyed last time I was there. There was still a hole in the wall where I'd thrown Henderschott through, though they had workmen patching the damage. I passed by without paying too much attention, trying to appear innocent.

I stopped at a lot of different stores, and I bought a few things. I had decided before I walked in that I was going to try and spend less than five hundred dollars, because even though I had ten thousand, I didn't ever want to be stuck in a situation where I needed money and didn't have it. I tried to find the bargain tables, checked the prices on everything before I bought it, and did the math in my head. It all worked out well and I found some very nice things (all of which were long sleeved and didn't show much in the way of flesh, because every inch of it I exposed was an inch that could kill someone) but that took my wardrobe beyond the dullness of Ariadne's. Not that it would take much.

I walked out of the store I was in, having stocked up on some professional-looking outfits and started to make my way back to the car. By my estimate, I was a couple hundred under my limit and quite content with that until I passed the store I'd gone by with Zack only a week earlier. The dress was still in the window, the red one that I had seen on the woman I had thought was my mom. I hesitated outside, staring. It was impractical. It wasn't for me. But I went inside, and they had it in my size.

I tried it on and stood in front of a mirror, staring at myself again. I looked...so different, now. I bought it and I couldn't define exactly why. Call it recklessness (even though I questioned whether I'd ever wear it in public), call it desperation (because to be able to wear it meant consequences that could be quite dire) or you could call it...hope. That things would change somehow, get better.

I was walking out of the store, lost in thought when a flash of red drew my attention to someone standing in my path. I looked up and found her staring at me, the woman from before. She still wore red, but it was a different dress this time. This one was cut to the knee, a little more conservative but not much. I could still see every curve she clearly wanted displayed, and it made me want to shrink away in envy. I tried to smile and go around her, but she stepped into my path. "Hi there," she said.

"Hello." I didn't know quite what to say. I could feel the hint of flush on my cheeks. "I'm sorry about last time, I didn't mean to scare you. I just...saw you from a distance and thought you were my mom." She stared back at me, impassive. "She's missing, so...anyway, sorry." I half-expected some soft, cooing sound of sympathy like I had heard from the women on TV. She didn't make a noise like that.

She laughed. "Don't worry about it, although you have to admit, it was kind of a foolish mistake to make." I feigned a smile and as I started to leave she blocked me again. "It's hardly the first time it's happened, though. I mean, growing up in the shadow of Sierra Nealon wasn't the easiest experience." My blood turned to ice at the mention of my mother's name and I locked my gaze on hers and noticed for the first time that her eyes were blue but flecked with green. She laughed again. "I had to find some ways to stand out from big sister." She ran a hand down the side of her dress. "See what I mean? Your mother would never wear this."

I froze and my shopping bags slipped from my fingers one by one. I knew the look on my face was pure shock and she reached out for me, grasping my arm, hooking it in hers and angling it so I didn't drop my bags. "You look surprised. I take it mommy dearest never told you about her little sister? That's all right. We're three of a kind—you, me and her." Her hand found its way to her chest. "But where are my manners? I'm your aunt, Charlene—but you can call me Charlie." Her smile was ten thousand watts, bright and vibrant. "I'm here to help you."

A Note to the Reader

I wanted to take a moment to thank you for reading this story. As an independent author, getting my name out to build an audience is one of the biggest priorities on any given day. If you enjoyed this story and are looking forward to reading more, let someone know - post it on Amazon, on your blog, if you have one, on Goodreads.com, place it in a quick Facebook status or Tweet with a link to the page of whatever outlet you purchased it from (Amazon, Barnes & Noble, Apple, Kobo, etc). Good reviews inspire people to take a chance on a new author – like me. And we new authors can use all the help we can get.

Thanks again for your time.

Robert J. Crane

About the Author

Robert J. Crane was born and raised on Florida's Space Coast before moving to the upper midwest in search of cooler climates and more palatable beer. He graduated from the University of Central Florida with a degree in English Creative Writing. He worked for a year as a substitute teacher and worked in the financial services field for seven years while writing in his spare time. He makes his home in the Twin Cities area of Minnesota.

He can be contacted in several ways:
Via **email** at cyrusdavidon@gmail.com
Follow him on **Twitter** - @robertJcrane
Connect on **Facebook** – robertJcrane (Author)
Website – http://www.robertJcrane.com
Blog – http://robertJcrane.blogspot.com
Become a fan on **Goodreads** –
http://www.goodreads.com/RobertJCrane

Sienna Nealon will return in

Soulless
The Girl in the Box, Book Three

After six months of intense training with the Directorate, Sienna Nealon finds herself on her first assignment - tracking a dangerous meta across the upper midwest. With Scott Byerly and Kat Forrest at her side, she'll face new enemies and receive help from unlikely allies as she stumbles across the truth behind the shadowy organization known only as Omega.

Coming August 2012

The Sanctuary Series

Epic Fantasy by Robert J. Crane

The world of Arkaria is a dangerous place, filled with dragons, titans, goblins and other dangers. Those who live in this world are faced with two choices: live an ordinary life or become an adventurer and seek the extraordinary.

Defender

The Sanctuary Series, Volume One

Cyrus Davidon leads a small guild in the human capital of Reikonos. Caught in an untenable situation, facing death in the den of a dragon, they are saved by the brave fighters of Sanctuary who offer an invitation filled with the promise of greater adventure. Soon Cyrus is embroiled in a mystery - someone is stealing weapons of nearly unlimited power for an unknown purpose, and Sanctuary may be the only thing that stands between the world of Arkaria and total destruction.

Available Now!

Avenger

The Sanctuary Series, Volume Two

When a series of attacks on convoys draws suspicion that Sanctuary is involved, Cyrus Davidon must put aside his personal struggles and try to find the raiders. As the attacks worsen, Cyrus and his comrades find themselves abandoned by their allies, surrounded by enemies, facing the end of Sanctuary and a war that will consume their world.

Available Now!

Champion
The Sanctuary Series, Volume Three

As the war heats up in Arkaria, Vara is forced to flee after an ancient order of skilled assassins infiltrates Sanctuary and targets her. Cyrus Davidon accompanies her home to the elven city of Termina and the two of them become embroiled in a mystery that will shake the very foundations of the Elven Kingdom – and Arkaria.

Available Now!

Crusader
The Sanctuary Series, Volume Four

Cyrus Davidon finds himself far from his home in Sanctuary, in the land of Luukessia, a place divided and deep in turmoil. With his allies at his side, Cyrus finds himself facing off against an implacable foe in a war that will challenge all his convictions - and one he may not be able to win.

Coming Fall 2012!

Savages
A Sanctuary Short Story

Twenty years before Cyrus Davidon joined Sanctuary, his father was killed in a war with the trolls and he has never forgiven them. Enter Vaste, a troll unlike most; courageous, loyal and an outcast. When Cyrus and Vaste become trapped in a far distant land, they are forced to overcome their suspicions and work together to get home.

Available Now!

A Familiar Face
A Sanctuary Short Story

Cyrus Davidon gets more than he bargained for when he takes a day away from Sanctuary to visit the busy markets of his hometown, Reikonos. While there, he meets a woman who seems very familiar, and appears to know him, but that he can't place.

Available Now!
(Free for signing up for Newsletter at RobertJCrane.com!)

The Girl in the Box

Contemporary Urban Fantasy by Robert J. Crane

Alone

The Girl in the Box, Book 1

Sienna Nealon was a 17 year-old girl who had been held prisoner in her own house by her mother for twelve years. Then one day her mother vanished, and Sienna woke up to find two strange men in her home. On the run, unsure of who to turn to and discovering she possesses mysterious powers, Sienna finds herself pursued by a shadowy agency known as the Directorate and hunted by a vicious, bloodthirsty psychopath named Wolfe, each of which is determined to capture her for their own purposes...

Available Now!

18127166R00130

Made in the USA
Middletown, DE
29 November 2018